THE
HERALDED SPY

AN IMMORTAL SPY NOVEL

K. A. KRANTZ

Mom
When I lost my love of reading, you helped me rediscover the joy.

CHAPTER 1

War raged throughout the Mid Worlds. Devourers from foreign galaxies assailed the new defense system Resen, determined to join their kith in overrunning the magic-rich collective. Netting woven of Mid World magic and yarns of Fate rebuffed the hungry foot soldiers, captured the enemy's midranks, and tracked their upper echelons, sending location data to mortal-manned security centers that then relayed the intel to armies of gods and Berserkers purging the infestation of anti-gods from the collective.

Thus, in the utterly inhospitable rocky moraine of Citlaltépetl, encroaching on the snowcapped peak of the mountain in the southern reaches of Mexico, troops from the four superpower races of the Consortium followed the leadership of Chimalma the Shield Hand, upper-ranking Mid World guardian from the Nahua pantheon and a beloved commander of great renown. Consortium forces had herded the Devourers away from the surrounding inhabited areas, toward the mountain range in a classic, albeit massive, pincer move. There was nowhere for the Devourers to go but up the dormant volcano.

Relentless gods from multiple pantheons presented as one army, wearing second-skin uniforms that covered them from crown to boot tip and left only their eyes exposed. The chameleon fabric blended with the grays, tans, and whites of the terrain, changing colors as the conflict moved from towns, to brushland, to the mountains. Woven by the Fates, the uniforms protected the gods from the scalding blood spatter of the anti-gods. Close combat employing fatal blows by god-forged weapons or greater magics was the only way to end an anti-god.

The gods were far from alone in the battle. The Angelic Host, who held dominion over all things air, leveraged brutal gales to corral Devourers into crumbling stony ravines made by the Dragon Horde, who defined all things land and sea. Dragons ensured the foreign invaders never stood upon firm ground, while more dragons carried gods upon moving—but stable—terrain to maintain battle formation enclosing the enemy.

Militaristic deities in their own right, the anti-gods quickly adapted. Every discharge of the Devourers' toxic gray magic blasted apart moving landscapes and immolated mortals, including angels and dragons. Gods tumbled from once-secure vantage points, too many of them breaking on the rocks, unable to regain their feet before the enemy was upon them.

This war had been a long time coming. Now that it was here, Bix couldn't wait for it to be over. She hated this part, the frantic, desperate scrabble for survival. It was one thing to test the Consortium, which was composed of this collective's chosen caretakers of dragons, angels, gods, and Fates. By introducing a foreign foe to the Mids, the Consortium had been mercilessly reminded of their hubris. They'd had to break their cycles of infighting and accept the necessity of collaboration. To the Consortium, defending the right to govern this collective was very much the why and wherefore of the conflict.

Bix knew better. This was a family matter. Her family. The first generation of cosmic entities born from the origins of all existence. The seven First Children of the Chaos and the Cosmos. Very few life-forms were aware that the First Children thrived as more than forgotten legends, and that was by design for the safety of the minor races who would perish in the presence of unrestrained primordial power. Unfortunately, this war in the Mids was the result of a tantrum being thrown by two of Bix's siblings.

The youngest twins, Tempest and Desire, embodied external and internal motivation. War was inarguably a motivating experience, which was one reason Desire had created the Devourers, while Tempest dictated their relentless assault on the Mids. Only the terrible twins could call off the anti-gods and ensure those armies would never return here. However, there was a price for salvation. A price Bix alone could pay.

To save her sanctuary, Bix had to murder her youngest siblings. That was their suicidal demand, not her vengeful whim. As First Children of the origins of all existence, death was something Tempest and Desire couldn't attain. Since achievements were the measurement of motivation, death's elusiveness made the youngest twins crave their permanent end more, and more, and more until it'd become their singular obsession. Bix's numerous refusals to oblige had only cemented their resolve. In fact, every time she'd said no, they'd redoubled their efforts and inflicted more pain and suffering upon her and hers. This attack upon her sanctuary was case in point. Their violent insistence epitomized privilege and entitlement. The consequences be damned, in their eyes. Why *would* they care? They weren't planning to be around to deal with it.

The consequences would fall on Bix. She was the youngest of the seven First Children and the only one without a twin because she'd been born equal parts Chaos and Cosmos, wild and structured. She was the cosmic entity of balance. The two-in-one. Whenever any of her siblings threw the greater existence out of whack, it fell to her to make the proper adjustments to restore balance. It'd earned her the dreadful moniker of High Executioner for All Worlds, which was admittedly better than über poop scooper.

There was some question—in her broken mind, at least—as to whether she truly had both the might and magics required to kill her brother and sister. They certainly thought so. She wasn't as confident. Regardless, doing so was out of the question. Morally, ethically, and practically. Removing all motivation from everything everywhere by eliminating the origins of it? That'd be straight-up stupid. Talk about ruining the balance of things. No matter how her siblings railed, bullied, and bludgeoned her, Bix would not end their existence.

That left her with the current problem of the Devourers and this damn war.

The youngest twins had bound her hands in the defense of her home. If she raised one thread of darkness or one ray of starlight against the army they'd dispatched to this collective, the pair would create nastier enemies, ones against whom there was no hope of survival. The terrible twins' rules of engagement were simple: Tempest and Desire wouldn't personally participate in the battle between the Devourers and the denizens of the Mids as long as Bix didn't either. Therein lay the slim hope that the Consortium could defeat the Devourers and preserve the Mids. Therein lay the belief that the underdogs could win.

Bix adored these hundred-odd Worlds crafted for her by the eldest of the First Children. She loved observing—and occasionally contributing to—the many chaotic lives within this collective who forever strove to be more and become better through means both ghastly and compassionate. There were individuals residing here whom she loved as part of her chosen family, just as there were friends and frenemies whose relationships gave meaning to her immortal life. Relationships mattered. The Mids were her sanctuary.

How could she make Tempest and Desire stop their attacks—now and forever—without giving them what they wanted? Figuring that out was her mission. Time was of the essence.

In order to move forward, Bix needed the final segment of her memories. It contained the finer details of how she'd fought the youngest twins previously and how those efforts had failed to shut down their antics. That portion also contained the reasons her other siblings wouldn't get involved and answered whether her parents ever had. Additionally, the last piece would unlock the rest of her arcane magics that remained just beyond the reach of her incomplete self.

Regrettably for the Consortium, the final, necessary, salvation-bringing segment was contained in the Mid World guardian Chimalma. To reclaim what was hers, Bix had to take everything from Chimalma and leave the venerated commander a hollowed-out husk devoid of even the most basic awareness of self. Not an ideal trade. Not ideal timing. But across the Mids, loyal friends, unlikely allies, and total strangers fought, bled, and died to protect Bix's sanctuary. They would continue to do so until she dealt with her irrational siblings.

Therefore, Bix lurked on the threshold of layered gates above the summit of Citlaltépetl, awaiting the precise moment to pounce.

"Five more minutes, and we'll have enough steam rising from Citlaltépetl to confuse both sides." Feng, the Phoenix in mostly humanoid form, quietly burned beside her while his magics awakened the volcano. An apex entity of the Mids, he was the lone angel-dragon hybrid and the living welfare gauge of native magic. Small flames danced at the feathered tips of his apple-red hair and highlighted the hawkish angles of his features. Even the point of his Van Dyke beard sported restless sparks. The reds and gold wreathing his head made his aquamarine eyes all the more arresting and exposed the wealth of past trauma still haunting their depths. Sure, his brown tweed sport coat and loamy brown slacks lent him the look of a subdued professor, but there was no disguising the taint of Devourer toxins creeping into his magical resonance with the proliferation of anti-gods across the Mids.

The more that taint grew, the worse the health of the Mids. Yet another reason Bix needed to solve the sibling problem sooner than later.

"Thank you for giving me cover." She offered an apologetic smile. "I know you'd rather be running rescue ops with our other team members."

"I'll sync up with them when we're done." He shrugged.

"Making sure you're ready for parley with the enemy's leadership is more important anyway. We grossly underestimated how many of their troops had made it into the Mids before Resen launched."

"There was no way we could've known. They shapeshift down to the DNA," Bix reminded. "Their poisonous resonance isn't detectable by anyone less than a superpower."

"Nevertheless, as invigorating as the skirmish we are witnessing may be, our side can't sustain this level of engagement across the Mids, nor can we replenish our resources fast enough." Feng glowered and flicked a hand at the battlefield. "We are at a compounded disadvantage when *we* are the only resource *they* need."

While Feng might not know the leadership of the Devourers were her siblings—she was disinclined to share that intel for many reasons—he was nonetheless right about the resource problem. Devourers came into existence fully grown and trained for battle as part of a hive mind. They fed on magic of any kind, which meant everything in the Mids nourished and sustained them. Buildings, boulders, plants, people, the whole lot was an edible feast for the anti-gods.

In stark contrast, the superpowers of the Mids—along with the myriad native magical races of Chwedlonol and the magic-grounding humans—had limited diets, limited magics, and limited environments in which they could survive. Their vulnerabilities ensured a symbiotic coexistence. However, intentional collaboration among Mids' species was a very recent and rather tenuous achievement. Even now, the ugly reality of the Devourers' invasion strained relations, particularly in communities where the shapeshifting anti-gods had quietly infiltrated months ago while the Consortium had been focused on individual power grabs instead of collective protection. The populace was not pleased with the Consortium, but was complying with the directives from their leadership. For now.

"Would you aim the steam clouds to our four o'clock, please? To the combat cluster approaching the volcanic vent? And, if you would, block the angels' efforts to clear the air around that area too." Bix jerked her chin to one of a dozen holes opening in the mountainside as pressure built beneath the summit. She had no intention of being around when Feng made it blow its top.

"How do you track Chimalma when the pantheons' uniforms make the gods look exactly the same regardless of height, weight, or build?" Feng harrumphed but did as Bix asked.

"She's carrying a piece of me inside her, which, when it comes to magical GPS, isn't all that different from me wearing your dewclaw." Bix tapped her pendant of a seemingly metallic angel wing soldered to a dragon's wing that hid one of Feng's golden dewclaws, all miniaturized, of course.

"Yes, but our connection has proven beneficial to both of us." He bumped her elbow with his. "Can you say the same for Chimalma's connection to you?"

"Pfft. Hardly. You've seen the madness that's befallen my other memory keepers. Chimalma simply has the benefit of war to hide the extent of her crazy." Bix deployed gates like stepping-stones, descending into the mist. She took her time while Devourers successfully separated Chimalma from her troops and lured the goddess into a ring of anti-gods disguised as rocks. To Bix, everyone stood out due to their resonances. Detecting an individual's unique energy had been a matter of survival when she'd been an amnesiac. Now it was an unconscious habit.

She was six stones from the Devourer's trap when fire raked across her chest from the dewclaw pendant. Feng's outraged keen blasted past the protection of the gates still surrounding him. Potent magic older than any World poured down the hill, raising goose bumps along her skin and setting her heart to wild thundering.

"Impossible." Bix pivoted sharply to behold the firebird fully ablaze and ensnared in an orb of...nonflammable woody vines?

Shit.

A giant, built like a coppery desert rose plant with every branch an arm, every leaf a finger, and every blossom an eye, dragged Feng from the cover of Bix's gates on roots that functioned as stout legs and pointy feet.

Chills of recognition snaked over her. The giant was one of her brother Desire's heralds, an entity wholly different from a Devourer and infinitely more powerful.

"Don't you dare," she shouted. Tentacles of shadows burst from her entire being and surged toward Feng.

The many eyes of the herald bobbed and blinked as though surprised. A breath later, the blinding copper magic of a First Child flared, engulfing the burning Phoenix and Desire's herald. When the glow faded, Feng was gone and so was the herald.

Stunned, her heart ceasing to beat and head spinning, Bix expanded her resonance search across the mountain range and beyond the battlefield. Nothing. No trace of Feng or the herald.

Had...had Desire just killed Feng?

Her hand closed over the pendant of the dewclaw. She kickstarted her heart and focused on that tiny piece of the Phoenix. A faint thrum. Not as strong as it should be and weaker than it had ever been. Not good.

The communications device clipped to her ear chirped. The panicked voice of the youngest member of her team crackled across the line.

"Bix? Bix? Something's wrong with Resen. The ley lines are spidering, the netting is fluctuating. The defense field is unstable."

Resen. Feng. The timing wasn't coincidence. It was causality. Damn it. Her brother was trying to get more of his Devourers inside the Mids. What to do? Husk Chimalma, regain her memories, but be offline for an indeterminate time while her brain sorted itself before she could take on her brother? Or did she answer the call of her teammates, find Feng, and try to shore up Resen first?

With a frustrated scream escaping through grinding teeth, Bix turned back toward Chimalma. The goddess stood defiant in a ring of decapitated Devourers and met Bix's gaze without flinching.

The answer was obvious. The Mids couldn't defend themselves if Resen failed. She had to let Chimalma be, for now.

Gates opened.

Citlaltépetl erupted.

CHAPTER 2

On a World dyed crimson by sunlight shining through red monoliths that enclosed the marketplace of the illicit, the indentured, and the addicted, Bix arrived unannounced in the upper chambers of a criminal syndicate's home base. Angels belonging to the choir of the disavowed shifted into their disguises of long-eared, hook-nailed green imps as they hustled down a central spiral staircase to the tempo of rapid clacking on a single keyboard.

Surrounded by floor-to-ceiling monitors displaying assorted Devourer conflicts and rescue parties interspliced by data streams and Mid World maps beneath the lattice of the Resen defense system sat a young human Sage with ginger hair flattened by padded headphones. His crystalized shoulders glowed in assorted hues beneath the loose drape of a too-large flannel shirt. The casters of his gaming chair crunched over the hard tips of his untied shoelaces as he coasted around the circular floor, green eyes tracking changes on the monitors while his fingers flew over his keyboard. His steady chatter into his boom mic revealed he was running overwatch for the multiple teams showing up on the monitors.

Of all the places in the Mids the kid could hole up during the cross-World war, Bix wasn't remotely surprised he'd chosen here. These angels had been his bodyguards for so long, he probably considered this place his third home. The Crimson Market wasn't an official data center for the defense system. Not only would the location have been a security nightmare, it would also have been a political disaster. However, the archangel of this disavowed choir spoiled the Sage by supplying whatever tech the kid could imagine. In exchange, the choir reaped the benefits of the kid's skills, accesses, and addiction to knowledge.

"Cian, can Resen locate Feng?" Bix closed gates behind her, dusting volcanic ash from her shoulders as she stepped fully into the syndicate's war room. Cian was one of the architects of the defense system and, like any creationist, had maintained a backdoor to the network.

"Hey, hey, hey. Bix, Bix, Bix, look, look, look." The kid sailed his chair over to her with a huge grin, rucking up his sleeve past his elbow. "Resen launched, and check out what appeared minutes later."

A fat oak leaf, lush green with pronounced lobes beneath a thin layer of crystallization, hugged the middle of his forearm. It was new. He had two others heading up toward his elbow: one a wilted leaf beneath a clump of crystal, and the other a smaller, but healthy, leaf sans crystallization. The inked leaves represented the grades of a completed trial toward full Fatehood and were bestowed magically by the Fates. The crystallization was an unfortunate side effect of magic passing through his body. He'd failed one test, passed two. Not a bad start.

"Resen's launch classified as a Fate test? Awesome." Bix applauded. "Congratulations, Cian. The size of that leaf tells me that was a BFD trial too. Good job. Well done."

"Man, I love being part of your team. You think I'd have had a chance like this without you and the other weirdos? Psht." The kid laughed, his attention bouncing around the monitors. His smile fell, and his brow wrinkled. "Wait. The something that's off with Resen might be Feng. Did you say you *lost* him? I thought he was with you."

"Operative word there is *was*." Bix couldn't make the jump that Desire had killed Feng. Every instinct within her said it was too...abrupt? Desire was capable of a lot of heartless and shitty things, but to send a herald to deliver her friend unto death? Right in front of her? The method was wrong. The audience wasn't, but the method was. Wasn't it?

"Okay, let's find Feng. Two secs." Cian pointed to a monitor with a map nearest Bix. "He should show up... That's odd. I'm getting a null result."

"In non-nerd, what does that mean?"

"It means Resen can't find him," answered a gruff polyglot rasp from the spiral staircase leading up to the archangel's bedroom. "The foundational elements of Resen can't locate the Phoenix. My ley line is freaking out. Other archangels are reporting the same distress from their lines. My guess? The kid's right. Feng's absence is what's wrong with the defense system."

Built brawnier than a comic book villain, Archangel Samael slowly descended the steps. One black eye rolled white, then black, then white again like an old flip clock, indicating the group mind-share with fellow archangels. His black burnout T-shirt painted every vein, muscle, and scarification. Black jeans and black jump boots were the same hue as his blue-black side fade.

"Oh my god," Cian gasped, blanching. "Is Feng...is he dead?"

"Kind of awfully hoping not. Not only is he our friend, but also when Feng dies, native magic drops from its apex to its nadir, which would mean Resen goes from increasing in power to minimum output. It wouldn't be able to stop the bulk of the Devourer army from entering the Mids anymore." Bix studied the purple and blue threads peeling away from the lattice of the defensive barrier as shown on the monitors. They appeared to be questing, much like her shadowy tentacles did when she cast them to hunt.

Was that her brother's goal? To weaken Resen? To see what she'd do to retaliate? She didn't know how far she could push back without Tempest and Desire blowing it all out of proportion by blowing up the Mids. Measured responses were necessary when dealing with megalomaniacs.

"The Phoenix isn't dead, but he's not in the Mids either." Samael flinched as he stood beside Bix. There was a time when being near any archangel had made her queasy due to the power disparity, but since she'd regained most of her innate magics, she was now the 800-pound gorilla making the superpowers uncomfortable.

"How is that possible?" Bix toyed with her dewclaw pendant. Feng, like Samael—like all angels, dragons, Chweds, and humans—was made of Mids' magic. None of them could get too far from the source of energy that had created them without dissolving. Gods, anti-gods, and Fates were Other World entities who could leave the Mids whenever they wanted. First Children were the makers of universes and all things within them. There was nowhere they couldn't go. Same for their heralds.

"Shouldn't be. The ley lines feel someone has pulled a fast one on them. Since they're sentient, they're prone to tantrums when tricked." Samael grabbed the back of Cian's chair. "Do a scan for pockets of Other World magic that appeared when Feng went off grid."

"You're thinking of the last time he went missing." Bix managed a half smile for the archangel. "When you and I started working together."

"Only other time a Phoenix has ever been lost." Samael returned her smirk. "Even then, however, the lines knew where he was. They just didn't care to tell us. This time, they really don't know."

Bix could go all überentity and hunt Feng, but if native magic couldn't find its creation, then he wasn't in the Mids, and if he wasn't in the Mids, then he wasn't alive. But the ley lines insisted he was alive, so something was wrong somewhere in the chain of assumptions.

"No anomalous records, but there are six reports of high-ranking Devourers getting past Resen and landing in hot zones in the moments right before Resen went wonky." Cian rolled to a triptych of screens changing data feeds. "System is still WAD."

"Working as designed," Samael translated, not that Bix needed him to. She wasn't a tech person, but she'd been around Cian long enough to pick up some lingo. Resen couldn't stop the big guns of the anti-gods from getting into the Mids, but it tracked them and told the good guys where to find the bad guys.

That was why gods like Chimalma were still necessary to the defense.

"Hey, Bix, Feng was with you when he vanished, right?" Cian asked distractedly as lines of data, or maybe it was code, slowed their scroll.

"Right." She didn't mention the herald or her brother because it would lead to problems that would result in all kinds of species getting themselves killed. Most myths and legends attributed the origins of creation to gods or titans. A token few ruminated on the existence of First Children. To many, Bix was a titan of destruction. That was as far as their minds could conceive, so she didn't correct them. Her existence didn't rely on the beliefs of the masses; neither did her ego.

"Okay, okay, okay. What have we all learned from weird shit going down when you two are together?" Cian questioned, though it seemed to be rhetorical as he kicked up the leg rest of his rolling chair and tilted back, words reduced to mutters interrupted by slurps from the straw in the huge tumbler affixed to his chair.

"I know you can hear him, but is he saying anything helpful?" Bix bumped Samael's elbow. Angels could hear a flea burrowing in a desert since they controlled all things air and atmosphere, which included sound waves.

"He's still giving guidance to the teams liberating prisoners from Devourer camps, but whatever he's typing has nothing to do with the rescues." Samael rubbed his neck. "My choir tries to keep pace with the kid's abilities, but ever since he danced with a ley line, his mind operates on a level none of us fully understand."

"He's an architect of Resen. There's no way the foundational elements—ley lines or the Fates—were going to let his brain be hacked, mapped, or cloned. Don't take it personally." She watched the kid thriving in his element with equal parts pride and worry. His life had changed drastically since he'd entered her orbit. There were so many paths he could take, so many ways he could develop. He'd endured so many tragedies already with so many more to come. She really hoped he stayed on the trajectory of being one of the solidly good guys.

"Resen doesn't show where *you* are at any given moment," Samael mused. "Feng's whereabouts only show when the kid actively looks for him. Anybody else on that exclusion list who might know what's going on?"

Yes, but it was someone who didn't much care for Feng and who was ass-deep in combating Devourers.

"Ah-ha! You think you can fool me?" Cian cried, fingers flying faster over keys. "Don't underestimate what a Sage can do."

Other World magic surged from two points within the angels' war room. A giant desert rose emerged from the wall behind Samael.

"Samael, behind you," Bix shouted, opening a gate to shield the archangel. The herald raised its leafy fingers and traced the edges of the gate like a curious child.

"Kid, move," Samael barked, calling forth a ball of angel fire.

Bix turned around as another herald leaned half out of the monitors in front of Cian. Before the kid could yelp, Bix opened more protective gates. A ball of angelic fire shot across the room. Copper magic countered, causing screeching blinding lights. The tower shook, smoke blossomed, and screams multiplied.

When the lights faded the heralds were gone. Cian too. His chair still spun. A hole twice the size of the herald yawned over the market. No tech. No walls. Nothing but smoky red sky.

Bix cursed under her breath. Yet again, Desire's herald had snatched someone out of her gates. How was that possible? And why send two heralds this time? To take a human teenager from a glorified computer lab? But only one to take Feng from a battlefield? There was something odd about Desire's means. Something she should recognize. The memory was…was like a word on the tip of her tongue, just beyond recollection.

Damn.

"What was *that*?" Samael bellowed, rushing to the section of missing tower and running his hands along the unburned edges of rubble. Members of his choir rushed up through the floor hatch in their guises of imps but armed with angel fire. "Damage assessment. Full World. Go, go, go."

As swiftly as they'd entered, angelic imps vanished, leaving a handful of the choir to gather debris and make repairs to the exterior walls. The tech was toast.

Every hair on Bix's body prickled as she stared at her reflection in the fractured glass screens that no longer displayed anything. Whatever Cian had figured out was gone with him. Was that why Desire had sent two heralds to grab him? Had Cian somehow provoked her brother? Or was this another attack on Resen?

Anger stomped up and down her spine, causing her darkness to writhe beneath her skin. With Cian gone, the rescue teams he'd been guiding were left in the lurch and fighting blind. Bix tapped the comm on her ear.

"Ashtad? You there?"

Labored breathing and a telling silence over the background of foliage rustling said her dear friend and former boss was there but couldn't speak.

"Feng and Cian have been abducted," she said softly so as not to alert whomever he was running from. "I think you're next. Exfil. Now."

Three heartbeats passed before the screen on her smartwatch brightened and streamed a live video up her sleeve. A static picture remained on the face of her tech beneath the watermark of a countdown timer. Ashtad had a preferred destination. Okay, then.

"Don't you dare leave without telling me what's going on,"

Samael threatened as he held a hand against the blasted opening of the tower. Native magic built around him as a dark blue glow. Red rubble flew up, in, and around, to fill the massive hole in the wall.

"As soon as I figure it out, I'll let you know. Promise." She offered an apologetic smile as she connected to a mote of darkness at the destination location glowing on her watch face.

CHAPTER 3

The tangy stink of overapplied disinfectants and electronically purified air engulfed Bix as she touched down in a familiar corridor of an infectious-disease development laboratory on a World she'd been in no rush to see again. Magics native and Other World greeted her in the expected surge and ebb of scientists at work. Beyond the shimmering curved white walls, null spots denoting a robust human population fanned around the massive lake in communities of quaint colorful bungalows and cottages. To the unfamiliar, the lab resembled a luxurious five-star resort with its long-windowed expanses ready to welcome the weary for indulgent rehabilitation. In truth, this was the last place one wanted to be a guest, much less a patient.

So it was with more than idle curiosity that she watched Ashtad's team of demigods race across the threshold of gates she'd opened at the far end of the hall, escorting a dozen Chweds, one dragon in humanoid form, and a pair of angels. No one was unscathed. Some were covered in blisters, others missing limbs. Many drifted in and out of consciousness. From multiple suites, dragons and upper-caste Chweds in humanoid form and covered from head to toe in PPE rolled gurneys to intercept the demigods and their cargo.

Loud crackling and bright bursts of electricity on the threshold marked Ashtad's arrival with a badly burned Fate draped across his shoulders in a fireman's lift. The son of a storm god, Ashtad Ba'al wielded energy with great precision, from a fingertip spark to a room-clearing bomb. As a demigod in the throes of his trials to full godhood, he continued to amass magics and power that would eventually define the type and caste of god to which he'd ascend. The challenges he, and all demigods, faced during this conflict with the Devourers would elevate them in ways their pantheons could only imagine. Might even create a new class of deity.

"Close the gates, now," Ashtad panted into the comm connected to Bix.

Bix obliged, keeping out of the way as the wounded were sorted by species, then carted off to assorted suites. Ashtad slid the comatose Fate onto a waiting gurney before making his way to Bix, hobbling all the way.

"Knee locked up?" she asked as he planted a bloodied and blistered hand on the wall beside her head.

He winced and nodded. A wealth of thick, ropey scars ran from midthigh to midcalf, rendering his knee unable to bend unless he maimed the leg again, which he tended to do before running an op. In his mind, his old battle injury was merely an impediment that made rising to a challenge all the more satisfying.

"I see your rescue op was a success. Congrats." Slipping into ancient habits, she covertly studied his magical resonance, noting the changes from years ago when he'd recruited her into the spy game. There were seedlings of magics waiting to blossom, waiting for the right combination of nutrients to catapult him to the next level. The growth and development of life-forms fascinated her. She wasn't a creationist, so observing the constructs her siblings used to make everything in existence, particularly the ones that permitted transformational development, was better than binge-watching anime.

"Once Resen came online, we were finally able to locate the family members of the assets the Devourers were leveraging to maintain their intel on our troop positions and Resen security centers." Ashtad groaned, attempting to flex his scarred knee as he wiped his grimy brow in his elbow. "Thanks for the evac, by the way. The anti-gods took out our original exfil site, so I'm glad you called when you did."

"Cootie lab, though? Really? You chose *here* as an ideal recuperation site?" She wrinkled her nose. "Since when do you offer up hostages as guinea pigs to designer plagues?"

"This place has a different mission these days." He flashed a weary grin. "We built a Resen data center at the bottom of the lake. The researchers here are studying the short- and long-term effects on Chweds and humans living so close to a constant feed of amped-up ley line and Fate magic."

Bix leaned back to snag a view of said lake through the long windows framing a research suite. What first appeared to be a rainbow rising from the heart of the lake was missing the oranges, yellows, and reds of a traditional color palette. The blues, purples, and greens of the foundational elements of Resen drifted in and out of sight as though dancing across dimensions. Fine threads of blue and purple, separated from the main arc, bowed and flexed, questing just like she'd seen on Cian's monitors.

"Take a look at the line to the data center." She retreated a few steps so he could see out the windows.

Hand over hand, he braced himself on the wall, then the window, dragging his leg as he did as she asked. His scowl intensified. "That's not supposed to look like that."

"Started when Feng was abducted. I think it's getting worse now that Cian's gone too." She'd almost forgotten how menace added golden depths to his cognac-colored eyes.

"Let's grab a conference room, then give me a gate to my bunker. There's tech I need to trace the problem."

Shadows slithered from her spine and bundled him up, carrying him to the nearest empty room. Fortunately, he was too worn out to decry the slight to his dignity. Something had gone more than wrong on his rescue op, and while she wanted to ask about it as any good friend would, her concern for Feng, Cian, and Ashtad kept her focused. She dropped Ashtad in one chair as darkness rolled another chair to support his feet. When he was situated, she opened a gate beside the armrest, allowing him to reach through to a desk in his supersecret bunker located Worlds away.

"Last time I checked in with Cian, he was running overwatch for Oracles and Sages out on rescue missions." Ashtad smirked as he plugged tech into tech and started typing in the air, sans keyboard. "Probably how I wound up with a Fate waiting for my team at the op."

Oracles and Sages like Cian were humans questing to become Fates. Oracles not only had the visions of legend, but they were also accomplished assassins. Sages were cunning thieves driven by their addiction to information that eventually turned them into living supercomputers. Like demigods, both underwent grueling trials that prepared them for ascension, assuming they passed. Cian was just starting his trials. The kid was so young. Why would Desire want him? To cripple Resen was the only logical answer.

Ashtad was one of the other architects of Resen. With Cian out of the picture, it was on Ashtad to figure out how to prevent further fraying of the netting keeping the Devourers at bay. It also made him another target for Desire's heralds, thus, Bix kept her darkness loosely looped around him. The other heralds had managed to snatch Cian and Feng from her gates. Snatching Ashtad from her extended person? She double-dog dared Desire to try.

"Okay, I've found the scripts Cian was running when he was taken." Ashtad cocked his head. Glowered. Typed faster. Widened his eyes. Chuckled. "That kid…"

Bix waited with bated breath for him to finish his train of thought.

"He's querying the Fates' weave, trying to bypass the Fates themselves in his search for Feng." Ashtad reached through the gate to his bunker again, stretching with a wince to grab a piece of tech that wasn't from the Mids. "His code is missing parameters to direct the Other World…"

Again, Bix waited while genius labored in half-uttered revelations. Ashtad was Cian's mentor in all things tech. Cian might have been on the road to becoming a supercomputer, but Ashtad had way more experience dealing with the Other World magic from which Fates drew their power.

"Can you tell if the kid is still alive?" she dared to ask into the tense silence, unable to hold back the burning question.

"Alive?" Ashtad flinched and tore his attention from his work. "Apologies, I was unaware that was a question. Yes. Both he and Feng are alive. That is a very clear message from the ley lines, and it's why the lines are spidering. They know their creations live, but they can't locate them."

That fit with Samael's assertion. The question then became for how long would Desire keep them alive? If his goal was to get Bix to kill him, murdering her irreplaceable loved ones would certainly motivate her.

"Bix." Ashtad tapped her darkness with his foot. "The kid wasn't asking *where* Feng was. He was asking *when*."

"*When?*" Bix's heart stopped. She wished that news lessened the knot of dread growing ever larger, but it didn't. "Searching the past will take too long, and searching the future is nearly impossible because of infinite timelines."

Time. Godsdamn it all, why did it have to be a question of time? Even if Desire kept her friends alive by keeping them in the Mids, taking them out of the moment could prove fatal. Cian and Feng were mortal. Aging ahead or in reverse was an issue unless precautions were taken. How long did she have before Desire started sending her the corpses of her friends?

When it came to her brother, time was not Bix's friend. Desire was the youngest son aligned to their father, the Cosmos. That side of the family were entities of order, of exclusion, of quantification, and of process. Time was a fundamental method of instilling order. Desire had the upper hand there. Sure, as equal parts Chaos and Cosmos, Bix could access the timelines of the present and past, but not the future. The future required creation. A skill Desire possessed and she didn't. Worse, if she, personally, traveled back in time, her chaotic half would erase the present.

"The Fates' weave is trying to answer Cian's query, but it's running into numerous issues." Ashtad plugged in another piece of tech and sat up straighter, his gaze riveted to his screen. "What can you tell me about the abductors that'll help refine the search parameters?"

"That Resen is programmed not to track them?" She closed one eye and braced for the rebuke.

He looked at her with his face blank before his eyes rolled and his lashes slowly flitted shut. He sighed and dropped his chin to his chest. "We excluded titans and above from the identifications to prevent Resen from burning itself out. Are you telling me that class is what we're up against?"

His words faded as the floor rippled. Bix's darkness snatched Ashtad out of his chair and held him aloft as leafy fingers stretched through the portal followed by blossoms of eyes as the herald breached the room.

Electricity reverberated through her shadows and tech flew into the bunker, landing with a clatter barely audible over the crackling of Ashtad's elemental defenses.

"Seal the bunker," Ashtad yelled, firing at the ceiling as leaves belonging to a second herald sprouted around fluorescent lights.

A passing thought closed the gate to the bunker a breath before a third herald pressed through dimensions to scrabble across the tiled floors on pointed taproot feet.

"You can't have him," Bix said to the heralds as she snugged Ashtad's back against her own, swallowing all but his hands and head in protective darkness.

The herald advancing from the wall paused, blossomed eyes focusing on Bix. Stout branched arms sprayed a nest of vines that tangled with the vines of the heralds rising from the floor and descending from the ceiling.

"Not this time, not this friend," Bix hissed. Her innate starlight brightened and twined with her darkness, forming a barrier of pure cosmic balance.

In that moment, she felt it, the skip in the timeline. A hiccup of seconds. The sudden absence of Ashtad from her darkness. The sudden absence of the heralds from the conference room.

He'd done it. Desire. He'd stolen Ashtad right from her arms. *How?* How the hell…?

Seething, she contained her darkness and bid her starlight to illuminate the timeline of the Mids. There. In the recent past and quickly fading shimmered a tangle of possible futures with the bright line of the actual past looped through it. She'd been cleaning up her siblings' messes long enough to know that futures didn't tangle, they branched…unless someone deliberately monkeyed with them.

Someone named Desire.

Her brother had planted a trap in the timeline of the Mids, a knot in the flow of the future. The present had raced right up to that moment of the perfect snare. An ambush not of location, but of timing. Bix hadn't seen it coming. Couldn't.

She stepped off the timeline and to the edge of the building. Her furious keen shattered windows and brought researchers racing from their suites. In the distance, green threads of the Fates' weave peeled away from the stream of Resen's foundational elements. Questing. Just like the blues and purples of the ley lines.

She was going to kill her brother, for real, but first, she needed someone to assuage the foundational elements before their hysteria weakened the barrier that prevented the bulk of the Devourer army from storming the collective.

Godsdamned emotional superentities.

CHAPTER 4

Colossal waves arched to foaming whitecaps that delivered howling Berserkers to the heaving decks of wooden galleons. The ships had been commandeered by Devourer troops who were still in the throes of shifting from their diminutive Klabautermann disguises into towering gray warriors with pewter horns and long black hair. Salt crystalized on the anti-gods' gleaming bronze uniforms as high-salinity swells washed the corpses of the sailors who'd been fooled by the shapeshifters overboard into the angry ocean. Brigantines under full sail aided by oars gleaming with green magic cut through the storm surges to surround the Devourers' galleons. Neon blue from the enraged Berserkers' eyes uplit the sails, adding to the eerie glow of the battle.

Blasts of toxic gray magic flew like cannonballs into the smaller ships while Berserkers boarded enemy vessels. Overhead, nimbi of blues, purples, and greens formed as the foundational elements of Resen responded to the summons of seven feet of big, blond, infuriated Berserker landing with a solid thud at the base of the mizzenmast of the centermost galleon. Five dark green circles spawned amid the nimbi, establishing the five points of a pentagram.

With a roar louder than the din of the ocean, Tobek,

commander of the Berserkers, raised his silver arm and pointed his broadsword at the sky. The blade shone with pristine white light so painfully bright in its awakened state that Devourers' eyes bled, causing the anti-gods to stumble away from its intensity. A song built in the heavens among the nimbi and was harmonized by the sword. At the klaxon climax, the foundational elements shot a beam of undiluted magics that connected to the sword. The engravings in Tobek's prosthesis flared pale silver, then bronze before deepening to hunter green and rotating, dancing as light flowed from sky to sword, to arm, to shoulder, to Tobek's full body. His long braids ignited, flaming green. From Tobek's entirety, arrows of dark green magic fired toward every Berserker on every vessel, creating a net of magics born of the Mids and many Other Worlds. The net hummed, the green deepened in hue, and the glowing blue eyes of the Berserkers upped their wattage.

Every Devourer caught within the net exploded. Great tarry black fountains of mortal divinity. *Pop, pop, pop.* The skin of the Berserkers blistered from the spatter, but the men roared with glorious victory.

On the threshold of a gate, outside the perimeter of the skirmish, Bix cheered. Her heart thundered. Her cheeks burned. Her stomach flip-flopped. Few sights were more intoxicating than her consort in the peak of battle. Good godsdamn, that man made death look…dirty.

Tobek lowered his sword, and its light faded to the dull sheen of tempered steel. The netting connecting the Berserkers winked out of existence. Tobek himself, for once, remained upright and uncharred. Considering his track record with potent magic had earned him the nickname Colonel Crispy, being whole and hale was quite the accomplishment.

The ocean calmed and the storm abated. The visible presence of the foundational elements dissipated, leaving a sunny sky to shine on the damaged vessels. Psychopomps arrived by the dozens to whisk away the gossamer souls of the dead sailors and deliver them to hungry gods fighting on other Worlds. Beneath the water, large purple dragons of various hues dove under the ships and circled the fleet, gathering the empty bodies of sailors and collecting the black blood of the Devourers in the center of a whirlpool.

Bix unmade the energies of the Devourers' viscera, erasing their taint from the World. Abiding by her siblings' rules of engagement, she hadn't lifted a finger in the battle. Cleanup, however, should offend no one's sense of fair play.

A cluster of small dark green swirls wreathed her head and whispered with Tobek's unmistakable gravelly rasp, "Enjoy the show?"

"I'm not one to ever complain about your performance," she purred. "Not in a few thousand years, at least."

His laughter could be heard from the ship without the help of magic. He raised his silver arm and motioned for her to join him on the deck of the galleon as Berserkers went about the business of clearing the galleons from fore to aft and all decks, looking for any survivors be they friend or foe.

"To what do I owe the pleasure of your company, sweetheart?" Tobek's smile reached his eyes and crinkled the corners.

"It's the foundational elements. They're..." She sighed, searching for the right words.

"Distraught? Throwing tantrums? Giving every dragon queen and archangel an earful? Yes, I'm aware." He sheathed his sword in a scabbard of dense ice protruding from his back. Tobek had been evolving for epochs from a demigod into a new class of Other that was yet to be determined or defined. His continuous development had recently provided him with a base state of ice to which he reverted when grievously injured. The unusual scabbard was as much to protect his men from the gruesome consequences of touching his titan-forged blade as it was to ensure the sword stayed with him even if he reverted to his base state.

"Any chance you can calm them down? The foundational elements? Because their distress is weakening the defensive barrier."

"I love that the inner workings of Mids magic continues to befuddle you." He thumped the end of her nose with a silver finger. "So ancient, so wise, but still there are things you've yet to learn. It makes me worry less about boredom in the endless future."

"Yes, I'm an old fart. No, you will never know everything, no matter how long you live." She pointed at the sky. "You've a knack for managing up. Care to make that literal?"

"Part of what you just witnessed was my invitation to the elements to blow off steam." He tucked a lock of hair behind her ear. "They obliged, but they will not be assuaged until Feng, young Ba'al, and the kid are returned to their protection. Now, I'm hoping you can tell me what it is the entire Resen Immigration and Defense Division has failed to identify and correct."

Tobek was the head of the newly formed RIDD. The Berserkers were the boots on the ground, while the staffers at the data centers ran the gamut of Chwedlonol races with a heavy mix of humans. Even more humans had been relocated to communities surrounding the data centers because humans grounded magic, thus were necessary to preventing the Worlds on which the data centers were located from being ripped apart by the direct feed of that much potent magic. Not only did Tobek have to keep Resen up and running, but also he had to ensure the Devourers were eliminated from the Mids. Her big blond bear had a lot on his plate.

"It's Desire," she confessed. Tobek was one of the few who knew of her family and her siblings. There wasn't much she'd hidden from him over the epochs they'd been together. "I think he took them out of the flow of time. I don't know to when. Until I do, I can't fetch them back."

"Your brother is behind this?" Tobek ran his natural hand over his face and exhaled loudly. "Sweetheart, if it's a matter of when, *you* can't be the one to fetch them back. You'll destroy time in the process."

"Yeah, well, I don't even know if he's holding them in the

same place at the same point in time, or if he's stashed them at separate points. Past. Future. Who knows?" She laid her hand against his soggy uniform jacket. "He's sent his heralds to weaken Resen by taking the architects and the welfare gauge, which means he's probably coming for you next, Mister Direct Conduit."

"Desire can take me any time he wants. He doesn't need his heralds for that." He moved her hand to cover his Eternal Knot hidden beneath layers of ink on his pectoral. "Any of your siblings can. That was part of the price of them binding me so that I could continue my evolution to becoming something closer to your peer."

"Stop being so nonchalant," she griped. "What will the foundational elements do if you're taken too? Do you think they'll actually hold the barrier? Or are the Mids going to be screwed? Am I going to have to erase time again to save you and our home?"

She'd done it before. More than a dozen rewinds, in fact. Each time the Mids had fallen to the Devourers, she'd erased time and reset the present far enough in the past for the denizens of the Mids to have a fighting chance at survival. This timeline was the first in which the Mids had managed to stand up a real defense against Desire's pet army. The tricky thing about erasing time was that the present could never be recreated in perfection. Her mother, the Chaos, ensured things always changed. For better or worse wasn't the consideration, just different. In other timelines, there hadn't been an Ashtad or a Cian. For those who existed across timelines, her relationships with them were notably altered, including the Berserkers and Tobek. She really, really, really didn't want to reset this timeline. Despite all the downs and the ups, her relationships with everyone in this present were better, stronger, and more in-depth than in other versions. Relationships were what mattered to her and her extremely long life.

"All right, let's think about this for a moment, okay?" Tobek pulled her close. "If it's a matter of when, me being taken is a good thing."

"Are you nuts? No. Not a good thing. It'd be a horrible thing."

She shoved against his chest, but he merely snuggled her closer until his clothes audibly squished along her front. Ha, ha, ha. So not funny.

"If they take me, I can communicate with the ley lines or the Fates' weave be it pre- or post-Resen to get a message to you."

"It wouldn't be a message to *me* since I can't exist inside the collective without you. I can only watch from afar." She tugged his beard, possibly a little harder than necessary. "I know it's been a while since we made the power-syphoning arrangement, but do try to remember I'm a First Child. The energy I naturally exude is too much for the Mids to handle. I'll dissolve Worlds if I get too close. I need my living cosmic sponge to sop up my excesses in order for me to live in my own home."

Tobek stopped breathing for five heartbeats.

"What?" She broke his hold and scanned the area for an influx of Desire's magic. "Do you see them? His heralds?"

"His goal in all this is to die, right? Still?" Tobek knocked away the ashes of the sleeve that once covered his silver arm, back before the simple fabric had been incinerated by puissant magic.

"According to his twin, yes. That's why the Devourers are here. To bully me into killing both Tempest and Desire." She'd already extended the offer to her brother, via his twin, to put them out of her misery. It was a bluff, yes, but she wanted him to face her. In person. He had yet to show. If he was so desperate, why was he dawdling?

"Let's assume your brother knows that you are not only morally resistant to ending him, but also that you *can't* do it yet because you don't have all your magics." He massaged his jaw. "If you were fully yourself again, would anything about Resen change? Anything that he or his troops would be able to discern? Something that would signal to him that you are truly ready for parley?"

"Uh, no? Resen is programmed to ignore me."

"Then why go after Resen at all? Could it be less about the defense system and more about the three mortals for whom you care deeply?" Tobek stared into the distance, surveying his men at work. "Strategically, if he's trying to motivate you, as his primary aspect would dictate, why bother to keep all of them alive? Why not kill one and deliver the corpse to you? It's a far more effective tactic."

"I know. I've been asking myself how long they have before he dumps their bodies at my feet," she whispered, and her voice broke. "I don't understand his game."

The air around them rippled, and four desert rose heralds emerged from the spaces between time. Their taproot feet clicked along the planks of the ship as the heralds surrounded Tobek and her. Piercing whistles went up from every vessel as Berserkers one and all took note of the new threat to their commander.

Tobek lifted a staying hand. He made no move on his sword. Instead, he hooked a metal finger under Bix's chin and tipped her head up to plant a memorable kiss. When he pulled back, his eyes held only the faint glow of banked passion, not rage.

"Four heralds to take me. None are necessary. It's relevant. Figure out the answer to counter his next move. I love you."

Another hiccup in time and he was gone. The heralds too.

Berserkers shouted questions, but Bix couldn't linger long enough to respond. Waves of immense power rolled off her, dissolving the planks beneath her feet, the looming mizzenmast, the decks below, and more as it flowed outward and overboard.

She reached for a mote of darkness beyond the Mids as gates delivered the Berserkers on the vanishing galleon to safe haven.

If Desire wasn't trying to tank Resen, but was, instead, after her friends, then her *best* friend was either gone or about to be.

CHAPTER 5

The convergence of labyrinthine passages connecting hundreds of Under Worlds throbbed until it hummed, causing the feral and forgotten of the pantheons to pause their brutal scrabbling for survival. The corallic structure of the massive intersection turned the hum into a song. It took a few haunting strains before Bix's almost-whole mind recognized the tune as an honorific greeting. Funny, she hadn't noticed it before. Perhaps it hadn't sung during her earlier visits because she'd been a feeble amnesiac with a fraction of the power she exuded now. Perhaps the convergence hadn't recognized her at her less than best, or perhaps it'd feared exposing her to her enemies. Whatever its reason for silence back then, its clear welcome took a smidge off the edge of her angry panic clawing for an outlet. Fortunately, the convergence had a blessed resilience to her unfiltered presence.

Unlike the Mids, everything in the Under Worlds was built from souls that'd been hollowed out by gods. Mortal experiences were the sustenance of deities, thus making souls, which contained said experiences, the currency of the divine. The Under Worlds functioned as treasuries for the pantheons. The gods presiding over the Under Worlds wielded the political influence of the wealthiest financiers. Curtailing their ambition, however, was their unenviable duty of being the ostiaries for titans. The Under Worlds had been constructed as the courtyards to the domains of titans. The gods of the Under Worlds had to appease the titans to ensure the big, big guys didn't run amok. While titans weren't anywhere close to being as powerful as First Children, their domains were designed to house exceptionally potent magics. Thus, Bix could move about freely here with a modicum of polite concern for what she touched and where she lingered.

She stayed in the convergence long enough to verify her best friend hadn't taken a wild hair to inhabit a reawakened, yet clueless god just for shits and giggles. A body thief of unmatched caliber, her best friend, Drew the draugr preferred to occupy the bodies of the dead, could—with much kvetching—occupy the living, and would gleefully test-drive a deity, in part to play with divine powers, but mostly to be the means of their humiliation. Drew had a vicious petty streak, but was unfailingly and fiercely loyal. The Under Worlds were the only place Drew could be independently corporeal, so Bix searched for her bestie along the path from the convergence to the Greek Under World, where she'd delivered Drew for necessary R & R after shit had gone very wrong on the last mission.

Souls that had somehow escaped their respective treasuries before being drained flitted from nooks and crevasses, swirling around her, desperate for her attention. She batted them away like the pests they were. If the soul wasn't stitched into a mortal body, thus becoming a living being, she had no use for them. She fed on gods and anti-gods, not their kibble.

The thundering of an approaching stampede shook the dimly lit passage. Advancing yapping and howling caused the unmoored souls to flee. Bix deployed a gate from throat to feet to keep from being bowled over as a pack of massive two-headed and tri-headed hounds intercepted her. Cold noses sniffed her head. Many tongues licked exposed skin, providing an abundance of giggle-inducing wet willies. Tails wagged hard enough to knock chunks out of the walls. Laughing, she uncurled tentacles of darkness from her spine that reached through the gates to pet each eager head and to nudge aside the hounds' thick, muscular bodies to clear a path. In the Under Worlds, the beasts tended to be as large, if not larger, than the gods.

"Hi, hi, hi, yes, I missed you too," she cooed. "Somebody didn't close the door to the Greek Under World all the way, did they? No. They didn't. No. No, they didn't. You scamps stay out of the Norse Under World, eh? I don't want to get blamed for another puppy boom just because you're too friendly with Hel's hounds."

"'Twas I who let the dogs out," drawled a shiveringly sinister voice from the shadows cast by the towering Doric pillars flanking massive ivory doors with gruesome reliefs of torments awaiting the unworthy on the other side.

"And now I have an earworm. Thanks for that, Phobos." Bix used her darkness to herd the hounds into the Greek Under World, pausing for a moment to glower at the Greek god of fear, who regarded her insouciantly as he pushed off the column and motioned her ahead of him.

Phobos was always so dapper in his three-piece bespoke suits and Chelsea boots. His dark hair lay in finger-raked layers swept back from his brooding aristocratic features. For a time now, he'd been her provider of food, clothing, intel, guidance, sanity checks, and whatever else she needed. He didn't have a choice in the matter since they'd both inadvertently charged into a codependent existence. As the greater power, and at the time not having a clue about said powers, she'd accidentally tethered him to her. However, in exchange for being her caretaker, he engaged in myriad novel experiences not afforded most gods, which were beyond priceless to immortals. Because of his time in service to her, he now possessed knowledge that eluded greater gods, an asset for any spymaster, but doubly so for him in this time of war.

"It was your arrival in the Under Worlds that set those hyper hounds to braying and pawing at the door. Such a ruckus is hardly productive to the leadership conference being held within."

Bix took the implied caution in stride. She considered a handful of Under World gods her allies. One or two she'd call friend. The bulk, however, she'd consume without a lick of remorse. They didn't much like her either.

"I'll do my best to steer clear. I'm here for Drew anyway." Bix tucked her darkness within her as the hounds bounded deeper into the vast Greek Under World.

That might prove problematic, Phobos said into her mind, using the telepathy common among gods. The reason for the mode switch became apparent as they crossed to a flatland expanse resembling formal Grecian gardens replete with columns wrapped in replicas of bioluminescent ivy that cast soft blues and greens to backlight lofted wrought iron braziers dancing with crimson and gold Under Worldly fire. Shrubs reminiscent of oregano and blooming tamarisk arranged in arabesque beds framed fountains bubbling with what passed for water. Stately simulations of olive groves waved from the distant sloping backdrop. At the heart, assorted citrus trees provided bold accents and refreshing fragrances that almost matched the real things from the Mid Worlds.

When Bix had lived here as a frightened and violent amnesiac, these gardens had been meticulously tended by minions forming souls into flowers and coaxing them into colors that suited Hades's whimsy. She'd watched the minions from afar, enthralled by their artistry. Today, however, those groundskeepers had been replaced by waitstaff catering to the two dozen Under World gods sitting around a massive round stone table.

The contrasts in attire made for an interesting study. Which gods kept themselves attuned to the modernity of multiple collectives? Which eschewed styles defined by anyone other than themselves? Which remained stuck in the fashions of their heyday? Hades had traded his usual loose drawstring pants and open-knit sweater for a tailored velvet sport coat and open-collar button-down in rich peacock hues. His shoulder-length dark locks had a windblown look about them. He stood from the table and granted her an indulgent smile that still carried all the gentle affection he'd shown her as her tutor and guide back when she'd barely known how to walk, much less feed herself.

Her reawakening could've taken such a disastrous path if not for Hades's intervention. She would always hold a deep well of gratitude and limitless respect for him.

"Mighty Chimera, welcome. To what do we owe the honor?" Hades bowed from the shoulders as his pack of exuberant hounds settled around the garden, steering clear of shaggier single-headed hounds and a few small hairless dogs. A veritable doggy daycare was happening at this conference of bigwigs. A few other male gods took the hint and also stood to greet her.

"My apologies, Hades, for interrupting your meeting. I was merely passing through to see a friend." Bix gestured to the plateau of a nearby hill hosting a plain hut and simple bench. It'd been her home throughout her tenure here and had since been a refuge to those she cherished who were in desperate need of the kind of help that she trusted only Hades to provide.

"If it is the draugr, I'm afraid it's been called into service." Hades stared pointedly at the white-haired goddess seated across from him.

The goddess's cheek braced upon her fist and her pale eyes narrowed on Bix. Her long, leather-clad legs dangled over one armrest. Her tall, spiked boots rested on the back of a large, shaggy, red-eyed hound, one of a dozen similar dogs sprawled around the garden.

Hel. Goddess of the Norse Under World and current head of the whole pantheon. While Hades had trained Bix to be a participant in society, Hel had drop-kicked her into the whirlwind of rediscovering all Bix really was. Hel merited respect for many reasons, but liking the goddess? Totally different story.

"Hel, where is Drew?" Bix asked, trying her best not to sound like a condescending bitch. The game was time, and Bix had none to waste on perceived slights. Plus, putting Hel on the defensive would blow up in everyone's faces. Hel was not the sort with whom one trifled.

The hound under Hel's boot lifted its head and whimpered.

"Unavailable for playtime, Chimera," Hel drawled, pressing a heel into the spine of the hound at her feet.

"I'm afraid neither of us gets to decide that today." Bix attempted a placating smile.

Hel's chuckle was low, long, and not amused. The goddess sat up and planted her feet on the ground with a singular loud clack. More than one god at the table shifted nervously in their seat as Hel slowly stood.

"I think you've forgotten I'm the one who created Anudrengr." Hel sauntered to Bix. The heavy chain hooked to her belt didn't clink or clatter like a regular metal. No, it echoed with tragic moans as it scraped along the seemingly stone patio. The hound at the end of the chain whimpered again. Of all Hel's hounds, it was the only one tethered. "Moreover, I think you've forgotten what sort of weapon the draugr is, particularly against the Devourers."

Hel towered over Bix, her intimidating height a result of being the daughter of a chaos god and a giantess. However, the last time Hel had pressed herself up in Bix's business, Bix hadn't backed down. That'd been before Bix had remembered the only entities more powerful than Bix herself were her parents. Hel, like every god, was merely a sentient storage container. It amused Bix to note the slight twitching of Hel's muscles caused by being too close to Bix's unfiltered presence. The goddess would be damned if she flinched. Hel's pride and position in her pantheon wouldn't allow it.

Read the room, Chimera, Phobos warned into Bix's mind as he blended into the shadows stretching from the garden's pillars. *Tensions were extremely high before you arrived. A set-to between you and Hel will damage the defense accords Hades is trying to negotiate among the leadership of the Under Worlds.*

Defense of the Under Worlds? From…the Devourers stymied outside Resen, presumably. Fortunately, Bix's pride wasn't rooted in scaring others. She actually had to work hard not to terrorize lesser beings. Instead, she let thin threads of darkness seep from the vee of her dress to skim over Hel's black leather vest, under the fall of Hel's long white hair, and around the shells of the goddess's ears so only Hel could hear what she had to say.

"I think you've forgotten the frightened child demigoddess who cried out to the vast starry night for help defeating the old gods determined to kill her and her brothers." Bix smirked. "I think you've forgotten the night answered and told you how to make that very special draugr."

Hel inhaled sharply and triumph gleamed in her gaze. "You remember. Finally."

"Thank you for sending Drew to look after me while I was broken," Bix said aloud, this time for the sake of their audience. "However, there is a great possibility you and I are no longer the only ones with a keen interest in our mutual friend."

"This third party motivates you to pay us a visit while war rages in your precious Mids? That is concerning." Hel introduced some space between them, then snapped her fingers. The shackled hound leapt over the table and a seated god to land in the gap between Bix and Hel.

"Bixie, babe," the hound breathed, red eyes staring up at Bix balefully. "Gurl, I've missed your crazy."

"Aw, Drew. I wish this was a reunion-party visit." Bix scratched Drew behind his floppy ear. "They've taken Cian, Ashtad, Feng, and Tobek. There's a strong chance you're next."

"They who?" Hel demanded.

"The whole gang?" Drew growled at the same time, curling a hairy lip. "Including my widdle herb nerd? Gimme a target, Bixie, and I will make them tear themselves apart."

"No carnage, Drew." Bix shook her head, ignoring the way Hel jerked Drew's chain. Drew's senses were muted inside a body, so the draugr didn't feel the pain of the choke collar tightening around his neck. As for the humiliation of being a dog on a leash? Drew had occupied far less noble creatures in far more embarrassing situations. This was performance art by both Hel and Drew for the benefit of the other Under World gods at the table. Bix didn't intend to ruin their act. "Your survival will depend on understanding them. But you *cannot* take them for a ride. You will be snuffed out."

"Chimera, Anudrengr's time is already spoken for. The draugr will be supporting a corps of Valkyries…" Hel didn't finish as the air around the garden rippled.

Six desert rose heralds crossed into the Greek Under World.

"Identify yourselves," a god shouted as the other deities at the table bolted up from their seats.

The heralds did not deign to answer. They merely advanced on the patio.

"Who are you? Who sent you?" barked another god, brimming with violence.

Too many gods were too quick to attack Desire's heralds. Weapons flew at the heralds, only to clatter to the ground, unable to pierce the greater entities.

Six heralds? One had come for Feng. Two for Cian. Three for Ashtad. Four for Tobek. Why skip to six? Who had been number five? Later. Ponder that later. For now, Bix had to convince the gods not to yield to their base natures.

"Gods, stand down," Bix shouted. "Do not attack them."

The gods with the greatest egos didn't heed her. They charged bodily at the heralds, only to vanish midflight in flares of copper magic. The gods with more sense than violence departed of their own accord. Hades settled in his chair, joining the few who were smart enough not to engage the enemy. Hel split her focus between the heralds and her hounds standing with spines bristling, teeth bared, and lungs vibrating with their growls. To their credit, the hounds didn't launch. They awaited their mistress's signal.

All but one hound, that was, who ambled to the nearest herald and sat before it.

"You want a piece of me?" Drew said to the herald. "I'll go without a fight if you take me to the young Sage."

The herald blinked its many floral eyes and laid a leafy finger against Drew's collar. The entire length of chain vanished in a curling copper wisp. Hel made no move to fetch her creation. The goddess simply considered the herald. Frigid interest tipped her head and thinned her lips. If it weren't for the ice spreading around her feet, one might think Hel was unperturbed.

"Chimera!" Phobos shouted aloud as sounds of a scuffle caused Bix to pivot sharply. Bundled in thorny vines, Phobos struggled against the herald dragging the god of fear out of the shadows.

"Phobos, yield to it," she cried, confusion escalating her rage and causing her form to phase between corporeal and native.

Time skipped.

Phobos, Drew, and the heralds were gone, leaving a furious Bix to face angry gods.

CHAPTER 6

Breathe. Slow counts of four in and three out. Breathe. Bix forced herself to exert control over the only thing she could control. Herself. She couldn't control Desire. She couldn't control his heralds. She could only control her reactions to her brother's instigations. Breathe. Think. Think clearly and beyond the influence of her foul temper. Think.

Six. The number was relevant.

Six friends taken. One herald to take Feng. Two for Cian. Three for Ashtad. Four for Tobek. Six to take Phobos and Drew together? No, better to think of it as five for Drew and six for Phobos. They'd been taken at the same time because they were in the same place at the same moment.

Six of her nearest and dearest.

Damn it. She should've anticipated six abductions. Six was Desire's sacred number. The heralds had always intended to take six hostages. Tobek had been right. This wasn't about Resen. This was about those closest to her. Figuratively and literally. The heralds had waited until her loved ones were with her to take them. Desire wanted her to witness their abductions.

Why? For what purpose? To what end? He couldn't possibly anger her more than he already had. If he returned one of them dead, she'd back up time until her friend lived again. Desire *had* to know that. He'd have to redo all his time traps, but he'd be at a disadvantage because she'd know to circumvent them…somehow. The two of them could play with a time loop endlessly, so, again, what was his reason for kidnapping her friends? What did he want with them and how did he want her to react?

If he wanted to die so badly, why didn't he show the hell up in person?

She was missing something critical in the details about her family and in the details about this prolonged skirmish with the youngest twins. Memories were relational, not linear, so what she needed, she straight up didn't have rolling around her brain. It was in the final segment held by Chimalma.

"Chimera, not to overstep our bounds, but perhaps you could explain what just happened?"

The gently posed question pulled Bix from her reverie. She knew the tone. Hades. It was his Handling a Hot Mess tone. He'd used it on her often enough when he'd been teaching her the basics of survival. She wasn't that frightened puerile immortal anymore, but she was scared. For her friends. However, she *did* owe Hades the courtesy of some sort of explanation, but there was only so much she was willing to share about her family, her youngest siblings being behind the attack on the Mids, and Desire's heralds' total disregard of boundaries.

Solidifying her form, she smoothed her skirt and blinked twice at the change in the pattern of her shoes. Gone were the griffins and wyverns, and in their place, assorted demonic equine heads winked. Some held one finger pressed to slightly puckered lips, while others cupped one ear. No, not cupped, pointed. Pointed behind their ears.

Phobos. A message from her caretaker. A message from a spymaster physically tethered to her regardless of place…or time. Phobos had met her other brothers and knew how to survive an encounter with a First Child. His panic with the herald had been a ruse. Whether for the audience here or the master of the heralds was of lesser importance. What mattered was that her youngest brother had taken an emotion god, specifically the god of *fear*.

Desire had stolen a Trojan horse.

A giggle-snort escaped Bix. Oh, how positively apropos. She could summon Phobos back to her right this instant, but she didn't want to get in a tug-of-war with her brother. No, better to give the spymaster time to gather intel. Phobos was immortal. His mind and essence were protected by his bond with her. He'd live no matter what Desire inflicted upon him.

Forcing a smile, Bix lifted her chin and surveyed the gods remaining at Hades's round table. She recognized each of them. Three had helped her on her path of rediscovery. Two she remembered fondly from days of yore. All represented different pantheons, different castes, and different relationships with the Mid Worlds and those inhabitants. Four of the five were actual gods. One was a titan, or, rather, a piece of a titan.

Ereshkigal, ruler of the Mesopotamian Under World, had existed before most deities who inhabited this sector of space, and had long defied categorization by even her own pantheon. She kept the bulk of herself in the lower realms of Irkalla, which masked the wealth of her magics. The extension of Ereshkigal seated at Hades's table, looking every bit a winsome woman of purest black from hair to hem, was more akin to one of Bix's shadowy tentacles functioning as an autonomous appendage. An adept of the Chaos, thus enmeshed with the eternal darkness, Ereshkigal had helped Bix rediscover her connections to her mother. The titaness and her consort had also been the first to recognize and name the Devourers as the enemy infiltrating the Mids while the Consortium had been gleefully ignoring the possibility of a problem.

Bix cast a thread of pure night to slither along the fine gaps in the patio stones as she approached the table. The titaness sent her own thread of night to greet Bix's and allowed joy to flow through their connection for seven beats before retreating.

"While the Consortium and mortals of the Mids have been fighting the invasion of the Devourers, I have reached out to those who sent the Devourers to the Mids." Bix inclined her head as Hades gestured to an open seat beside him. "What you just witnessed was part of their response."

"Those overgrown weeds were messengers from the Devourers' command element?" Hel asked, disbelief heavy in her tone. "Never in all my previous encounters with the old foes have I met the like."

"Then you weren't dealing with the very top of their command chain," Bix said, shrugging.

"You're trying to get their leadership to call off the Devourers?" The goddess Setesuyara of the Balinese Under World tapped her long spiral nails on the table. Precious gems gleamed within the twists and hissed like an army of serpents with each strike upon the table. "How soon? We need to know how soon. The titans are awakening, and too many of them with bloodlust."

"The titans?" Bix hesitated a beat with her butt hovering over the seat, deliberately not looking at Ereshkigal. "Was that the reason for the meeting of the Under World gods? The titans?"

"Though the Devourers are being rebuffed by Resen, their reinforcements are still arriving in droves," Hel explained, returning to her chair. "Since they occupy the space around the Mids, they are encroaching on the borders of the Unders and Uppers."

"This is despite the coordinated efforts of the pantheons to keep the Devourers away from those collectives?" Bix asked. She'd recently witnessed the gods of the Uppers and Unders going on the offensive against the Devourers once the anti-gods had lost their hiding place.

"Reinforcements arrive faster than we can kill the ones already here." Hades sighed. "Their numbers continue at net positive growth."

"We can feel their presence intensifying from deep within our respective Under Worlds. Their toxicity builds like a thick miasma and seeps into domains unseen by the naked eye, thus alerting and annoying the titans." Mictecacíhuatl, goddess of the Nahua Under World, gripped the arms of her chair until her knuckles whitened, causing the intricate paintings covering her hands to leap in stark contrast.

Fear of the titans rising explained how Hades had been able to gather so many fractious gods of the Under Worlds for a meeting. Ereshkigal didn't leave Irkalla unless there were extenuating circumstances. Same for Mictecacíhuatl. The titan that Mictecacíhuatl and her husband guarded required constant surveillance. It had quite the bone to pick with just about everyone within its awareness, including Bix. The sentiment was common among that group of superentities. Titans, on the whole, were extremely bitter about being the unwanted and discarded toys of the First Children. Bix understood their plight as well as their greater purpose, which was why she'd never ended them en masse despite their destructive proclivities. Many were serving rehabilitative sentences to which *she'd* condemned them, sentences that required them to stay far away from the fragile collectives. No bulls in china shops. If the Devourers were baiting the titans to break out of rehab, then the situation was about to go from horrible to catastrophic.

"Even the titans who aren't bent on mass destruction still pose more danger to the collectives than the endless army of Devourers." Setesuyara stopped drumming her nails and laid her hands flat on the table as she sat forward. "So, forgive my impertinence, mighty Chimera, but to negotiate with the titans for whom we are responsible, we need to assure them the old foes are truly departing. They will know if we're lying."

"And if they're not leaving now, then *when*," Hel added.

Everyone at the table stared at Bix expectantly, and the longer she took to answer, the higher tensions rose.

"That's, uh, yet to be determined," Bix hedged.

Mictecacíhuatl appeared completely flummoxed. "Why? You're the Chimera. Why don't the Devourers' commanders yield to your will?"

Bix didn't immediately answer. There were too many ears in the Greek Under World. Again, confirming the existence of First

Children to gods was akin to inviting the lesser entities to their doom. They were power hungry by nature, and her siblings didn't have the same patience for them that she did. Heck, her eldest brother played with deities the way a rambunctious kid played with action figures, dismemberment included.

"Oh, for fuck's sake," Hel cried with exasperation. "You're not yet whole, are you? What is the holdup?"

Bix's hackles rose and her darkness rippled beneath her skin. "Hel, I understand your position, but—"

"The holdup is the Mid World guardian Chimalma, the final keeper of her memories," a quiet feminine voice interjected from the cover of a flower bed. "The Chimera must husk her memory keepers to prevent their madness from worsening. However, this last keeper is pivotal in the defense of the Mid Worlds. Thus, the Chimera hesitates to reclaim what is hers."

Bix's heart stilled and her throat closed as she stood to behold a goddess with riotous red curls separating from a bed of tamarisk. With a height comparable to Hel and a body lithe like a prima ballerina, the goddess didn't remotely resemble the petite curvaceous blonde bombshell she'd once occupied. However, there was no mistaking the goddess of healing's resonance.

Mirri.

Former Norse ambassador to the Mid Worlds and Bix's ex-girlfriend, Mirri had survived brutalities that had left her in a coma with a shattered mind. Bix had stolen her from Hel's harsh care and hidden her away here in the Greek Under World with Hades to nurse her back to health.

On the one hand, Bix was thrilled to see how far Mirri had come in her recovery. On the other hand, Bix's feelings for Mirri were…complicated. When they'd dated, Bix hadn't had a clue about her own past, about Tobek, or about being the Chimera. Mirri had never let on either. Bix wasn't certain Mirri had known Bix was the Chimera, but, then again, Bix wasn't certain Mirri hadn't known. Then there was the not-insignificant fact that Bix was the reason Mirri had been horrifically assaulted, so…baggage. They had some.

"Drew told me everything," Mirri said by way of explanation as bright red spread across her cheeks and down her neck. She fiddled with the pleats of her long green dress, refusing to look Bix, or anyone, in the eye. The younger goddess kept two flower beds between her and the outer ring of sleeping hounds. "We have a wager over whether you'll spare Chimalma."

"A wager over whether I'm ruthless or merely self-absorbed?" Bix sighed, utterly unsurprised that Drew had blabbed. Bix had expected as much. Indeed, she'd planned for it. She'd hoped that Drew being a friendly presence Mirri would recognize and Drew sharing stories about folks Mirri knew would aid both their recoveries. Drew needed interpersonal connections as much as Mirri needed a lifeline to good times. Mirri being coherent was the unanticipated part.

"Chimalma the Shield Hand being husked is a problem. She and her forces are working in tandem with other war gods to wipe out Devourer troops using pincer strategies in certain theaters." Mictecacíhuatl snapped her fingers. A hologram of the Mids appeared and zoomed past the Primary Mid World to a World twice the size of the Primary and covered in dense jungles where Chimalma's troops could be seen setting up camps. "The chairman of the Consortium is relying heavily upon our pantheon, and upon Chimalma specifically."

"War in the Mids is going to be moot if the titans rise and the Chimera can't stop them," Hel reminded. "Gods get sidelined in battle all the time. The reason doesn't matter. Taking out Chimalma should be no different."

"I concur." Ereshkigal gave Bix an apologetic look. "The Chimera needs to be whole. The justification for sacrificing this Mid World guardian reaches far beyond our little sector of existence."

"I'm sorry to agree, Chimera, but you were unable to stop lesser entities from abducting your friends. It does not bode well for any of our futures should the war escalate." Setesuyara crossed her arms and grunted as though her input was the final say.

Sadly, Setesuyara was right. As it stood, Bix was probably on par with the heralds when it came to greater versus lesser entities. If she were one hundred percent herself, she would've been able to smite the heralds without effort.

"I side with the Chimera on this. Chimalma is critical to the war in the Mids. The Mids are critical to our food supply. The priority should be to protect the Mid Worlds," Mictecacíhuatl argued. "Some of you will just have to try harder to appease your titans."

"If this were just about the Mid Worlds, then we wouldn't be—" Hel started.

"All it takes is one titan loose on this side of the galaxy—" Setesuyara said louder and at the same time.

"Just because Chimalma isn't part of your pantheons, doesn't diminish—" Mictecacíhuatl shouted over her peers, which caused her hairless dogs to yap incessantly, which caused the large hounds to bark, which set the multiheaded hounds to baying.

Louder the goddesses yelled, over each other and the dogs, with increasingly vicious attacks that provoked their magics to spark and crackle around the table. Soon, words weren't enough. Actions escalated from fist pounding, to standing, to pointed fingers zapping not wholly harmless energy.

Flames from the braziers leapt and fire beasts roared, drowning out the bickering.

Everyone stopped and stared at Hades, who, throughout the confrontation, never so much as batted an eye. He quietly cleared his throat and stared at each irate goddess until she took her seat and mumbled an apology.

"Has anyone *asked* Chimalma her opinion on the matter?" He looked to Bix expectantly.

Bix shook her head.

"Perhaps you should?" Hades dangled a hand over the side of his chair to scratch one head of the ever-faithful Cerberus. "I've found asking women if and how they'd like to be involved often yields delightful success."

"Wise as ever, Hades." Bix rolled her eyes, taking the chastisement in the friendly manner it was intended. "What woman can resist, 'Excuse me, after I consume every part of you but the seed of your divinity, would you prefer to be left a husk or unmade altogether?'"

Hel snorted, and Setesuyara muttered something decidedly tawdry.

"Surely there are other options?" Mictecacíhuatl scoffed, unable to hide the concern in her voice. "Must you destroy her to regain yourself?"

"Historically, it's proven necessary." Bix was loath to speak of the process, but it was hardly classified intel. After all, Hel and Ereshkigal had helped her extract her first two memory segments from divine keepers. "However, the challenge, at the moment is that I can't stick so much as one tendril of night beyond the protective layer of a Mid World without destroying the World. Thus, I cannot pull Chimalma aside for a bit of girl talk."

"Ah, yes. The downside of becoming more fully yourself," Ereshkigal whispered sympathetically.

Bix braced for another round of censure from the other goddesses, but received only their expressions of confusion. Eh, skip it. She wasn't going to explain Tobek to anyone.

"I'll go." Mirri stepped closer to the table, but not close enough to breach the ring of hounds. A shaggy two-headed pup surged up from its resting spot and scrambled to her side, pawing at her skirt. She cupped a hand around one head and absently rubbed the pup's floppy ear. "I'll go to the Mid Worlds and ask Chimalma to join us here."

Hel snorted derisively. "You're afraid of your own shadow and have yet to venture beyond this tiny section of Hades's home. The situation calls for someone who leans toward temerity, not cowardice."

Mirri opened her mouth to argue, but Hel cut her off.

"Don't think that because I'm not here, I'm unaware of your status." Hel raked Mirri with disdain. "I'll send a few of the Valkyries. They're on rescue ops near there anyway. They can be quite convincing when necessary."

"No," Mirri blurted. "No. I was the ambassador to the Mids once. I know how to negotiate with gods from other pantheons."

"Chimalma is an army general in the throes of battle. She has no time to cater to the whimpering of a wilted flower," Hel snapped.

Mirri lifted her chin and finally looked at Hel fully. "I'm going. I'll be back shortly."

Mirri vanished in a cloud of honey-colored mist, taking the two-headed puppy with her. Hel hid a smirk in her fist and glanced at Hades. His eyes crinkled at the corners.

"She named the dog Thárros." He chuckled. "It means courage."

CHAPTER 7

For purely selfish reasons, Bix hoped Mirri was successful. Not only did she want her ex to have recovered the confidence necessary for a simple messenger mission, but also Bix wanted her own memories back. She wanted to be whole. She wanted to end the war in the Mids. She wanted to keep the titans tucked in bed. She wanted to bring her loved ones home safely. She wanted an end to this fucking game with Desire. She wanted it all, and she didn't want to pay the cost of further derailing the Consortium's battle to save its own turf.

Sadly, there were always costs.

She paced beyond the gardens of the Greek Under World, a hound of Hel and a hound of Hades at each side. A curved panel of viewing gates allowed her to keep an eye on Resen in its entirety. So far, the foundational elements had kept their questing threads within the barrier and the barrier was holding. Now and again, rogue green threads of Fate poked up, as if testing the distance to the Devourers' camps. While that feature hadn't been part of the original build specs, she wouldn't be surprised if Ashtad or Cian had made the modification. After all, knowing how far the enemy was from the front door was useful.

A second curve of viewing gates set at a greater distance

from the Mids provided a clear map of the enemy army amassing like spawning rings of Saturn, pushing ever outward toward the Uppers and the Unders. A third set of gates watched the route the Devourer reinforcements were taking through neighboring galaxies to get to the Mids. The pantheons' ambushes had negligible effect on the anti-gods' steady march.

"What is it your brother wants that he sends his heralds to take rather than to train?" Ereshkigal asked as the titaness pulled herself together from the shadows thrown by the viewing gates. "After all, heralds are meant to teach supplicants how to survive the presence of a First Child. They then shield the supplicant from the energies of the First Child during that meeting. They are not meant to be weapons."

"I wondered if you recognized them," Bix admitted. Ereshkigal had notably not spoken up during the shouting match among the other goddesses, nor had she moved to intercept the heralds.

"I was there when you came into existence, child. Desire was immediately smitten with you. He doted on you in your infancy. Everything you know about drive and tenacity, you learned at his knee." The titaness stroked Bix's hair, arranging it down her back as a mother would. "When you rebelled against your father and struck out on your own path, Desire was your loudest cheerleader. What happened between you two?"

"He is in pain," Bix murmured as a dribble of sorrow leached into the persistent burn of rage. "Beyond that, I need the final part of me to fully understand."

"If there is anything I can do, even if it is simply to listen, I am here for you." Ereshkigal took Bix's hand and squeezed.

Bix rested her head on the titaness's shoulder. "Thank you. That means a lot."

The hounds woofed and trotted to the garden as divine resonances blossomed at Hades's round table. Time flowed differently in the Under Worlds than it did in the Mids, so it didn't seem like it had taken long for Mirri and her hound to return… with Chimalma. Mirri literally glowed with triumph. The younger goddess sought everyone's gaze and partnered it with a brilliant smile. Her hound sat on her feet and thumped its tail, tongues lolling from its mouths. Alas, Mirri couldn't quite meet Bix's gaze. Mirri's regard made it as far as Bix's pendants, but not to Bix's face.

Bix didn't take offense. Regardless of the baggage they still needed to unpack, Bix was truly happy for Mirri. Completing one's first solo mission was a big deal. Bix remembered the elation of that. She was glad Mirri got to experience it too. Empathy. Bix was capable of it. Now.

"Chimalma, thank you for coming," Hades greeted. "We appreciate the delicacy of the situation you've left in the Mids."

"The Chimera calls. I answer. It's that simple." The Shield Hand's speech was slurred, not as though inebriated, but rather as if there were some sort of physical impediment. Chimalma removed her second-skin hood and face mask, revealing sagging muscles along the left side of her face that caused her eye and half her mouth to visibly droop. Her thick, dark hair had been braided and wound into two knots that sat at the edge of her forehead like horns. The wide band of olive-brown paint across her eyes had deflected the glare of fighting in the snow and sun. Small blisters from Devourer blood spatter dotted the paint band where the uniform had been unable to protect her skin, though the wounds healed fairly quickly for a Mid World guardian. "I would've answered at Citlaltépetl, Chimera, but you seemed to have more pressing issues."

"The fluidity of priorities in times of conflict," Bix dismissed as she studied the guardian for indicators of the madness of a memory keeper. The facial imperfection was odd, since gods were notoriously vain and despised physical flaws. Those who were scarred or maimed had suffered the injuries when they were demigods, thus still mortal and vulnerable. But what sort of injury would cause half of one's facial muscles to fail without leaving scars on the skin?

"In times of conflict, priorities should never be fluid. Changes like that diminish the confidence the troops have in their leadership. It screams indecisiveness, which weakens the support from the rank and file, particularly in the long term." Chimalma gripped forearms with Mictecacíhuatl as the two Nahua goddesses exchanged greetings.

Bix caught the amused grunt from Ereshkigal and the approving nod from Hel directed at Chimalma. Rolling with constantly changing goals—and masters—was a core difference between spies and soldiers. Bix knew that from living among the Berserkers. Under normal circumstances, she would've been glad to hear Chimalma's rebuke. As it was, that clarity of conviction made Bix sad for having to remove everything that made the general a worthy leader.

"I assume you've called me here to take back what is yours?" Chimalma widened her stance as the other goddesses and Hades took their seats at the table.

"It needn't be done in front of an audience." Bix had no intention of going through the final assimilation around any living thing. She lost lucidity during the process, which permitted her subconscious to run amok. She had a habit of stealing things, moving people, and unmaking countless creations, including Worlds. More than once, her elder siblings had had to intervene to contain her instinctual chaotic half.

"I'm not ashamed of the commitment I made to you, so witnesses make no difference to me." Chimalma shrugged.

"Mighty Chimera, if I may, once again, ask you to reconsider what you're about to do," Mictecacíhuatl pleaded. "The Mids need her. Our pantheon needs her. Her army needs her."

"My seconds have prepared for my departure ever since the Chimera returned to the Mids reawakened. The United Mesoamerican Army will continue without me. It would be poor leadership indeed to make oneself the single point of failure in any movement, much less the defense of an entire collective." Chimalma spared a half smile for her advocate. "Thank you, though, Mictecacíhuatl."

Previous memory keepers had had different reactions to Bix

coming for her displaced bits, though every one of them had been hostile. Some had been more manipulative than outright combative, but none had faced the inevitable with such practical calm as Chimalma. Was her composure masking the goddess's madness? Was all this spoken devotion to leadership just an act? Would Bix reach inside the goddess and feel the corruption of Chimalma's mind as she had with the others?

Bix would know soon enough. Without further ado, she reverted to her amorphous native state of starlight and midnight. Amid the gasps of awe from the gods of the Under Worlds, she enveloped Chimalma and took the Mid World guardian far from any inhabited space.

CHAPTER 8

In a place without time where stars had yet to reach, Bix allowed Chimalma to drift independently of her. The red aura of Chimalma's divinity bumped up against the glow of Bix's starlight, offering the only illumination for hundreds of thousands of miles.

"Is there a place or a person to which you'd like me to return your husk?" Bix asked.

Chimalma combed her fingers through the weighted night, wonder finally cracking her stoic mask. "When you've taken everything from me, Chimera, I ask only that you fully unmake me. I do not wish to be reborn into fairy tales of the goddess I once was. I would have my loved ones remember me as they knew me. I do not want them burdened by persistent disappointment for me never becoming that woman again."

A curious answer for a deity. Then again, most hadn't known until recently that they weren't truly immortal. Ending them was something only Bix could do as the High Executioner. Historically, she'd limited herself to merely husking gods. She couldn't remember why she'd stopped there, though. These days, she had a "grown-ass adult" policy, which meant she'd oblige reasonable requests as long as she was willing to accept the foreseeable consequences.

Consequences were what made Chimalma's request different from Desire's.

"Fine, if you're certain?"

"I am. I've had plenty of time to think about it." Chimalma took a deep breath and spread her arms wide. "I've lived an adventurous life. I am content."

Bix didn't believe the equanimity of the goddess, not one bit. The complete and total acceptance, the very *embrace* of death? Had to be false bravado. Even mortals who knew their end was inevitable fought it tooth and nail. Not that Chimalma's truth mattered. Bix would allow the goddess to die with the dignity of performative peace.

"Then I thank you for your sacrifice," Bix murmured and cast seven spears of night into Chimalma's body.

In previous reclamations, Bix had feasted on the god's essence first, then culled their memories for any useful intel, and finally drained them of all but the seed of their divinity as she summoned her displaced bits home. Once she pushed past the outer shell of the deity, their insides were a jumbled slurry devoid of organization of any sort, which was to be expected. They were entities of chaos, after all.

Chimalma was different. Within her confines, the seed of her divinity had sprouted a web, segmenting part of herself from the whole…

No. Not herself. On the other side of the web, the auroras of Bix's displaced memories undulated. Chimalma had successfully partitioned that which was Bix's from the rest of herself. But how? Every other memory keeper had mixed Bix's bits with theirs. It was the cause of the madness and corruption of the gods. How could Chimalma have segmented herself without exposing herself to the fragments of Bix's memories?

Leaving everything exactly as she'd found it, Bix pulled out of Chimalma's body.

"You've kept my parts separate from yours," Bix said, her astonishment obvious to even her own ears. "Who helped you?"

"I realized the instant you implanted your memories in me that the temptation to tap into the power innate to those pieces would be my undoing," Chimalma admitted warily, her drooping eye twitching. "It was not a challenge I could meet on my own. Thus, I asked the Mid Worlds that had chosen me to be their guardian for help. Over the centuries, they continued to oblige me, to strengthen that separation whenever I faltered."

"Are you telling me you've *never* tried to read my memories? To glean information? Access my magics? Reveal my secrets?" Bix pulled her form into something resembling humanoid, but not of flesh.

Chimalma lowered her arms and tipped her head to the side, a hint of sympathy in the parts of her face that could show it. "Chimera, when you came to me, I saw you were in a hollow place that I too had been. A place beyond pain, beyond grief, beyond rage and hate. A place where emotions had to be shut away in order to function—if not from a state of benevolence, then from a state that did no harm. Whatever your reasons for divesting yourself of memories and magics, I had no desire to intrude on your suffering."

Bix inhaled sharply. The reason for that pain and suffering could only partially be blamed on Tempest and Desire. The bulk of it tied in to a greater family issue.

"Chimalma, I am going to inspect this barrier Mids' magic helped you form. If, in fact, it has prevented my memories from corrupting your being, then I have no reason to husk you, much less end you. Is returning to the Mids wholly yourself minus my memories something you would want?" Bix had to ask. If Chimalma was truly at peace with dying, then not dying could mess her up.

The goddess retreated a few steps, mouth moving without forming words.

"That is a big *if*, Chimalma," Bix clarified. "So much as one fissure, and I will assume the worst and end you."

"Gods, Chimera," Chimalma breathed, one hand rubbing

the lax muscles of half her face. "Living longer as me…that is…that is not a possibility I ever entertained. I couldn't. That way lay foolishness and irresponsibility."

"There is nothing to say I wouldn't end you in the future should your behavior merit it," Bix cautioned, and her starlight danced. She wasn't sure either of them should consider Chimalma returning to the Mids whole and ready to resume battling the Devourers as a merciful act, but the possibility of putting an important player back in the game had definite appeal.

"Yes," Chimalma blurted with a croaked giggle. "Yes, I think I would very much like to return to my life as me, as the goddess I worked hard to become."

"Then let us both hope for the best." Bix clutched the goddess in her darkness once again and penetrated the divine shell.

There. Just as Chimalma had described. Skimming above the red web of divinity shimmered filaments of blue. The chaotic half of Mids' magic, the half created by Bix's eldest sister, Movement. Had Movement helped the goddess, or had it been the ley lines? Movement via the ley lines? Why only this one guardian? All her memory keepers had been Mid World guardians. Perhaps Chimalma had been the only one to ask for help? Perhaps Chimalma had been the only one who didn't want Bix's power?

Some poking, some whacking, and some intense inspection confirmed Mids' magic had indeed protected Chimalma from Bix's memories. There was bound to be a cost for mercy somewhere down the line, but it might not be as high as the price of ending Chimalma.

Ah, the joyous unexpected. The delightful confirmation of the eternal existence of the Chaos.

Bix altered her approach to her memories within Chimalma's body, coming for them from the other side of the separation. The lights of her memories blossomed like happy daisies as they found their way home. Pixels of pictures. Nanoseconds of sounds. Scents. Sensations. Emotions. Intuitions. All the everythings, all the missing details in a life older than the concept of age.

As the effort to organize her mind took its toll on her lucidity, Bix withdrew from Chimalma and returned the goddess to the Greek Under World. The goddess could get herself back to the jungles of the Mids from which Mirri had escorted her.

CHAPTER 9

All the discomforts Bix had assumed were part of existing no longer existed. She was whole again. At last. At long fucking last. Each network of starlight. All undulations of darkness. Everything in perfect glorious balance. Not an ache. Not a pain. Not a throb. Not a vacuum or pocket of missing anything. She knew everything she knew. Those things she didn't know, she had educated guesses that had their own PhDs. From the minute details of her childhood to the gargantuan mess still consuming her entire family, she finally possessed all the clues.

Not necessarily all the answers. She still didn't know why Desire had taken her friends, nor what reaction he expected her to have to the affront. She still had to figure out how to put him and Tempest out of their misery without permanently ending them like they desperately wanted. She still had to get them to call off the Devourers and any other creations they thought to send her way in the future. She was, however, very clear on every action she'd taken in the past to mollify the youngest twins and the reasons those efforts had failed. Not going to lie, she wasn't entirely proud of those past actions.

What was now wholly unambiguous was the nature of her brother Desire. Yea, though she loved him dearly, he'd become the worst type of villain. The type who played upon every emotion yet allowed none to color his own existence. A skilled actor who could mimic empathy but discarded actual feelings before they invoked his conscience. He was personal motivation incarnate, the origin of ambition, the root of selfishness, the cause of lying for gain. When he was balanced, he was equal parts good and greedy. Both aspects were necessary to the greater existence. Alas, he hadn't been balanced in a long time. For a child aligned to the Cosmos, the origin of order, Desire's prolonged imbalance had turned toxic. It wasn't destroying him, he'd welcome that; it was forcing him to devolve and dragging his twin down with him. That was what Bix had to undo. That was easier said than done.

Upshot, she was finally mentally and magically equipped to tackle the challenge of the youngest twins. Armed with the histories of her failures, she could establish better plans, missions, and actions. The first was getting her friends back to their proper place and time. That began with the god lurking in her shadows.

"Hello, Phobos," she greeted.

The Greek god of fear stood as small as a dust mite within the vastness of her natural unfettered state. Sighing with the delight of being whole again, she compacted herself to her preferred humanoid form. Phobos flicked his wrist and attired her in the fashions he deemed appropriate. A teal wiggle dress with high collar and sweetheart neckline shifted hues until it adopted the exact shade of her sacred color. The long sleeves came down to widow's peaks on the knuckles of her middle fingers. Her favorite part? Her shoes. The holographic pattern of broken analog watch faces made her chuckle.

"Behold, the mighty Chimera in her complete glory." He pressed a hand over his heart and bowed. "Congratulations."

"I couldn't have done it without you." She grinned as his magic arranged her hair in cascading pin curls. "How was your trip to me?"

Because of their bond, her subconscious summoned him

to care for her in times of need, usually provoked by her pain threshold being exceeded, such as during a memory assimilation.

"Far more direct than the journey away." He brushed the metallic half-moon behind his ear. A gift from one of her elder brothers that allowed him to travel across or outside time to be with her. Flakes of dried ichor shimmered on the half-moon's surface. Closer inspection revealed traces of dried ichor in his hair and on his clothes. He'd tried to hide it from her.

"You bled," she stated baldly as irritation at her brother stirred. "What did Desire do to you?"

"When his heralds couldn't remove it, he took a shot at it himself." Phobos waved off her concern. "Enlightening to discover that your elder brother made this tamperproof, regardless of how much of my skull may be intact."

"Desire tried to steal a time-travel implant? To keep you from leaving?" She hoped Phobos didn't notice the inhuman snarl in her voice as irritation leapt to rage, causing threads of darkness to whip from her spine. "In the process, he tortured you. Yet again, I must apologize for the boorish behavior of my siblings."

"It has taught me to value your restraint," he drawled, dusting off his shoulder and restoring his attire to its customary pristine condition. "Though, I'm surprised one of your siblings didn't attend you during this final realignment. I'm equally surprised that we didn't ricochet around the greater existence as has been your wont during prior memory merges."

"I came home to she who created me." Bix gestured to the pitch-black night surrounding them. "Phobos, may I introduce you to my mother, the Chaos?"

The god of fear blanched past pasty to porcelain. This was a sight few ever encountered, this unspoiled stretch of the eternal darkness, this unmarred expanse of the Chaos, this pristine patch of the feminine origin. True, Bix's mother existed everywhere, always. The Chaos was the womb in which all creations came into being. What most entities were accustomed to seeing, however, were the places where creations existed. In those places, there was also the Cosmos, the masculine heart of order, the light of conception, the essential exclusion of community. Bix's father literally outshone her mother. This place had yet to know her father's influence.

Phobos audibly swallowed and bowed so deeply his forehead touched his knees.

Bix patted his back. "Up, up. Obsequiousness is unnecessary. We are outside time here. Our presence is a fleeting moment in her awareness."

"That's not wholly reassuring." He glanced over both shoulders as he stood.

"After the last assimilation, I had enough of my memories to theorize a means of protecting the greater existence from the pandemonium caused by my chaotic half while my ordered half is busy reassembling my mind. With any luck, when we return to the flows of time, we'll discover that entangling my chaotic half in the Chaos herself worked."

"So to prevent yourself from being a destructive dervish, you simply needed to hug your mother? Is that how a peon like me should interpret that?" Phobos arched a censorious brow.

"There are worse interpretations. But enough about my mother. What I need from you, dear spymaster, is a briefing on my brother and, more importantly, my friends. Were you able to locate them? Are Feng, Cian, and Ashtad alive? How fare Drew and Tobek? Is everyone together?" She looped her arm through his and gave him time to adjust to the influx of power. When she was corporeal, her body was a sheath for her potency. It didn't block all her innate power; it just softened the ooze a bit. As her bonded caretaker, Phobos was uniquely capable of enduring direct contact with her. Lucky guy.

"Your precious mortals *are* being kept together in the Mid Worlds. Although, I was only with them for a short period before my implant was discovered. I was subsequently removed from their tiny commune and trapped on the other side of the World." Phobos brushed his hand down the arm onto which she held, and his sleeve added quilted layers of something denser than fabric, as if trying to protect himself from her touch. She made to let go, but he patted her hand, keeping it in place on his arm. "I did not see the original Berserker, though I did detect his presence. Safe to assume we were all prisoners on the same cell block, but not sharing the same cell."

"Figurative cell block?" She had to ask because Desire could create an entire prison World with a passing thought. Nevertheless, it was reassuring to have the confirmation that her team was in the Mids as the ley lines and the Fates' weave had insisted. Trust but verify, as the saying went. It meant that a rescue was absolutely possible.

Phobos grunted the affirmative. "The mortals live in a fairly symbiotic relationship in which the Phoenix manifests Mid World-grown food for the Sage and the demigod while feeding off the emotions of the Sage. He also provides fresh bodies for the draugr to occupy. The shell of Hel's hound did not survive the early days."

"Drew probably made sure of that, shedding it in hopes of leaving a clue for Hel to find." She smiled, imagining Feng rising to the call of benevolent provider. It was good for him to be needed and appreciated, but not revered. That balance would help him cope with the trauma of being abandoned and tortured for years, trauma that understandably still haunted him. "You said 'early days.' How long do you think you've been gone?"

"When dealing with the future, it is impossible to tell the difference between now and then."

"The *future*?" Bix echoed, horrified…and a little amused. Her team didn't necessarily get along. They played well together for her sake, but it was mission-based cooperation, not gleeful cohabitation. Unable to escape each other for an untraceable amount of time? Talk about mandatory team building with all the potential to go fatally awry. Gah.

"Indeed. Even with my implant, time seemed to be muddled." Phobos shook his head and his brow wrinkled. "I would guess by the tragic state of our environs that it is a future in which the Devourers have had plenty of time to feast and destroy."

"Cian was right. It wasn't a question of where but when," she murmured as appreciation for the kid's wit warmed her heart. Alas, it was chased by the chill of cold resolve. Jumbles. Tangles. The when of their situation was inside another one of Desire's accursed time knots. That significantly complicated the rescue. High risk. No wiggle room. Not impossible, though. "Desire thinks he took you out of my reach. To the one place I personally can't get to, the future. That's good. He's underestimating me. Has he done anything to inhibit anyone's magics? Feng in particular?"

"Not that I'm aware." Phobos pulled the fob of a still-beating heart from his vest pocket and massaged the filigree cover with his thumb. "Be warned, Chimera, irrespective of the exact time apart, your brother and his heralds have learned quite a bit about your dearests. Similarly, your mortals are very much aware of the existence of your family now. The Sage forced a retreat of the heralds simply with his endless questions. I believe branches wilted under the boy's onslaught."

Bix laughed. Oh, she could imagine it. As Ereshkigal had said, a herald's primary job was to prepare a supplicant for a meeting with a First Child. Answering questions was part and parcel. Cian was an information addict, a side effect of being a Sage. She actually looked forward to the interrogation Cian was sure to levy on her once she got him home.

"Did you get any sense of why my brother took you or what reaction he's expecting from me?"

"From my position as a spy, it's obvious he's fishing for intel on you. He's specifically interested in what's changed since you broke yourself into pieces. That was the question he feared I would discern in what he wanted me to perceive as amiable and idle conversation."

"After he'd tortured you, of course." She tsked. "Though it is a fair query. I have the same question about him. It's been three hundred years since I monitored his behavior. It's not a long time for a First Child, but then again, it was long enough for me to evolve my capacity for empathy."

"As a member of a large family of emotion gods, many of whom are fond of life in the extremes, I can say with confidence that your brother not only lacks empathy, but he also actively rejects it." Phobos curled a lip.

"Emotions are considered problematic by the men on that side of my family." She smiled ruefully. "There was a time when I too buried my emotions in the false belief that it allowed me to be impartial when I rendered my judgments in the course of my eternal duty of balancing the greater existence."

"You misunderstand me, Chimera." Phobos shook the heart fob at her. "You *suppressed* all emotions. Your brother *replaces* them. What should be joy is envy. What should be love is possession. What should be curiosity is hostility. Empathy can only exist in a consciousness of 'we.' Your brother isolates himself in a state of 'me.' In the terms of popular culture, he is a psychopath."

"Sociopath," she corrected with resigned sadness. "He has a conscience. When I was a child, he listened to his and taught me how to listen to mine. Something happened to change him, though. It's contorted his primary aspect of personal drive to the point that he considers his sense of right and wrong to be an impediment to achievement."

"That is not a trait that can be fixed, Chimera. It doesn't matter what type of entity one may be." Phobos regarded her with commiserating resignation.

"Not quite accurate. The pantheons' histories are chock-full of psychopathic and sociopathic deities," she reminded. "Some of those histories even mention how the deities were cured of their antisocial personalities."

"The cure? You husked them," he scoffed. "Are you planning to do the same to your brother? *Can* you? Is it even possible to husk a First Child?"

"That's the billion-dollar question, isn't it?" She groaned miserably. "I've tried everything else."

"Then you're going to need much more than a summary from me." He tucked the fob into his vest pocket. "It's been too long since I had a decent meal. Robust souls have been in shockingly short supply in the future. If we may return to my home, I will happily tell you *all* I gleaned from my time in the company of your brother and his heralds."

"Oh, geez, yes, you must be starving. My apologies." She opened gates to an Other World far from the collectives of the Mids and Unders. "One burning question? Were you able to discern what it is my brother fears most?"

"His greatest fear, Chimera, is that you will give up on him."

Bix's eyes flitted shut, and her fingers curled at her sides. A sneer twitched. Give up on Desire? Give up?

As if that merciless jackass would let her.

CHAPTER 10

Armed with the intel Phobos had gathered from his time as Desire's prisoner, Bix left him on his home World to recuperate while she returned to the Greek Under World. She had lots of incomplete thoughts about Desire and his reason for taking her friends, but first things first. It was time to bring her loved ones home, and to do that, she needed worker bees.

She found Hades and Cerberus strolling along the banks of the fiery River Phlegethon that wended its way toward the realm of the titan Tartarus. The souls carried along by the river had been misanthropes so full of hate that their enmity burned as red-orange flames. Hades had once described their flavor as a fine wine improperly corked. The Phlegethon cooked off that excessive bitterness, making the soul more palatable before being stored in the pantheon's treasury.

"You needn't lurk, Chimera," Hades called out. "You are always welcome in my home, be you broken or whole."

"Sometimes, I like to watch you at peace before I ruin it." She perched on a large boulder as the barking of happy hounds warned of the imminent arrival of the welcoming committee.

Hades spread his arms wide and laughed. "Peace is boring if it isn't balanced by disaster. Speaking of which, you have a new ardent fan in Mictecacíhuatl. Seems the return of Chimalma in a condition better than when she left has the whole pantheon reconsidering their dislike of you."

"However will I maintain my bogeyman reputation?" she asked with mock affront. Though, hearing that Chimalma was doing better without Bix's memories was reassuring, depending on how a god defined "better." They were a capricious lot by design.

"We're not done with the war against the old foes, so I'm sure there's an opportunity somewhere in there." He ambled up the hill to join her on the boulder. "What can I do for you?"

"I need a base of operations until I can return to the Mids." She batted her lashes and offered a cheesy grin.

"Of course. Whatever you need. Ereshkigal will be disappointed you're not using Irkalla, though." He gave a boost to a puppy whose heads were too wobbly and legs too short to scramble up the curves of the rocks. Runt of the litter by the looks of the rest of the pack playing with Cerberus.

"Plans require a bit of a revolving door, and Irkalla is rather locked down." She scooped the runt into her lap and rubbed its belly while its sharp little teeth gnawed on her impermeable skin. "Oh, and is Mirri still here, or did Hel send her back to Asgard?"

"I believe she's training Thárros by the River Lethe." He hopped off the boulder.

"Does she know your service dogs are the means by which you keep tabs on everything and everyone? Unders? Uppers? Mids?" She handed him the runt and dusted its fur off her skirt. "The more often they breed, the greater your reach? Your cute, cuddly swarm of spies?"

"Whether consciously or not, I suspect she finds that part reassuring, just like you did whenever you took my hounds exploring." He set the pup on Cerberus's paw, then offered her a hand off the rocks. "Feel free to use the western garden for your base. I've left it as a conference area until this matter with the titans and Devourers is put to bed. I've already alerted the staff to cater to your requests."

"Thank you." She accepted his help and ambled with him toward the garden. "I mean it, Hades. Thank you for everything you've done for me. Now that I am whole again, I better understand the costs you paid for helping rebuild me."

"No cost was, or is, too great, considering all you'd done for me." He slid his hands in the deep pockets of his loose drawstring pants. "After all, I am the only one of my siblings you haven't husked. When the point came that I decidedly deserved it, you instead granted me mercy with a choice between rehabilitation or rebirth."

"You chose the more difficult path," Bix recalled. "Your siblings wanted the easy out, as most gods do."

"Rehab was the right choice for me." He smiled and looked away, possibly to a far distant place and time. "When my hounds informed me of your arrival in the convergence, I rushed there. I wasn't the only one coming for you, naturally. However, I'd convinced myself that I alone could preserve your merciful aspect because I had thrived under it."

The warmth of comfortable camaraderie suffused her. It was nice, that emotion, that unencumbered casualness of friendship. Whole as she was now, a large part of her resisted it. It wanted to seek out the flaw, the manipulation, the trick. Distrust was a defense that had been her default for so long that she had to exert an effort to hold fast to the better emotion. She had to work to trust her newer instincts, the ones birthed and honed while she'd been broken.

It wasn't to say that she ought to be naïve or gullible.

No, this was about recognizing and embracing the nascent bonds of a relationship. As old as she was, those routine behaviors that had forced her to suppress her emotions still had to be overcome. Especially now that she was fully herself. It was going to take time for the original Chimera and the reawakened Chimera to achieve balance within her. If she wasn't careful, she'd slip back into old habits, into being who she once was, a cosmic entity so overwhelmed by life that she had to break herself into pieces and rebuild from scratch in order to change how she engaged with the greater existence. These relationships, particularly with lesser beings, they were important to that new approach. They mattered. She had to allow herself to be vulnerable enough to nurture them. That was the nature of *her* rehabilitation. She wasn't done yet. Far from it.

She returned Hades's smile. "You succeeded better than you know."

"Sending me your cherished ones when they break brings me the joy of deep satisfaction. I'd dare say divine pride is involved too," he confessed with an exaggerated false humility that made her laugh. He paused at the edge of the garden and smothered his grin as Mirri bolted up from a seat at the otherwise empty round table. "I think I'll inspect the Acheron now. Call if you need me."

Before Bix could say goodbye, Hades phased out, leaving her alone with Mirri…and the dogs. Always with the dogs.

"I'm sorry. I'll go," Mirri blurted and made to run for it, but her pup, Thárros, got tangled in the pleats of her long white dress.

"Mirri, wait. This awkwardness between us is unnecessary." Bix crossed her arms over the high back of a chair, keeping the huge table between her and her ex for the goddess's sake. Mirri looked like prey desperate for an out. "We're immortal. It's not like one of us is going to drop dead and make our baggage die with us. Let's get the weird out of the way, shall we?"

Mirri stepped behind the chair she'd vacated and fluttered her hands along the top. "I didn't know you were the Chimera. Not back then. I swear."

"Okay. I believe you." Bix grinned, guessing that wasn't quite the root of Mirri's discomfort. It was, however, a starting place. "But Hel did send you to the Mids to be my honey trap, right? The position of ambassador was the price you demanded."

"Why else send a goddess of healing to speak for the Norse? I was hardly qualified to maneuver in that kind of political arena, but I was confident I could learn to do it if given the chance." Mirri tapped her nails along the back and sides of the chair in a tune reminiscent of the wailing River Kokytos. "I knew when Hel agreed to my ridiculous demand that you had to be someone important, but she never told me your name or your origin. All she gave me was a case file number from the Chwedlonol spy guild. Get the file, identify the target, get promoted from acting to permanent."

"So your primary mission was to find, seduce, and turn me to the Norse cause?" Bix tipped her head past her shoulder, trying to snare Mirri's elusive gaze. Bix didn't hold any animosity for Hel or Mirri in this case, not at this distance from the acts. She didn't even need the restoration of her limitless history to bear no ill will. She'd be a hypocrite of the worst sort if she did. After all, seductress was but one of many roles she'd played during her own tenure as a spy under the yoke of the Consortium. Frankly, she was worse than Mirri. She'd had the gall to crawl into Mirri's bed after each of those assignments as if monogamy really had been on the table.

"To heal you. Hel told me you were powerful but broken. I assumed you were a greater goddess who'd run afoul of the Chimera and been husked." Mirri chuckled glumly. "Oh, what an idiot I was. I never ever entertained the notion that *you* were the Chimera. I didn't believe it even when my captors rubbed my face in the evidence. I couldn't believe the woman I loved was the monster feared by every pantheon. My heart still refuses to believe."

Mirri spoke the last words so softly, Bix almost missed them. Almost. Bix certainly didn't miss the ragged rise and fall of Mirri's chest.

"Is that why you can't look at me, Mirri? Because I'm the bogeyman?" Bix searched her normally wild emotions for something akin to dismay, annoyance, or even bittersweet resignation. There was nothing but serenity. She was oddly at peace despite the tumult that had characterized her relationship with Mirri. Maybe it was because she was older than time and possessed the full experience of immortality. Maybe it was because she wasn't properly connected to her emotions, emotions that might be riotous for someone else. Maybe this was what was meant by moving on and getting over it.

She wanted Mirri to be able to move on too.

"Because I know about the original Berserker," Mirri blurted in anguish. She finally looked at Bix, eyes brimming with tears. "Drew said he's been your consort longer than I've been alive. That's not a passing fancy. That's an unusual commitment."

Was Mirri actually angry that Bix had fallen into her honey trap? No. Surely not. Maybe Mirri was embarrassed for thinking she could have a place in Bix's life despite Tobek? Or was this what it looked like to be on the losing end of jealousy? But jealous of what? Of Tobek? Of an enduring partnership? Of having to put up with Bix's crazy for eternity?

Gah.

Gently managing other people's emotional turmoil was not something Bix was remotely qualified to do. She would never apologize for loving Tobek. He and she had worked too damn hard for their happiness. But, it didn't mean she wanted to further contribute to Mirri's pain. Mirri deserved better.

"I'm sorry you're hurting because of my relationship with Tobek," Bix said, choosing her words carefully. Allowing even a micron of false hope would be cruel. "He wasn't a factor in what was between you and me, though. I didn't remember him at all when you and I were together."

Mirri's hands stilled, and she tsked as tears dribbled over her pale cheeks. "But you did. You may not have remembered his name or his face, but you knew your heart belonged to someone who wasn't me. I tried to cling to that fact as if it could save me from falling for you."

"Didn't work, eh?" Bix teased. Were they at the point of humor yet? Could that help lighten the mood? Maybe stop Mirri from tearing herself up? Mirri had come so far in her recovery that the last thing Bix wanted was to cast the young goddess into a spiraling relapse. She'd hoped to give Mirri closure by forcing the confrontation, but she was having serious second thoughts about the wisdom of doing it now.

Mirri's hound leapt up into the chair and furiously licked at her falling tears, causing the goddess to laugh, a wet, rueful sound. "It's not your fault. You never promised me a happily ever after. You didn't even promise a happy for now. I knew I was in a doomed relationship. For Hel's sake, you were my target, not my wife. You're just…you're just a hard woman to get over."

"And because you loved me, you fought for me. You fought to clear my name after I was exiled. You fought impossible odds against horrific enemies and paid a very steep price." Bix wanted to hug her, but it wasn't appropriate. It wasn't an act that could be taken as it was meant. Lines with exes had to be firmly drawn and never crossed. It wouldn't be fair to Mirri to offer her physical comfort. "I saw. I noticed. I valued. Grateful isn't the word you want to hear, but it is the right word. Without all you did, I'd still be languishing as an amnesiac and the Mids would've already fallen to the Devourers. You're a hero, Mirri. It's past time someone told you that."

Mirri let loose a laughing wail and cuddled her dog close. "Damn you, Bix. Stop making me put you on a pedestal."

"Is it a rickety one? Big crack up the side? Crumbles around the base? One pitiful sneeze will send me tumbling on my ass?" Bix added a bit of wry to her smile, wanting humor to finally work. She didn't want to cut Mirri completely out of her existence, but she would do it in a heartbeat if it helped Mirri get her life back. A total exorcism was often the only way to heal, but Bix was selfish enough to want to be friends with Mirri, to build a new and different relationship. If they went forward, it would have to be Mirri's choice, with Mirri's full understanding that their friendship would never again grow beyond those parameters.

"I still want to help," Mirri sniffled. "If you'll let me. I want to help. You. The Mids. The original Berserker."

"You don't mean that last one." Bix closed one eye and wagged a finger.

"Not really, no. But I do get that he's important to the Mids and its defenses, so I'll suffer his return to your arms." Mirri peered between the split of the dog's two necks and rolled her eyes, letting reluctant mirth infuse her expression. "Just don't expect me to like him."

"Fair," Bix conceded, the knot of dreaded confrontation finally passing. "But if you are serious about helping—"

"I am," Mirri interjected.

"—then I have a very important role for you to play in what will be a huge spell," Bix continued with a half grin. "Are you sure you're ready for something like that?"

"It wasn't the spell that did me in," Mirri whispered. "It was knowing the bad guys wanted to vivisect you, and I couldn't do a thing to stop them."

"No blood spells this time," Bix assured with a pang in her heart. Wanting to protect your loved ones, yet not being able to? Bix was intimately familiar with that wild, desperate, hopeless fear. As crazy as it might seem, though, she was happy to be reacquainted with that powerful emotional combo. It was part of the bad that, in the long run, was very good for a First Child. "But it will take place in the Mids, after I make the necessary arrangements."

"Consider me eager and intrigued." A honey-colored cloud surrounded Mirri for a brief count of five, and when it dissipated, she was attired in jeans, boots, blouse, and blazer. Her hound wore a sparkly harness and matching leash. "Whenever you're ready... mighty Chimera."

Bix inclined her head and reached for the second of two pendants she wore, this one a metallic gargoyle. A gift from a god who was now the chairman of the Consortium.

"Oh, Ogun," she sang out. "I need an audience. Now."

CHAPTER 11

The Chairman of the Consortium appeared first as a hologram before solidifying as the real deal. He wore the same Fate-woven camouflage uniform that Chimalma had. As a god of war, specifically the technologies of war, it was hardly a surprise to find him armed with cutting-edge weapons he'd likely forged in his office at Consortium HQ. Droplets of Devourer blood beaded on his sleeves and torso. His deep brown eyes narrowed on Bix as he holstered something akin to a laser cannon.

"Didn't we have a discussion not so long ago about summonses and how inappropriate they are?" Ogun fumed.

"Silly you, giving a greater power the means of direct contact." Bix flicked her gargoyle pendant. "And as I recall there was also something about allies, collaboration, and defense systems. Speaking of which, how *is* Resen?"

"Where is the man I put in charge of ensuring the damn system works as designed?" Ogun widened his stance and crossed his arms. "None of his men can answer that question."

"Same place as the system architects and the Phoenix."

"Which is?" he groused, clearly short on patience.

"With the leadership of the Devourers." Bix perched on the lip of the table as Ogun choked on a breath. "Would you care to get them back? Before the foundational elements of Resen have a complete meltdown? I certainly would."

His whole body twitched, and a scowl could be seen despite the face mask of his uniform. "You want them back, but *you* can't get them back? How is that possible?"

"Because it's a matter of when, not where, thus the superpowers of the Mids have to do the deed."

Part of the duty of the caretakers was to anchor the Mids' timeline in a linear manner, to maintain the rails through which time glided. It was a feat of balance. Dragons were the natural opposite to angels, Fates the opposite of gods. All four races were necessary to access the guide rails.

"Godsdamn Fates," the Chair muttered. "They knew about this and didn't step forward? They badger me with demands yet shirk their responsibilities. What the hell good are they?"

"Good for things like this. You're going to need six of them, Heads of Houses specifically. One from the past, one from the present, four from the future." Bix examined her nails, letting Ogun glare at her to his heart's content. "You'll also need six dragon queens and six archangels, none of them born with the same ley line."

"I will, will I?" His voice dropped into that demonic range that gods loved to use to scare the shit out of people. Alas, Bix was not a people.

As much as Tobek gave her grief over not understanding the intricate details of how Mids' magic worked, she'd been used often enough as an ingredient in Mids' spells that mucked with time that she'd learned a thing or two. So had Feng. So had Tobek. Which was why she had faith that if the caretakers of the Mids could open an access point to the timeline in the present, the Fates of the Future could hook a thread to the beacon that would be sent from a hot spot of Tobek's magic in the present to Tobek himself somewhere in the future. Feng did the actual traveling along the timeline. She'd seen him carry two people while doing it, but she didn't think he could transport more than that in any one session.

So the caretakers would have to hold open the access point long enough for him to make two trips to bring the whole team back.

It was a risk with many opportunities for failure, but she couldn't participate in spells that involved the future. Those required creationists, which the four races of caretakers were.

"Oh, and of course, six Mid World guardians, one of whom must be Chimalma." Bix swept her hand in a wide circle, opening viewing gates overlooking the Mid World collective and Resen, another set of the galactic view showing the army of Devourers expanding between the Uppers and Unders, and a third set with a close-up of the Virginia side of the Washington, DC metro area, Primary Mid World. "They will need to assemble as close to the Berserker main base as possible without breaking the base's wards."

Ogun took in the sights offered by the gates, sighing with disgust at the Devourer army, then pausing to study the worrisome fluctuations now visible in Resen. It was a few moments before he approached the gates showing the Consortium's side yard.

"That puts dragons in the Potomac River, angels on the Parkway, gods in the historic district, and Fates at the airport?" He pointed at the locations as he spoke. "Four corners to peel back the layers protecting the timeline, I assume. The Berserker's base as the landing zone?"

"Just so," Bix confirmed. "They have to act in total unity. If one side fails to pull their weight, they break the timeline and propel our guys to a different branch, possibly stranding them in the future."

Stranding her team in the future was why Bix couldn't reset the timeline. There were no second chances if they broke the flow during this rescue attempt.

"Give me a few hours in the time of the Mids to shuffle resources and backfill the positions our spell casters are currently holding." Ogun rubbed his head, bald beneath his hood. "How much intel do we think the leadership of the Devourers has gleaned from them?"

"I suspect whatever intel the other side thinks they've gathered will only sabotage their efforts. Lying and obfuscations come easily to their prisoners." Bix chuckled, imagining the shenanigans of her team once they'd figured out Desire's goal in taking them. "While Cian is the only one who hasn't endured protracted torture, as a Sage, he is a fount of useless information."

"You and your cabal of spies." A shimmer of mirth made it to Ogun's eyes. "I'll trill the pendant when we're ready."

"Keep your eyes on the Berserker's base. They'll let you know when they're ready on their end."

"Understood. Anything to shore up our defenses." Ogun faded to his holographic state before vanishing altogether.

"Chimera, what is it you want me to do?" Mirri asked, stepping from the cover of a kumquat tree.

Bix almost commented on Mirri's impulse to hide from Ogun, who doubtlessly had known she was there, but thought better of it. Mirri wasn't a hundred percent yet, but the goddess was doing her best. The best was all one could ask.

"I need you to go to the Berserkers' base, shown there on the monitor. You will be blocked by wards. The moment you feel them firmly obstructing your path, you will be registering on their security system. That is good. I need you to ask for Gurp."

Mirri's face lit. "The goblin? Drew told me all about the marvelous majordomo. I should be delighted to finally make his acquaintance."

"Plain paper and a pen, please?" Bix called out to whomever Hades had listening in on the conversations. In an instant, a stack of legal-size paper and an assortment of colored markers and pens appeared beside her on the table. She scribbled instructions to Gurp on one page, wrote his name and Tobek's in large letters on another, and on a third sketched a sunburst with six squiggly rays and a dot in the center. "Gurp will need a few minutes to modify the wards so that you can get on the grounds of the base. Do not assume you can get in any of the buildings, though. They'll still be off-limits."

"Got a thing against gods, do they?" Mirri joked, sort of.

"It's not just gods." Bix winked and slid the picture of the sun to Mirri. "Gurp will gather representatives from the six lowest races of Chwedlonol. They are to arrange themselves in this manner. You are the dot in the middle."

"If they're Chweds who barely have any magic, how are they going to broadcast the beacon?" Mirri stroked her wriggling pup before setting it on the ground.

While the Consortium made Chweds and humans as dictated in the Cycle of Souls contracts, the seeds of the lesser races' origins came from Desire and Tempest. The order of Chweds balanced out the chaos of humanity. That was the contribution of the youngest twins to Bix's sanctuary. The less Mids' magic the Chweds had, the more brightly the glow of their innate order would shine with the aid of the beacon, thus cutting through the time tangle Desire had made and illuminating the path home.

"They're not casting the beacon, Mirri, you are." Bix gripped the pendant containing Feng's dewclaw. "The magics in this pendant are muted by their proximity to me. The moment I take it off and put it in your hand, expect to be overwhelmed by the Phoenix's power."

Mirri's eyes widened, and she retreated a step. Stopped. Squared her shoulders. Took two steps forward and raised her chin. "If that contains Feng's power, then it can't last outside the Mids without your protection. Too far from the source of Mids' magic, it'll disintegrate."

"Exactly, which is why I need you to be stepping into the Mids while this is still between our hands. There can be no detours, no hesitation. I will have to let go before you cross Resen. You should expect Mids' magic to have a reaction to you showing up with a piece of Feng. It might not be welcoming." Bix wondered if she spoke too sternly when Mirri worried her bottom lip.

"Do you think he'll recognize me, my call, because of the time we spent together as captives?" Mirri whispered, her voice so small.

"I do. Enduring the horrors you two went through together forges an unbreakable bond. Down here in the Under Worlds, you've stretched that connection so thin that you probably can't find it within you. But once you reenter his Worlds, it will not be hard to locate." Bix used her magic to unmake the loop that secured the pendant to her braided necklace. The seemingly metal chunk dropped into her fist, audibly throbbing now that it was free from some of the spells Tobek had used to contain its magic. Mirri's dog quietly howled to the tempo of the pendant. "Feng will not initiate contact for fear of causing you further harm. You must find your internal connection to him and leverage the power contained in this pendant to blast your call far into the future in hopes of reaching him. It's the only way he's going to know the rescue is underway and that he needs to do his part."

Mirri folded the papers Bix had marked up and tucked them in her blazer pocket. "The rescue isn't a sure thing, is it?"

Bix snorted. "They never are."

"Then thank you for putting your trust in me." Mirri picked up her dog and extended her hand to Bix. "Let's bring our friends home."

CHAPTER 12

Bix released a painfully pent-up breath once the viewing gates showed Mirri's arrival in the Mids still carrying Feng's dewclaw. The goddess manifested a small, thin, hollowed-out cluster of obsidian etched with runes for healing and protection. She tucked the dewclaw pendant into the lumpy box and strung it on a cord around her neck that was long enough to hide the box in the valley of her bosom. With her hound, Thárros, trotting happily at her side, Mirri emerged from a budding thicket and made her way along disused railroad tracks toward the twenty-five-acre renovated coal plant sitting across the river from Washington, DC, Primary Mid World.

The Berserkers' main base had sustained damage during the last DC skirmish and was running on a skeleton crew while units were deployed battling Devourers. However, it remained one of the safest places to be during any war. According to protocol, Gurp should've returned to the coal plant to coordinate a search via the magical underbelly the moment Tobek went MIA. The goblin was far more than the majordomo of the battalion, he was the third member of Bix and Tobek's tiny family. Gurp understood the intricacies by which Tobek wielded Mids' magic, which was why the goblin's participation was essential to the spell working. He knew better than she how to prep the base to anchor the retrieval spell.

The wards around the coal plant flashed hunter green against the dreary skies of a cloudy spring day as Mirri approached on foot via the railroad tracks that had once carried coal to the plant. Thárros paused every other rail tie to sniff the strange new-to-him domain until the poor thing bounced off the invisible barrier, triggering another flash of green wards. Bix laughed aloud when the dog peed on the nearest ward.

It was a good thing she'd cast these gates to be picture only. Thinning them enough to allow sound might permit too much of her magic to brush the Mids, which she had to avoid until Tobek was ensconced in the collective once again. Phobos had said Tobek was being held on the same World at the same time as her mortal team. With any luck, Tobek's connection to the Mids would alert him to the rescue underway and he could either get to the others or Feng could loop back and pick him up on the second trip. Yes, it was a stretch. Yes, she dared have hope.

Mirri held up the paper with Gurp's and Tobek's names written in extra-large print. Since time moved more slowly in the Unders, it seemed as though Mirri's unusual knock was instantly answered, only not by Gurp. Tobek's second-in-command, Xipil, who looked like a teenager with a penchant for vests and collarless dress shirts, yet was one of the oldest Berserkers, met Mirri at the border of the wards. He latched a silver bracelet around Mirri's wrist, then motioned for her to follow. The bracelet glowed green as she passed through layer after layer of barriers protecting the base. They made it as far as the parking lot outside the body modification shop Dysmorphic before Gurp intercepted them.

The Gordian knot in Bix's guts loosened fractionally. Gurp was home. Good.

Mirri handed the squat potbellied goblin the three sheets of paper. Gurp's expression darkened as he read, then it brightened, then his nose bobbed and his belly quivered. He ate two of the pages and handed Mirri back the third, presumably the one with the drawing. A moment later, he disappeared inside the shop with Xipil on his heels.

Two beats after that, a trio of Berserkers emerged and escorted Mirri to a park bench in the middle of the largest green space at the compound. The parade ground, the guys called it. They set a bowl on the grass for the dog, opened a patio umbrella over the table, then sat down and chatted up the goddess.

The guys might have been soldiers who were fueled by rage during battle, but Bix had yet to meet a Berserker who wasn't also a gentleman when he wished to be. Watching Mirri give them a genuine smile loosened Bix's coil of anxiety a little more. Mirri no longer looked ready to bolt, and Thárros was wandering at the end of the leash instead of being plastered to Mirri's leg, which meant the dog didn't sense any panic from its mistress. Excellent. Two critical pieces in position and full cooperation from the Berserkers.

With preparations in Gurp's very competent hands, Bix zoomed out from the viewing gate and cast tendrils of shadows to keep watch for the arrival of the superpowers in the area.

Other World divinity rippled as a mulberry cloud appeared beside her. When it dissipated, Phobos, hale, hearty, and vibrating with anticipation gave her a pointy-fanged sinister grin.

"Am I too late?" he asked, scanning the viewing gates. "No, I see. The party is just getting started. Outstanding."

"I was unaware you were interested in bearing witness," Bix bald-faced lied, knowing perfectly well he'd asked Hades to summon him once the rescue started.

"And miss the fully restored Chimera's attempts to architect a Mid World magic-based rescue when the targets are in her brother's arms? I would never forgive myself." There was a borderline sensual tone to his murmur. He leaned closer and inhaled deeply. "I want to see if your fears come to fruition."

The snarky retort died on her tongue. Of course he sensed her fear. She might be a cosmic entity capable of playing with time, but there were mortal lives involved in this, lives that couldn't be flawlessly restored or replaced if something went wrong. There were multiple points of potential failure in this rescue, so yes, she was afraid.

Barking announced the arrival of Hel, Mictecacíhuatl, Setesuyara, and all their respective hounds. The resonance of Hades with his dogs was fast approaching, as was the resonance of Ereshkigal's animated extension. Apparently, a watch party was about to be had.

Definitely a good thing that the viewing gate didn't permit sound to transfer from either side. Bix was fairly certain the Under World gods would not be able to resist running commentary. Voices from her side coming through the gate would freak out the human-centric World with the whole "voices from on high" thing. Humans on the Primary Mid World were still adjusting to the recent revelation that magic and magical beings were real.

"Desire knows we're coming," Bix admitted to the god of fear. "Benefit of existing in the future with an eye on the past. To what extent he allows the rescue will define how violent my next steps are."

Phobos leaned back and gawped at her before letting loose a malevolent snicker. "Violent, eh? How delicious."

"You spent time with him. Do you think he'll try to stop it?"

"Depends on whether he's gleaned all the intel he needs from his prisoners." Phobos pivoted slightly to study the gates overlooking Resen. The security netting developed more questing spikes the longer her team was gone. Not reassuring at all when it came to the defense of the Mids.

"I mean, do you think he'll kill them rather than let them return to me?"

Phobos inhaled deeply and tapped his lips with a finger. "Strategically, that would be foolish. He's identified the ones who mean the most to you. If he kills them, he loses leverage."

Bix tried to take comfort in that, but it bothered her that she still didn't know what sort of reaction Desire wanted from her for abducting her friends nor why he was declining her invitation to his theoretical execution. If he'd taken her friends to figure out whether she'd really kill him, then why hadn't he already returned with them to the present? There was something she was missing, and it was making her queasy.

"I see bottom dwellers," Setesuyara called out, nodding to Bix as she laid a platter of curiously shaped, vibrant souls on the round table. "A strange army to be assailing the Berserker's base."

"They're not attacking. They're part of the spell," Bix assured with a brittle laugh as the viewing gate showed Gurp warmly greeting the leaders of a motley group of lesser Chweds before handing them off to the Berserkers entertaining Mirri in the parade field. Chweds weren't blocked by the base's wards. Sections of the base had been built to harbor them during times of war among the superpowers. All Chweds were welcome; naughty ones would be squashed.

"Oh, I do love a surprise slaughter." Mictecacíhuatl set a serving bowl of lush, iridescent souls on the table. Smaller bowls manifested around the larger, along with a spikey ladle.

"This isn't a blood spell. Mids' magic wouldn't cooperate in the manner needed if it was." Bix rubbed her palms together, willing the knot in her gut to cease its sudden tightening as six dragon queens in their base form, though sized to fit, took up staggered positions in the war-altered river and along the reconfigured DC waterfront. The queens' ever-present enforcers perched atop the nearby ruins of monuments, ready to respond to the slightest threat. Six archangels with wings wide alighted on mushroom-capped monoliths that had sprouted along the George Washington Memorial Parkway as defensive structures during the last skirmish.

Ten formerly human Fates, each with a visible physical flaw, rode on the shoulders of massive ogres clambering over the vestiges of what had once been Reagan National Airport. One advantage of the war with the Devourers was the Consortium finally repealing its ridiculous laws about Chweds having to assume humanoid forms whenever they were in the Primary Mid World. Magic was real. Humans were not alone, nor were they the top of the food chain. Surprise. Why had the Houses sent *ten* Fates, though? The spell needed six, no more, no less. Too many and it wouldn't work. Then again, Fates, being able to see into the future, probably knew four extras would be needed for something Bix hadn't anticipated. Best not to question the Fates unless shit went sideways.

"Isn't that your girl Chimalma and her posse down by the broken fountains?" Hel asked, holding up a bowl as Mictecacíhuatl ladled souls into it. "Her face has improved."

To the south, in the heavily damaged historic district of Old Town Alexandria, six gods arrived at the all-brick Market Square wearing combat uniforms. Four of the gods had their masks off and hoods back, Chimalma among them. As Hel had noted, the drooping half of Chimalma's face no longer drooped. The old affliction must've been caused by the webbing that had separated Bix's memories from the goddess's essence. Once the divider had no longer been needed, the goddess must've restored herself, vanity being a deity-defining trait after all.

"I'd say with the forming of the sunburst eye, they're ready to go." Hades held up two glass orbs and projected the sights and sounds as perceived by Thárros's two heads. The dog sat with the Berserkers who stood by with stretchers and medic bags in the shadows thrown by the wrecked parking garage. Gurp's unique garble carried clearly through Hades's orbs as the last of the Chweds followed the goblin's directions and assumed their places in the six rays around the oval eye centered in the middle of the compound. As the iris of the eye, Mirri stood alone, obsidian locket in her trembling hands.

The gargoyle pendant Bix still wore vibrated against her skin. Ogun's signal that the superpowers were ready. Gurp raised his fist, thumb up.

And so it began.

Archangels aglow in hues of blue cast six streams of pure native magic across the skies, stopping dead center above the Berserker's base. Dragon queens engulfed in undulating shades of purple threw back their heads and roared amethyst flames that collided with the angels' streams over the base. From the north, six—and only six—Heads of the Houses of Fate seated atop their ogre perches raised their hands. Rainbow-colored yarns shot from their palms to join the convergence causing ripples in the atmosphere. Mid World guardians steepled their hands in front of their lips as red auras built around them. Red ribbons rose from each god, flying in a unified arch to form the final connection. Nimbi built from the rippling currents, circling and swirling.

"Someone's not pulling their weight," Bix shouted at the pendant molding to her thumb as she pinched it tightly. "Godsdamn it, Ogun. Those churning clouds show weakness. They'll only rupture a hole in Resen. Everyone has to give everything they've got to rip through the barriers shielding the timeline."

"It's the guardians." Hel wagged a finger at the viewing gates overlooking the area around the base. "They're holding back so they'll have something left when they return to battle."

Tentacles of night seeped from Bix's spine. Responding to her rage, they surged around the viewing gates of Alexandria and poked at the picture, trying to get to the other side.

"Either they give their all right now, or I end them permanently," Bix snarled.

Mictecacíhuatl pulled a skull from thin air and stared into its hollow eye sockets. "Chimalma, hear me. Give everything. Leave nothing. I will bring you a feast when it is done. You will heal. Demand nothing less from your peers. Absolute power drain, now. So commands the Chimera."

On the viewing gate, Chimalma could be seen stiffening, lungs expanding, mouth moving. As one, the reds of the guardians deepened in saturation. At the convergence, the nimbi consolidated into a tight lollipop-like structure and sprouted four monstrous claws from its center. The claws pushed outward, tearing open the layers protecting the timeline of the Mids and offering a glimpse of the orangey gold shimmer of the timeline in motion.

"It's open," Setesuyara cheered. "And it is glorious."

"Come on, Mirri," Bix breathed. "This is your moment. Cast the beacon. Shine, literally."

Mirri's hands shook so badly, she dropped the locket. Twice. Thárros bounded to her side and retrieved the box.

"Will the hound be hurt sitting in the center of the spell like that?" Phobos rasped, tugging the fob of a still-beating heart from his vest pocket.

"Depends entirely on the internal conversation between Mirri and Feng once she casts the beacon." Bix practically rubbed the skin off her hands as she brought her rage to heel and her shadows to calm. "I apologize in advance, Hades."

"I doubt there'll be a need for that." Hades chortled, then sat forward. "She's got the box open. Here we go, folks. Moment of truth."

Bix gripped Phobos's arm with both hands, her attention bouncing among all the displays of up close and far back. "Come on, Mirri. You're stronger than you know. Believe."

Mirri pressed the pendant of Feng's dewclaw to her brow and closed her eyes. A honey-colored cloud built around Mirri and the dog seated on her feet. Seconds passed like eternities. Red zipped through honey, twirling.

"There's our girl." Hel applauded. "Tapping into the core of her divinity, finally. That is where her tie to the Phoenix is anchored."

Flames red and gold burned blue and purple as they engulfed Mirri. Feng responding. A funnel of copper magic leapt from the Chweds and swallowed the flames along with Mirri. Magics of the Mids and Other Worlds roared toward the sky with enough ferocity to shake the orbs in Hades's hands, shattering the glass. North of the coal plant, four ogres held the four extra Fates high overhead. Rainbow threads, finer than the yarns used by the other Fates, merged with the pillar of copper and flames.

Guiding threads, of course, to form the linear slide down which Feng would travel to return to the present. Without them,

Feng could get lost in any number of timeline tangles Desire threw into his path.

Threads pulled taut. Too taut. Fates scrambled to hold on to their threads.

Something was wrong.

Immobile wings of fire emerged from the access to the timeline. Threads of Fate hooked into Feng's fiery arches hauled the massive body of the firebird fully ablaze through the hole. The Phoenix barely squeezed through, scorching the monstrous claws holding open the access and turning them into ash.

"No," Bix gasped, and it was echoed throughout the Greek Under World. "No, no, no! Don't close. Don't close! He needs to make two trips. Four people. He has to bring back four people! He can only carry two at a time. Don't close, damn it!"

Too late.

CHAPTER 13

T he colorful convergence of the magics of the superpowers in the sky over the Berserkers' base faded away, leaving nothing but dismal gray. Archangels crumpled atop the mushroom monoliths, then were swept up by their choirs. Dragon queens fainted into the arms of their enforcers. Ogres carefully cupped unconscious Fates in their huge hands. Mid World guardians teetered and wobbled, barely upright. Psychopomps arrived by the dozens with fresh souls for the gods.

Bix's gaze was glued to the scene at Berserker central. Feng, still burning in his massive firebird form, had crashed atop the parking garage, barely avoiding crushing Mirri and the Chweds in the center of the parade field. Berserkers hustled up the rubble, vibrant blue eyes brightening.

Rage? At this point? Why? The Berserkers' rage was tied to Tobek's rage. If Tobek got mad, every Berserker got mad, no matter the distance. Could the same be said for the distance of time? Or had Feng brought Tobek through on the first round? No. Impossible. Tobek wouldn't let himself be first out, not unless he thought an enemy more dangerous than the one holding them was waiting at the other end. Besides, he hadn't been in the same location as the others. That was why she'd hoped Feng could've made a second trip. For now, Tobek was stranded in the future. She had to get him back soon. *Had* to. Yes, Tobek was immortal, but his mind was as vulnerable as any other entity's, and Desire was a ruthlessly abusive shit.

What about Ashtad, Cian, and Drew? Which of them had made it back? Feng had had to make a devil's choice. He definitely would've brought Cian back on the first trip. The kid was the most mortal among them. The others would've insisted. Ashtad and Drew would've bickered over who had the right to stay behind. Ever the elitist, it would've been a matter of honor for Ashtad to send Drew back with Cian and Feng. Ashtad would've viewed surviving in the future as one of his demigod challenges. Drew would want to follow the kid to protect Cian, but was more resilient than Ashtad, so the draugr would've played some trick that would've forced Ashtad to go first, but Ashtad would've anticipated it, so...Feng would've had to make the final decision.

Whichever way it'd gone down, until the Phoenix's magic-fueled fire went out, no one could get close enough to help him or his cargo. Bix had zero doubt there *was* cargo. Feng wouldn't turn his back on the team. She was, however, very concerned that Feng wasn't moving. He should've been able to make the journey, yes, with effort, but it shouldn't have taken everything from him. Had Desire tried to stop him? Was Feng, in fact, injured? The more she thought about the numerous ways Desire could've harmed her friends for trying to escape, the more rage meshed with fear.

"Should we be worried about that storm moving in? Doesn't look deity born." Setesuyara asked before draining a soul.

Clouds of blue, purple, and green gathered above the Berserkers' base. They rolled like a northern storm front and less like a midwestern tornado.

"No, that's the foundational elements of Resen welcoming the Phoenix home," Bix answered with distraction as rain fell across Alexandria and greater DC in fat drops of azure and plum, extinguishing Feng's fire. Once the flames were out, Berserker medics swarmed the Phoenix, Gurp and Mirri at their fore.

Wait. Mirri leading the charge? Then again, she was a goddess of healing, and she had a now-proven connection to Feng. That must've been enough to shake off the aftereffects of the spell, or she was running on instinct and adrenaline. Probably the latter.

It warmed Bix's heart to watch the Berserkers heft Feng's huge wings and the Chweds who'd formed the symbol now scurry beneath those wings to drag two bodies from the plumage. Mirri was on them so quickly, Bix barely caught a glimpse.

Ashtad and Cian.

"The architects. He brought back the architects. Good, good." Bix glanced at the view of the greater Resen netting around the Mids. The defense system finally looked less like an angry porcupine. The foundational elements were appeased, which meant Feng would be on the road to recovery soon.

Part of her was relieved and part of her was sad. She had four out of six of her friends back, including the two who couldn't survive beyond the Mids. She had a Plan B and Plan C to retrieve Drew and Tobek, and, frankly, those plans involved events that Ashtad might not have survived. Drew would likely have to spend a little more time in the Under Worlds for R & R, but her bestie would bounce back. Assuming Desire allowed Drew to live, that is.

Phobos sharply cleared his throat and stared pointedly at his arm. Bix looked down and groaned. She'd gripped his forearm so hard during the spell casting that it was nothing but dust in a sleeve. Horrified, she let go, caught his detached hand, and started to apologize.

"I'm a god," he reminded as his arm rebuilt. He angled his hollow cuff her way, and she slid his hand down his sleeve until it met resistance. He grunted with satisfaction and waggled his fingers. "You need to steady your fears. You are too mighty to allow your subconscious to react to emotional provocations. Imagine if I'd been your precious demigod? Or worse, the Sage?"

She accepted the chastisement. He was mostly right. He'd helped her test and train herself after her memory assimilations, so she recognized that he wasn't remotely mad, just concerned for her.

Magic rippled, and all the hounds barked.

Mirri appeared in the garden carrying Ashtad across her arms. Thárros busily licked Ashtad's dangling limp hand. Bix lurched for her erstwhile mentor, but Mirri warned her off with a look.

"Phobos, if you would please help me steady him on his feet?" Mirri's voice quavered.

"I can…I can do it," Ashtad wheezed and struggled to raise his head.

Phobos was at their side in an instant, lifting the demigod from Mirri's arms and setting Ashtad on his feet. The god of fear kept a firm grip on Ashtad's shoulders, though.

Ashtad tried to focus on Bix, eyes narrowing repeatedly with excessive blinking. "Get it out."

"Get what out? What did he implant in you?" Bix hissed as her temper spiked. All her brothers had a yen for implanting things in her toys. Phobos had come out of his first meeting with her eldest brother with quite a disturbing quantity.

"Out. Out. Out. Get it out." Ashtad wobbled, and Phobos braced him.

"Hel, we need your help." Mirri's worried gaze remained fixed on Ashtad as her faithful hound leaned against her legs. "The trip through time, it's done something."

Hel grunted with annoyance but joined the other gods around Ashtad. Hel barked a single note of mirth and jabbed a hand into Ashtad's side. Ashtad screamed in agony as blood spurted. Bix dug her nails into her palms and willed her darkness to remain calm. These were allies trying to help her dear friend. Just because Hel had an atrocious bedside manner didn't mean she wasn't helping.

"Please be careful. All is not as it should be within him," Mirri blurted a breath before Ashtad's eyes rolled and he collapsed into Phobos's outstretched arms, leaving an unconscious giant icy-blue malformed wolf hanging from Hel's fist.

Drew. In the draugr's native state. Drew could only be

corporeal in the Under Worlds; otherwise, that icy blue was mostly gaseous energy.

Bix couldn't believe what she was seeing. Ashtad, who held no love for the draugr, had let Drew occupy his body for the sake of the journey. Feng had brought all three of them back to the present. Tobek was alone with her brother in the future, true, but Drew, Ashtad, Cian, and Feng were safely returned to the present. All hail the team. Bix had to lock her knees to keep from fainting from joy and gratitude. Now that she was at her full power, if her brother dared to send his heralds after her friends again, she'd unmake his lackies in less than the blink of an eye.

"We should take the demigod back to the Mids so that he may complete his trials without further undue interference," Hel said as ice flowed down her arm to encapsulate Drew. As Drew's creator, Hel had the power to heal the draugr. Bix didn't, so Bix beat back the urge to snatch her best friend away from Hel's cruel but restorative grip.

"No." Mirri fished in her blazer pocket before extracting a scrap of printed linen. "This is from the Fates. It says he should go to Irkalla. It has something to do with what's wrong inside him."

Everyone who was still lucid pivoted toward Ereshkigal, who had remained silent throughout all the drama.

The titaness threw up her hands and gasped with delight. "The young Ba'al, cherished friend of the Chimera, in my home? Under my care? What a curious request. I accept."

Bix wasn't sure that was a great idea, but, then again, the Fates knew more than she did about what he'd endured while with Desire. Ereshkigal knew how important Ashtad was to Bix, and the titaness would be highly insulted if Bix was anything less than enthusiastic about the arrangement. Upsetting a titan, never a good idea. Besides, gods of assorted sciences abounded in Irkalla. Perhaps there was something the Fates wanted Ashtad to learn from them or from Ereshkigal herself. The titaness was exceptionally wise and had long been one of Bix's confidants.

"When he's coherent, I'll need to talk to him about his experiences in the future," Bix said instead.

Ereshkigal gave her a knowing smile as threads of the titaness's darkness coiled around Ashtad. Within a count of seven, his resonance departed the Greek Under World.

"I'm going to return to the Mids to look after Feng and the Sage boy," Mirri announced to an oddly quiet garden. "Chimera, how should I reach you to let you know when they're able to recount their stories?"

Bix pointed to Phobos. "He'll know how to reach me. I still have one more team member to bring home. I can't thank you enough for what you did, Mirri."

Mirri blushed three different shades but smiled. "It felt good to be useful and competent again. Thank you for giving me an opportunity to which I could rise."

"Hades, goddesses, my gratitude for your assistance as well." Bix said, closing the viewing gates. Tobek was still in the future, and she needed him home. However, before she went off half-cocked, there were experts far beyond this galaxy she ought to consult.

"We still need an estimated time of departure for the Devourers, Chimera," Setesuyara reminded. "The titans must be appeased, or they will rise."

Bix resisted voicing the first dozen responses that leapt to mind. She was fully the Chimera of lore once again. If any titan so much as poked a finger into an occupied galaxy, particularly the one housing her sanctuary, they'd have the High Executioner to answer to. However, she understood the gods' concern and respected it. They had a job to do and needed either information or marching orders to do it. Bix had neither to give, so she said nothing. She simply mocked a salute as she opened a gate to someone who would love to play with naughty little titans to break up the monotony of his incarceration.

CHAPTER 14

Bickering, loud and forceful enough to shatter collectives, carried down a hallway so massive, it could store a hundred sprawling castles. Glossy black gables and baseboards reflected distant flares brighter than sunlight that were instantly swallowed by swirling darkness. Panes of long arched windows rattled in their frames, threatening to shoot shards into nearby nebulas. Wide doors along the corridor swung repeatedly, slamming shut then popping open. Triangular red garnet tiles vibrated as they pivoted beneath Bix's feet, guiding her closer to the conflict.

It'd been ages since she'd last caught her eldest brothers in the throes of a heated argument. Since this was a prison for only one of them, she had a good guess as to who'd started it and who was enjoying it.

Bix rounded an atrium hosting a massive waterfall. Terrariums of different environments trapping a mixture of gods and anti-gods jutted out from the falls on cliffs of ever-changing terrain. Now and again a terrarium would tumble from its perch and disappear into the water, only to pop up at the top of the falls and tumble again, bouncing off cliffs and other terrariums like a pinball. Sometimes it dislodged another terrarium; sometimes an unseated terrarium managed to land on a new cliff.

Ah, the entertainments of bored First Children.

Farther down a few more winding corridors, Bix came upon her favorite place in the entire prison to visit: the solarium. Today, however, on one side of the mostly glass room, a vortex of darkness spun. Specks of red glitter winked from its stormy churning. Across the large room, an array of bursting suns exploded in patterns older than Morse code. The darkness was her eldest brother Eko, also known as Knowledge Innate or Instinct, in his irritated native state. The suns were his twin Esiw, also known as Knowledge Amassed or Experience. Eko was the son aligned to their mother the Chaos, Esiw to their father the Cosmos.

In comparison to her brothers, Bix's preferred humanoid body was the size of the tarsal hook of a flea. She could, of course, match the elder twins size for size, but it would be much more entertaining to deflate them and their tempers. Thus, she cast threads of contrasting messy night into Esiw's ordered arrays and spears of organizing light into Eko's swirling shadows. Within the sacred count of seven, she'd rearranged their bits.

Esiw caterwauled as his suns dimmed to golden stars and sorted themselves into the outline of a large four-tailed fox. As the fourth child of the Chaos and the Cosmos, four was his sacred number. Thus, four sacred beats passed as the fox sprouted white fur for its giant body and yellow fur for its socks, ear tufts, and tail tips. Stars remained in his eyes as he cast a reproachful look down at Bix.

At this scale, she was a bit more akin to a Bichon. An unrepentant Bichon, mind.

Eko's angry bellow ended with hoots of laughter as he condensed his form into that of a massive black three-toed minotaur. His spiraling black horns veined in red glitter prevented his wild mane of cherry-red hair from falling in his broad, square face. The fire of his eyes danced merrily as he patted Bix on the head with the tip of one of his three fingers.

"Little sister, you are whole now," Eko cheered, nudging her into the palm of his hand. "I no longer sense your broken places.

This is wonderful. Esiw, look, little sister is herself once again."

"She may have all her parts, but she is hardly the same as she was." Esiw sniffed with disdain. "The sister I raised would not stoop to interrupt a discussion with childish pranks."

"When you behave like a child by cornering Eko in his prison to deride him for his natural chaotic tendencies, then I will take that as a sign that we are all to behave as if we lack impulse control and an awareness of Other." Bix planted her hands on her hips and mirrored Esiw's censorious expression. "You know how much I love a good game."

"You *dare* lecture me on impulse control?" Esiw cried indignantly.

"This time, she would be correct to do so, eh, brother?" Eko guffawed as he wiggled the fingers of his empty hand, casting a whirl of red glitter that pulled on the minor energies in the room to form a plain black table scaled for the solarium. He set her on the matte surface, then manifested a simple three-legged stool for himself beside the table.

Lips twitching to fleeting sneers, Esiw appeared to be choking back a retort. Eventually, he snapped his tails, and a large yellow pillow poofed into existence beneath him. Clearing his throat, he kneaded his pillow with his front paws before casually sinking into a lounging pose, stoic composure regained. "Please do not allow the lives of others to interrupt the flow of yours. To what do we owe your company, little sister?"

"Don't be a dick, Esiw." She expanded her form to be on par with theirs. Sometimes, Esiw needed the subliminal reminder that just because she was younger didn't mean she was dumber. He'd raised her to hold her own against him and anyone else who would try to use intellect to bully her. She loved him for that now, but she'd had to become an adult before she'd appreciated his efforts. "I'm here about Desire and what he's been up to during the three-hundred-odd years I didn't remember you guys existed."

Eko smirked at Esiw, as if she'd just asked the guy with crumbs on his face who'd eaten the last cookie.

"You need to be more specific," Esiw said, ignoring his twin.

"Desire recently abducted my favorite toys and tried to put them some place I couldn't reach. He did that instead of confronting me directly. Desire is many things, but never a coward. I don't understand why he's hiding from me." Bix swung her legs, studying her eldest brothers. Something was off with these two. Eko usually was the cat swallowing the canary, and Esiw the rat threatening to narc if he didn't get the bribe he wanted. Today, they'd swapped roles.

"Why didn't you come to us for help retrieving your toys?" Eko asked, obviously offended.

"As generous as you two are, you would've told me how to do it and stopped there." Bix tapped her temple. "I knew the how. At this point, I don't understand why he let them live, nor why he is refusing to meet with me. Both are out of character for him, so something must've happened while I was broken. I need to know what that was so I am prepared when I attempt to convince him to evict his Devourers from my home permanently without further bloodshed."

"You've been trying to reach him, yet his only response is to steal from you. How curious." Eko stared at his twin, sarcasm tingeing his tone. "I wonder what is keeping him."

"Last I remember, you two and the eldest two had turned your backs on Desire. Shunning him. You'd had it with his antics." Had Bix not been focused on getting Tobek home, she would've loved to pick apart this peculiar interaction between her brothers. Tobek might be resilient, but Desire was devious and cruel. She didn't trust her youngest brother with the man she loved.

"Desire is a snollygoster. He refuses to accept responsibility or accountability for his actions," Esiw growled with disgust. "Of late, he's chosen to pursue an obsession that, by all rational standards, is unattainable. He confuses himself with being one of our creations rather than a First Child."

"He wants to die. That's why it's odd he's refusing to meet with me, the High Executioner." Bix wondered how much Esiw knew about the lengths to which Tempest and Desire had gone to achieve their goal. The eldest son, aligned to order, tended to perceive more than he ever let on. "Has he asked you two to help him?"

"Such a pursuit is absurd," Esiw insisted. "Even if we wanted to, we couldn't. He knows that, yet he blames *us* for his failure. Look at what he is doing to your home and your favorites."

Bix allowed the generalization of "we." Fact was, she *could* kill her brother. She knew that now with absolute confidence since she had all her memories sorted and settled. However, doing so didn't save the Mids nor did it return Tobek to her side. Then there was the problem that would be caused by Desire's absence, which would amount to the absence of all motivation from the greater existence. Sloth would no longer be a character flaw; it would be the default for every creation of every type. Life would come to a grinding halt rather quickly.

"We are always available to encourage each other and help each other grow. That is what family is for." Eko smiled and patted her knee. "But there comes a point at which assistance creates dependency, and that dependency creates false expectations that suffocate all involved. For our own well-being, we could not allow him to use us to foster his desperation."

"And that still holds true to this day? For all of you? Hard line, cut direct, yes?" She noticed Esiw's hackles rising and pondered the reason for his unusual response. Esiw was the king of not letting things visibly get to him. It was why Eko took perverse delight in needling him. Esiw being the aggressor in the squabble she'd interrupted earlier was not normal for him.

"More so than ever. When death eluded Desire, he infected Tempest," Eko added sadly.

Bix stiffened. Had they finally noticed? Could they finally see what had been happening under their noses since Bix's childhood?

"When you say Desire is infecting Tempest…" She let the question hang.

"She, who was once his only bastion of sanity, has been

corrupted by the miasma of his folly." Eko stared at the nebulas winking beyond the glass ceiling. "As a daughter aligned to the Chaos, Tempest is more susceptible to the irrational. The only thing she wants from us now is to pressure you into killing her and her twin."

Holy shit. They did know. All these years. They finally saw it.

"You don't blame Tempest? Even though her behavior is equally atrocious?" Bix couldn't overlook the last three hundred years of Tempest's unrelenting violent nagging, which was peculiar for a chaotic entity. They didn't maintain focus for that long. It went against their nature. They were very much the children of "Squirrel!"

Was that what had caught Eko's and Esiw's attention? Tempest's sustained determination despite Bix's incapacitation? Prolonged pressure was a tactic of a child aligned to order. It was why Bix had zero doubt that the bulk of Tempest's unfaltering hostility came from Desire through their twin bond.

Yet another reason Desire's current avoidance of Bix was bizarre.

"Tempest can't escape his influence, and he's forcing her to carry the burden of both their obsessions. It's nothing less than protracted abuse," Esiw admitted. "So, while she has attacked each of us, yes, I can forgive her. I even pity her. I have told her and Desire repeatedly that their relief is solely under Desire's control."

Bix relaxed a little. Tempest and Desire's toxic linkage being stronger than ever was the foundation of her revised plan to rescue Tobek. The rest of what her brothers confirmed was the core of their family problem that had to be corrected in order to save the Mids. Upshot, at least Eko and Esiw *saw* the problem now. She no longer had to convince them, which was a new development.

"Tempest refuses to do anything to stand up to Desire, still?" Bix grimaced when both brothers nodded. It would be so much easier if Tempest *wanted* to stand up for herself. Despite their history, Bix would be right there to support Tempest's efforts. Together, they could disarm Desire permanently. Alas. "Does she give your advice a passing consideration? Or does she brush you off as some clueless overbearing fuddy-duddy?"

"She accuses me of favoritism. She believes I am only concerned because you are the target of their ire. She insists I always place your well-being ahead of theirs." Esiw looked away and softly spoke those words.

"Yes, because I had your undivided attention when I was your pupil and she had to share you with Desire." Bix snorted. "She never understood the benefit of not owning your singular focus."

That elicited a tiny smirk from the eldest son of order. "She didn't like sharing Desire's affections with you either. She gives in too easily to jealousy. It's rooted in insecurities that Desire's selfishness fostered during key developmental periods."

"She's always felt like she was being left out and left behind." Eko shook his head. "Movement and I tried hard to guide her out of that poisonous aspect, but…"

Movement was the firstborn of the First Children. She was the first aligned to the Chaos. She wasn't a warm, fuzzy, maternal sort, far from it. Loud, acerbic, abrasive yet demonstrative. Movement was as quick with a left hook as she was with a hug. Unpredictable by nature, Movement didn't offer stable ground. One had to have a strong sense of self to have a healthy relationship with her. For someone like Tempest, who sought a constant to be her source of affection and inclusion, the attempts by two other chaotic entities could never be enough. Tempest needed the continuity that came from the siblings of order, that *should* have come from her twin. Unfortunately, Desire's primary aspect was personal drive. His approach to life was very "me, me, me." Anything that got in the way of his goals was ruined, including the needs of his twin.

"Since Tempest and Desire are at odds with the entire family, why did they help make this prison for you, Eko? You were gloriously free before I gave away my mind." Bix still needed to understand why Desire showed up to help the others, yet refused to meet with her when she alone could give him what he wanted. "Someone extend an olive branch?"

Eko hung his head and picked at his pant leg. His three tails tucked under his stool.

"They understood the implicit danger Eko's action presented to the greater existence." Esiw glowered at his twin. "There was no negotiation required."

Bix wasn't a hundred percent sure what Eko had done to merit incarceration, but she had an inkling. His freedom relied on her, and she had until the Devourers were gone from the Mids to confirm her suspicions. After that, she'd promised to spring him. If she was right about the incident that had scared the bejesus out of her family, then, well, all that was a conversation to be had between the two of them in private after Desire's toys were out of her house.

"How did you reach Desire? He was being actively ignored by everyone. After all, that was the reason I didn't come to any of you when he and Tempest had pushed me too far. For all intents and purposes, you'd given him what he wanted, he was dead to you." Bix knew that being ignored sent Desire into conniptions. Attention was a quantifiable thing, and he was the root of greed. He tried to accumulate attention always. His siblings ignoring him meant he'd failed.

"Tempest," Esiw sighed. "Movement went to Tempest. Tempest summoned him, just as she did when it came time to bind your favorite toy to aid in his evolution into an undefined Other."

"So back then, he was still answering her." Bix's mind raced. Desire hadn't responded to Tempest's recent invitation to death, or so Tempest claimed. Then again, it was possible Tempest was lying. "Why did they help bind Tobek? What did they demand in exchange?"

"They made no demand," Eko grumbled. His three tails whipped along the floor, cherry-tuft tips glimmering in the light cast by Esiw's entirety. "They'd figured out that by binding your favorite toy, they'd have constant access to him."

"We all do." Esiw turned a paw up and bared his claws. "Never forget that."

Tobek had reminded her of their access just before Desire's heralds had taken him from her. Any of her siblings at any time for no better reason than a whim could snatch him. Thing was, Tempest *hadn't* done it. Even when Bix had provoked her. Desire, on the other hand, had taken him, but he'd used his heralds. Four of them. Which had meaning. That she didn't understand yet.

There was a huge chunk of What the Hell that was eluding Bix. It wasn't based on what had been. She had all those details. Something had changed with Desire and Tempest while she hadn't been paying attention. Something was amiss between them. She needed to apply more brainpower to the conundrum, which her gray matter was unwilling to oblige until she had Tobek safe, sound, and in her arms.

"So, Tempest has positioned herself as the gateway to Desire. She's making you all go through her to get to him. That is inordinately useful information." Bix hopped off the table and smoothed her skirt. As a gatekeeper, Bix knew the trouble that came with that position. Unfortunately for Tempest, her sister was about to get an unpleasant education.

"Little sister, what is it you're planning to do?" Esiw prompted warily.

"Get my favorite toy back from Desire, of course." Bix wondered if her brother had missed the entire purpose of their conversation.

Eko dropped his head in his hands, shoulders quaking. He practically burst trying to mask his merriment, for which he received a droll scowl from his twin.

"As always, dear brothers, thank you for your insight. Try not to annoy each other too badly while I'm gone." She tapped the tip of her nose and bestowed a mischievous grin on Eko and Esiw. "Don't worry, I will be back. I'm dying to know what it is Esiw has done that both of you are hiding from me."

CHAPTER 15

In an undeveloped galaxy abutting that of Bix's sanctuary, sentient night offered a pathway of pewter pinpricks down which the reinforcements of anti-gods marched. Out here in the vast nothingness, the miasma of the Devourers' toxicity flowed around them like gossamer robes.

"Don't think because you're tiny, I can't sense you, bratling," Tempest hissed, the warning carrying throughout her native state of darkness.

"Where is your twin, Tempest?" Bix brightened the stars that composed the half of her that was aligned to order. She didn't change her form or go supernova, but the light was enough to cause the advancing army to pause and point. "He's refused my invitation for so long now that I'm beginning to think Desire doesn't want to die anymore. Did he leave you alone to wallow in your suicidal fantasy?"

"He's busy in the future finding ways to torment you. How *are* your favored toys, hmm? Hear you're still missing one." Tempest condensed her state into her preferred form resembling a hybrid of a cephalopod with the core of a human woman. Her headdress of black tentacles layered over her lower body of more black tentacles, all emblazoned in pewter iconographs of arcane languages. Sharp pewter hooks sprouted from the tentacles in place of suction cups. Haughty disdain oozed from her like the cloud of toxins from the Devourers.

Once upon a time, Desire had created the Devourers as a peace offering to Tempest after she'd tried to assert herself and break his hold over her. As part of his manipulative apology, he'd made the anti-gods bear a strong resemblance to Tempest so she wouldn't refuse them. In Tempest's twisted mind, using Desire's creations to attack Bix's sanctuary was a perversely satisfying means of lashing out against both Desire and Bix. Bix could follow the insanity of passive-aggressive petulance, even though she didn't subscribe to it. It wasn't that Bix didn't have her own brand of crazy, but hers was rooted in learning how to process and responsibly respond to her own feelings. Bearing their unfiltered burden was new to her, and it wasn't going smoothly. She was an emotional powder keg. It made her unpredictable, which was advantageous when confronting a chaotic sibling.

"No, he's not busy. He's hiding," Bix taunted. "What happened to your great urgency? You've been in such a rush, demanding I kill you now, now, now, but I can't unmake you without him. You're two sides of the same sheet of tinfoil. He's the shiny side, while you're quite dull. Still, you have to be unmade together or not at all."

Tempest invaded Bix's personal space and bared the sharklike rows of her teeth. "The Devourers will continue to assail your fragile home until we're dead. It matters less to me how long he takes to get here, since it allows me more time to watch you squirm and cry over the slow demise of your precious playthings."

If Bix had needed confirmation that Tempest wasn't as suicidal as Desire, it couldn't get much plainer than her sister placing Bix's misery higher than her own release. Which then made Bix wonder if Desire was losing his cruel hold over his twin. Was all his time hiding in the future giving Tempest space to think for herself? Tempest was a victim, true, but there were two types of victims. Those who vowed never, ever to be like their abuser, and those who found victims of their own to torture. That was how abuse propagated. Tempest, as the origin of external motivation—of peer pressure, family expectations, social obligations, etcetera—easily expanded upon the abuse she endured. She fostered all those heavy, stifling factors to crush more often than to guide or uplift. And Tempest had the gall to be annoyed that the masses kept calling out for help to unburden themselves.

"Tell me, sister, at what point does the victim become accountable for allowing their abuse to continue?" Bix feigned a look of deep concern. "At what point do you accept responsibility for being just as bad, in fact worse, than Desire?"

Tempest jerked back. "What are you talking about?"

"You're his emotional waste bin," Bix jeered with a sneer as her chaotic half reveled in the frothing of acute, hostile fear every moment Tobek lingered in Desire's pernicious clutches. "When you got too full of his shit, you didn't throw it back at him. You didn't stand up for yourself. No, you buckled and became his mimic. Yet you have the audacity to pule about the family not loving you enough. You are just as guilty as Desire for shirking the responsibility for the isolation you've brought on yourself."

"It is *your* fault I have been isolated from the family." Tempest jabbed a sharp nail into Bix's shoulder, clawing out a chunk of flesh-coated midnight. "To this day, our siblings are so worried about the novel two-in-one, trained by our father to be an obedient killer who might end us all. Yet the one time it would be a massive benefit to the greater existence, you refuse to do your damn duty."

Bix no longer knew how much of that sentiment was Desire's toxic implant and how much of that was Tempest's favorite excuse. End of day, some people delighted in being assholes. Their backstory didn't matter; their behavior wasn't going to change. The only thing Bix could control in this relationship at this time was the number of fucks she had to give for the terrible twins. As long as Tempest kept commanding Desire's Devourers to consume the Mids and as long as Desire had Tobek, Bix had zero guilt about what she planned to do next.

To borrow a phrase from her best friend: Sometimes, bullies gotta get beat.

"It's funny how bold you are." Bix let a sinister smile spread, one that would make Phobos proud. "Reminding me of my training. Begging me to kill you. It's almost like you've forgotten that *you* were the one who taught me how to find everyone's boundaries."

"Don't threaten me, bratling. The reason you force me to continue my miserable existence isn't to punish me. It's because you're a coward." Tempest spat on Bix.

Bix ignored the clump of gummy spittle sliding down her cheek and danced her fingers along one of Tempest's tentacles. "You positioned yourself as the gatekeeper between Desire and our other siblings. Movement had to beg you to bring him along so you could all bind my favorite toy."

"We had to bind your toy to force you to break your ties to him." Tempest knocked aside Bix's hand. "An act I knew would cause you great suffering even in your doofus state. And you know me, anything that causes you pain, I'm in."

"Yeah, I know. That jealousy Desire implanted in you makes you vulnerable, stupid, and useful."

Bix didn't give her sister a chance to react. She exploded into her native state and violently pierced her sister's body with all the force required to keep her sister off-balance long enough to find the thread connecting Tempest to Tobek. Exploiting that connection would be more than a little bit excruciating for Tempest, the kind of agony Bix wouldn't willingly inflict on their older siblings.

Tempest didn't fully understand the ties that bind. In fairness, neither had Bix until she'd reclaimed all her wits. While she'd recently severed her direct connection to Tobek, it wasn't the same as severing their connection altogether. He and she remained indirectly linked through her siblings.

Tobek's current evolution into an unknown class of superentity required his aspects to be constrained by greater powers so the various magics he absorbed were trapped within him, forcing all facets of him to continually develop. These days, the only powers significantly greater than his own were First Children. Bix couldn't create the necessary bindings. That was beyond her ability. In fact, her destructive skills made her an unwitting detriment to his bindings and his evolution. She would be forever grateful her siblings had stepped up to help him.

At the moment, she was also grateful that she and her siblings maintained direct connections to each other. All hail the filial bond. The swirls of the children aligned to the Chaos were braced by the rays of the children aligned to the Cosmos, which created the constantly changing web that supported the greater existence. Bix, as the two-in-one, realigned the structure as needed, untangling knots or expanding spaces in between. It was her business to be constantly up in their business, though she usually wasn't quite so literal about it.

Usually.

There was a reason no creation could hide from her. While she preferred to use her network of spies to locate someone, sometimes she had to follow the path of the creators to get to the creation. In those rare instances, she used a subtle thread that passed beneath the awareness of her siblings as it passed through them to walk the chain of creations. Normally, she was hunting for a location. Once she had that, she'd retreat from the personal invasion, her sibling rarely the wiser. This time, however, she was bringing back more than information. She intended to bring back the man himself. She'd never done it before, but she couldn't use gates to reach into the future and she couldn't be there herself. She had to stay tight to the part of Tempest that bound Tobek. Bix had to hide within that tie of a creationist that could exist in the future and travel as fast as she could along the chute before Tempest realized what she was doing and expelled her.

She was using seven percent of her awareness to make that journey; the rest of her was actively engaged in physical combat with her sister as they shifted in and out of native and preferred states, trying to get the upper hand. Playing mercilessly upon Tempest's weak spots and egging on her sister's jealousy, Bix sustained blow after blow and gave back as hard as she got. They'd both trained with Movement. Tempest had had Desire as a sparring partner. Bix had had Movement and only Movement. There were advantages and disadvantages to both, but there was nothing Bix wouldn't endure to save Tobek from the cruelties of her family.

She'd seen the condition in which the rest of her team had returned to the present. Desire had done something bad to them, probably in trying to keep them with him. Feng should've been able to make that trip to the present no problem. Sure, he might've been tired, but no way should he have been catatonic. That Fates' threads had had to haul him down the line and through the access point? That the ley lines had had to extinguish his flames because he couldn't? That Mirri had had to bring Ashtad and Drew to the Under Worlds because they were both so damaged? That Ashtad's best hope for rehab was in the care of a titaness? All of it was definitive proof that fuckery had been afoot. She was terrified to think about Cian's condition. The kid had what they jokingly called an "allergy" to magic moving inside his body, the kind of allergy that would turn him into a fist-sized crystal thanks to an infection caused by Desire's toxic toys.

So while Tobek was the most resourceful and powerful among her friends, she didn't trust Desire to refrain from devising innovative ways to punish Tobek for the rescue of Bix's team. Thus, she refused to let up on Tempest, Desire's victim and accomplice.

In the fragment of her awareness hurtling down the tie to Tobek, she collided with his resonance. Weak. But undeniably Tobek's. She cleaved herself in two, separating her darkness from her light. She pushed her light down the tie crossing time and left her chaotic half in the present. She stopped fighting her sister and twined with her, becoming stickier than wet toilet paper.

Tempest shrieked and thrashed. "What are you doing? What are…you…? What trick are you playing, bratling?"

Bix didn't resist Tempest's movements. Instead, she flowed with her in the dance of chaotic violence. This was the advantage of functioning wholly on instinct. Tempest had been her antagonist for so long, there was little Bix needed to anticipate. She felt like a ballerina in the throes of her hundredth performance with years of practice conditioning muscle memory. While the entirety of her starlight of order was busy spreading along the Eternal Knot that anchored her siblings' ties to Tobek, it left behind no glimmer of structure attempting to improve Tempest, to balance her sister as Bix's dominant aspect demanded. Chaos moved with chaos in the present as starlight expanded around Tobek in the future and dragged him up the binding tie toward Tempest.

The tethers of time resisted her efforts. Tethers that…that didn't belong to Desire.

The hell?

Esiw. Damn it. *This* was what he was hiding from her?

Stunned, Bix lost her flow with Tempest. Her sister shoved her away. Mostly. Almost. Bix's rage woke within her lights of order, feeding Tobek's primal rage that was the root of his magic. Together, they broke free of the tethers of time and rocketed up the final distance to the present.

"I suggest you revert to your native state, dear sister, lest you discover what it's like to give birth to a fully grown man through your eye socket," Bix snarled as she pulled away from Tempest. Starlight filled her being as her other half returned to the moment.

Tempest burst into gray-streaked night just as Tobek breached the opening of the chute. He tumbled into vacated space, glowing hunter green through fractals of ice spawning over his battered and bleeding body. Bix quickly enveloped him in protective midnight and starlight as she assumed a form somewhat feminine but wholly cosmic.

"How dare you?" Tempest seethed quietly. "How dare you violate me? How dare you use me as a godsdamned passageway?"

"You wanted to play doorman for Desire. You enjoyed the attention it got you from the others." Bix's chuckle was full of the malice fomenting within her. "All I did was step through another door, one of billions within you that you never protect or even notice."

"My body is not your toy," Tempest screeched. "I am no one's toy. I am no one's pity party. I am no one's victim. I am the godsdamned fifth child of the Chaos and the Cosmos. I am all things motivation. I am the nightmare that plagues you in every aspect of your existence until you give me what I demand."

"Tempest, your hypocrisy is truly astounding," Bix derided, letting her malice transform the soft contours of her darkness into hardy thorns and her starlight into prickly burrs. "Besides, you're so consumed by your hate for me that you can't detect the real reason Desire hasn't shown up in the present."

"I cannot hear him above the din of trillions of incompetent, sniveling creations begging for guidance, begging for aid, begging for a miracle so they don't have to put in the effort themselves," Tempest wailed, her darkness turning to tentacles that lashed about wildly. She sobered quickly and fumed, "However, I can assure you the only reason he's not here is because he knows you aren't going to deliver until I apply more pressure."

"Desire is a prisoner, my selfish sister," Bix said with all the pity she felt, which was precisely none. "I've left you a clue how to free him. Up to you if you leverage it to rebuild your backbone."

CHAPTER 16

The hospitality Mid World welcomed Bix and Tobek with cooling breezes through dense, color-changing forests that cast fragrances lush and spicy across a wide clear lake. At the center of the lake sat a small island speckled with fruit trees, shrubs bearing edible berries, and multiple tiers of a thriving herb garden surrounding two adjoining wattle-and-daub yurts. On the western side, a silk hammock swung over grassy slopes leading down to a blush-pink sand beach where a driftwood kayak rested upon hewn-stone racks. On the southern side, a firepit with three stump seats awaited the evening as the three crescent suns inched toward the twilight horizon under the undulating auroras of Resen celebrating Tobek's return to the Mid Worlds. Three full moons rose from the opposite horizon, shifting shadows, altering the calls of the creatures living deep in the woods, and luring aquatic beasts to play among the changing currents.

This World was one of the original three created by her eldest sisters Movement and Music to be Bix's sanctuary. This World was older than anything in the Uppers and the Unders; indeed, it was one of the first planets in this entire galaxy. Yet, until Bix had turned Tobek into a magic siphon for her cosmic excesses, she'd only been able to watch this place from afar. He allowed her to exist within the Mids, to experience the lives of lesser beings firsthand, to be something less than cumbersomely powerful.

Extracting Tobek from the safety of her native state, she set him upon the hammock. A notable part of her calmed. She had her big blond bear back, but judging by the thick frost coating his body, he was either injured or rapidly evolving. His growth into a different class of Other required prolonged exposure to myriad magics of increasing potency. Spending time in close quarters with Desire absolutely qualified. She waited with bated breath for him to show signs of a growth spurt or to revert to a solid block of ice. The latter would confirm her suspicions of extensive physical damage.

Neither happened. Tobek groaned and winced, stretching. Patches of frost melted, exposing his fully inked torso and curiously fashioned pants. He thrust his silver hand in her direction. "Get over here, sweetheart. I've a primitive need for some personal contact."

"Don't know how much comfort I'm going to be," she cautioned, consolidating her form into her preferred state. Because he loved her, she allowed herself to be fragile in his presence. Gods did she feel fragile right now. She was teetering on the edge of going nuclear. Her emotions ricocheted through extremes at a frenetic pace.

"Excellent. I promise not to be much better." His laugh was wicked, and his eyes glowed with his Berserker's rage. "The infusion of your wrath was the catalyst I needed to shield myself as we broke free of that cursed spell. Lie by me. Let's be angry together."

She hesitated going to him. She was just too prickly to be pleasant company, and he was wounded, though she couldn't tell how badly.

"Okay, I'll come to you." He rolled off the hammock, planting his big bare feet in the fragrant grass. His knees buckled. Gates caught him and dropped him back in the hammock.

"Tobek, you just traveled through time. That takes a toll. Let your body and mind have a moment to reconcile the journey."

Hanging his head, he stuck out his natural hand. "Please?"

Oh, who was she kidding? She needed him as much as he needed her. She clasped his hand and slid onto the silk weave, wriggling until she'd affixed herself to his side with her head on the fleshy bicep of his otherwise silver arm. The sigh of contentment and relief that flowed from her was not remotely a human sound.

He burst out laughing. "I missed you too, sweetheart. More than you can imagine."

"How long has it been for you?" She scanned his body for clues to the passage of time, but he'd stopped physically aging a long, long while ago.

"Well, let's see, you left me just under three and a half centuries ago, so—"

"Not what I meant, and you know it." She smacked his thigh. "To you, how long has it been since Desire's heralds took you?"

His lips puckered amid his frizzy facial hair. "I've no idea. I can't track time differences like you. It's all a bit new to me."

"Don't think it was your lack of experience. Phobos had a similar problem." She sighed. "It has to do with the time trap in which you were entangled."

"It feels like it's been more than months, but I can't be more specific," Tobek admitted with an annoyed grumble. "I kept trying to break the spell and get back to you, which caused me serious damage, so I'd freeze up. Then when I woke, I'd have no sense of how much time had passed, and your brother wasn't exactly forthcoming on the matter. Reverting to my base state shoots my circadian rhythms to hell. Something changed near the end, though, Desire seemed restless."

"The rescue of my team, probably," she guessed, skimming her fingers over his Eternal Knot that was still exposed amid his layers of ink due to the active magic of First Children flowing through it, fighting to protect his evolution from her. "Phobos said the heralds separated you from the others. Why? What did Desire do to you that he didn't want the others to see?"

"Unlike the others, I suffer no ill effects from being in the undiluted presence of a First Child." He manifested a light blanket to cover her naked body, ever considerate of her modesty hang-up. "Mostly, your brother wanted to talk. He was particularly interested in the loss of our child."

Disbelief stopped her heart and her senses until she couldn't contain her outrage anymore. Her flesh gave way to darkness flying upward in a torrent of thorny vines as her starlight screeched like fireworks to explode above the tree line.

"He *dares*? He *dares* exploit our tragedy? He *dares* attempt to break you by using our dead daughter?" she howled, the disembodied sound traveling across the World and sending creatures of land and sea diving for cover. "That is it. I have *had it* with him. That is too far, even for a First Child."

"He doesn't seem to have a sense of boundaries nor a concept of his actions having any sort of consequences that might come to bear on him." Tobek rolled to his knees in the middle of the hammock, vibrant eyes glowing brightly with his reawakened rage as green magic sparked around him.

"He's never had to face the godsdamn consequences because they inevitably *fall on me*." Bix's chaotic rage whipped through the forest and across the lake, causing trees to bend and snap while whitecaps crashed over the shorelines to erode beaches and banks. "Desire's actions have brought about the end of the Mid Worlds *forty-two times*. Forty-two times I have reset the godsdamned timeline to save my home, my friends, and my loved ones. Forty-two times, Tobek. Do you know that the past is never recreated in perfection? That is forty-two different lives I have led that no one, *no one* but me remembers. The consequences of his actions are forty-two different relationships with you, with the Berserkers, with the Consortium, with the gods, with the Devourers, with my entire godsdamned family. I *alone* remember it all. Me."

"Forty-two? Oh, sweetheart," Tobek howled like a wounded beast and laced his fingers behind his head, lifting his rage-bright gaze to cut through the storm of her midnight fury, to openly share his pain with her. "You never told me."

"You have no idea how many times I *did* tell you, because those confessions were erased in the reset." She realigned her starlight and her midnight, coalescing into cosmic femininity as she ruthlessly bid her temper to refocus its target. Tobek wasn't it. He hadn't done anything worse than live and love her. "I have watched you die numerous times because in those timelines, you never evolved to immortality. A thousand years, three thousand, thirteen thousand. I have lost track of the short resets, but the long ones are pikes skewering bleeding collectives in my memories. Collectives destroyed by Desire's godsdamned toys and his singular obsession with death."

"How alone you must feel," he rasped, his voice breaking.

"You want to know why he's so interested in the death of a child I failed to bring into existence? Because our daughter who never was achieved what he craves," she cried, tearing at her own incorporeal belly. "It is a small mercy that you and I only had to experience a miscarriage once and not forty-two times. Once is already too much."

He opened his arms to her. "Tell me what I can do to ease your pain."

"Nothing, love, nothing." She cradled his head in her ethereal hands. "You are magnificent as you are right now, in this moment, in this timeline, in this order of events. You are everything to me. That *you* live despite their machinations is the sweetest Fuck You to Tempest and Desire. That you've evolved the furthest you have in any prior timeline is our reward for perseverance. Who you are keeps me fighting to save this timeline from their determined self-destruction."

"It's not self-destruction if what you've destroyed is the timeline and not them," he countered, pressing his cheek into her palm.

"Oh, my heart. You think me better than I am." She smoothed his long hair over his broad shoulders. "I am not an entity of benevolence. I am an entity of balance, as much chaos as order."

"I know exactly who you are. I shy away from none of your

truths because they make you the entity to whom I am totally committed, the entity I love." He didn't hesitate with his response, nor did he hold back on the vehemence of his sincerity. "I know you so well, sweetheart, that I see you're struggling with guilt. What did you do?"

"I killed them." She smiled softly as the memories of those moments washed through her with renewed emotions. Deeply satisfying emotions. The guilt she felt wasn't for her actions, it was for not having a lick of remorse for those actions. "I have killed Tempest and Desire six times. My own siblings. Dead. Unmade. Erased from existence. Six glorious times."

Tobek leaned back, bracing on locked arms. Zero judgment bled through the rage they were feeding each other. One of a thousand things she loved about him. He understood hard, ugly choices had to be made. He understood the unpopular and ethically difficult decisions were the price of power. He understood some people were simply beyond help. He understood she was the High Executioner and that she owned every consequence of her actions.

"Six?" he asked, lips twisting into a vindictive smirk. "Did you change your mind afterward? Reset time to restore them?"

"Not I," she refuted bitterly. "My parents. The only entities who, when working together, can reset time. Since that's my trick as the two-in-one, I am not only aware of when they do it, I remember everything from those undone periods. My siblings do not."

"So, Desire has gotten exactly what he wanted from you *six* times. What an ungrateful little shit," Tobek teased, merciless mirth enhancing his rage-bright eyes.

Bix laughed loudly and obnoxiously. She was riding a wave of mania brought on by the return of her consort to her side and the freedom of confession. Somewhere there was a fleeting thought for the crash that would inevitably come, but for the moment, she reveled in reliving her destructive prowess.

"Your malice," Tobek mused, stroking his beard. "The one

emotion you left yourself when you sacrificed everything. Your parents are the root of it. They refuse to let you have peace."

"They punish more than me." She spun away from him, cackling like the mad woman she was. "They torment each of my siblings. Desire and Tempest may be the Legos under our feet, but we are all in pain. My parents will not permit me to heal the siblings I adore. I'm so beyond hate, yet so far from numb."

They fell into a prolonged comfortable silence while each wrangled their rage into something less destructive. Bix focused on the first time she'd unmade the terrible twins. It'd been an accident. She'd been horrified. They'd pushed and pushed. She'd only meant to take them to the edge of death, to scare them with the reality of potential success. But she was very good at ending things, too good in that instance. The second time they'd pushed her too far, she'd done it with a heavy heart but full intention. After that, the act of unmaking them was easy and came without remorse. Why should there be when her parents would just erase her accomplishments? They wouldn't help Tempest and Desire fix themselves, but they wouldn't relieve any of their children of Desire's misery either.

"Before you claimed the last of your memories, you were determined to spare Desire and Tempest. Where do you stand on that now?" Tobek's gravelly rasp pulled her from her mental meandering.

"Killing them is pointless. Instead, I'm going to break them, like I broke myself." She threw up her incorporeal arms. "How, I have no idea. I haven't been able to let myself think about the details until I had you and the gang home safely. You were and are my priority. Always."

"And if Desire sends his heralds after us again?"

Bix waved off his concern. "He doesn't need to. He most likely got what he wanted from each of you, while I got his coded message thanks to you."

"A message? Why didn't he simply have his heralds tell you?" Tobek sat forward and slapped his hands against his legs. "Forgive my incredulity, but I damn near came apart at the molecular level every time I tried to break out of that time prison. I'm not eager to go back."

"He took six of my nearest and dearest because six is his sacred number and straying from that number agitates him as a son aligned to order. He didn't know which of you would motivate me to react the quickest, but he knew I'd come for all of you at some point. In so doing, I'd discover the truth of his predicament: his bolt-hole in the future has been turned into his prison." She huffed as Tobek grunted with surprise. "All of you have been damaged in some way, but you weren't outright killed, not yet, at least. Part of that is a lingering threat and part is that he needs me to spring him before I kill him."

"Not. Yet. Killed," Tobek echoed and arched a brow. "Phobos and I are immortal. What happened to the others?"

"I don't know. Persons better qualified than I are looking after them." She hated her voice quavering, but she was crashing off the emotional high as she acknowledged her fears. "I'm scared, Tobek. I'm scared they're not going to make it. I got them back as fast as I could, but…"

He crawled to the edge of the hammock and held up his hands to her incorporeal state. "Take me to them. Let me see what I can do."

She backed up. "No, you need to rest and recover."

"I'm too fired up to rest. All I want to do right now is fight." He coiled his hair at his nape and stretched his neck from side to side until it popped.

"Don't even think about taking on my brother," she cautioned.

"I'm not. That's a fight I cannot win, even in my own timeline." He scratched his jaw. "Though, I've dealt with plenty of entities like him. Are you open to hearing advice?"

"I'm on my forty-third go-around with him, so I'll take all the suggestions you've got." She drifted toward Tobek, nudging him to the center of the hammock lest the tirelessness afforded by a Berserker's rage fade and he face-plant off the edge of the bed swaying in the winds of her ire.

He patted the fabric beside him, but she shook her head. They were both too wound up, and her chaotic half kept her shadows in thorny vines instead of soft tentacles. Shredding the hammock was highly likely.

"Master manipulators, like your brother, create an emotionally vulnerable situation to solicit what they want. Especially when they believe they're the cleverest turd in the toilet." Tobek settled in the middle of the hammock, sitting with his soles pressing together and his knees wide.

"Did you defeat him with rage or by being a curmudgeon?" She absently cast a shadow to retrieve the kayak her own temper had beached on the far side of the lake while the sounds of the forest repairing itself offered crackling chastisement.

"I didn't defeat him. My rage is my strength and my weakness. However, there *are* two ways to thwart a sociopath." He held up a silver finger. "The first is to be equally emotionally detached."

"The me I used to be," she agreed. "The me I've worked hard to no longer be."

"Just so." He held up a second silver finger. "The second is to be so unhinged that your emotions defy logic or predictability. The latter is infinitely harder than the former to feign and harder still to recover from."

"He can't control me if he can't anticipate my reaction." Bix pondered that for a moment. "He's a son aligned to order. He seeks the pattern in pressures and responses so he can use it to his advantage."

"Sweetheart, when you broke yourself into pieces, you threw him for a loop, a very big one. He did not anticipate any part of that. You won the battle, though at great cost." He sent a stream of green magic to dance around her incorporeal fingers, to hold her hand.

"The loss of our child was the moment I became fully unhinged. He and Tempest applied pressure at precisely the wrong time." Bix wove starlight around his green, creating a lace of magics. "I flipped from unhinged to an emotional void in a nanosecond."

"Exactly why he's wary. He doesn't know where your mind is or how you think anymore." Tobek tugged gently on their weave. "He is your sibling, but he is a creator. He doesn't need to emulate a pregnancy when he's capable of giving physical birth anytime he chooses in any form he wants. Thus, he can't understand the gutting loss of our fetus or the tumult of a miraculous conception that should never have been possible because you and I are sterile. Yet it happened."

There were no such things as miracles when dealing with First Children, but that was neither here nor there at the moment.

"He took my closest friends to learn how I've changed since then, to regain the upper hand." Bix groaned and stared at the three full moons whirling slowly in the sky, throwing an undulating glow of a triskelion beneath Resen's lattice. "I wonder if he got what he needed?"

Tobek barked a laugh. "I have been your consort for ages and physically attached to your emotions for the better part of it. Even I can't predict what you'll do, especially when you're up to something. I only know if and when you *are* up to something."

"I miss having that emotional bond with you," she confessed. "It's hard feeling all the things without you there to guide me back to equanimity. You were exceptionally good at that."

"Whenever you need me, reach for me. I will answer. Always." He held out a silver hand and green fireflies hatched in his palm to then launch into the air and dance around her. "That said, before you engage your brother, you must face and process all the emotions you suppressed throughout your relationship with him."

"That's my entire life," she whimpered, emitting starlight to accompany his fireflies.

"*Including* the parts only you remember," Tobek added. "Not dealing with your feelings for your brother, complex though they are, gives him multiple openings to exploit. You *must* be prepared for him to push every button. This type of battle prep will not be easy, especially for you, but it is necessary to win."

"Grueling battle prep is next on the docket." She grimaced,

knowing Tobek was absolutely right. If she didn't deal with their tumultuous history, Desire would use it to keep her off-balance until she stumbled into his trap. It'd been the leading cause of her repeated defeat. "Breaking my mind and magics into pieces wasn't easy, and that was on my own self while I'd shut down every emotion. Doing it to Tempest and Desire will be hella complicated and possibly impossible. I can't allow them to turn me into a vacuum of empathy, not again. Then there's the not small matter of where and how to store their fragments so they can't reassemble themselves or each other. They're creationists, which would allow them to bypass the trials necessary to curing themselves."

"Meaning they could rebuild themselves from a fragment without needing the whole." Tobek whistled a note of caution. "That could make our current situation look like a godsdamn utopia."

"The idea is fraught with multiple points of failure," Bix admitted. "I also have to figure out how to sell my other siblings on the plan and pray my parents will let this solution stick. Otherwise, this option is…is the last one I have, really. I've exhausted all others."

"How can I help?" He scooched to the edge of the hammock again. "No way am I letting you bear this alone. Tell me what I can do."

"You can rest and recover so that when I actually know what to ask of you, you'll be up for the challenge." At his raised eyebrows, she hastened to add, "No offense to the evolving wonder that is you, of course."

"If that's the case, then I need to be in the heart of the battalion so I can reconnect to my personal network. My time away from my men taught me my evolution has made us more symbiotic than I'd realized." He laid his hand over his Eternal Knot. "It seems they are the storers of my magic. Recycling centers, if you will. I am far from balanced at the moment."

"Oh, shit. Of course. I didn't think…" Flummoxed, Bix threw open gates to the coal plant. "I'm sorry. This island was our default once upon a time. I'd foolishly assumed…"

"And it will always be our private haven. Never apologize to me for doing what you think is best, particularly in these times of uncertainty." He smoothed a hand over the hammock, leaving a trail of green magic that solidified into suitable public attire for her corporeal form. "I don't like leaving you alone when you hurt this much. Come with me to the coal plant. We can stay in the apartment in the basement. All I need is proximity, preferably to both you and my men."

"Go to them, Tobek," she urged, not emotionally stable enough to be fleshy. "They need you as much as you need them. Besides, I'm too volatile to be in a populated area right now. I'll find you after I've worked through the truths of my relationship with Desire. Fair?"

He scowled. "I feel guilty."

"Don't. I never want you suffering for my sake." She stroked his cheek with a mote of starlight. "I'm a big girl. I can have a tantrum, or twelve, without supervision."

Sighing, he nodded reluctantly. "Answer me one thing before I go?"

"Anything," she said.

"Why you? Why did Desire, who has been your greedy adversary for ages, bait you into rescuing him from a prison in the future? That's not your playground." Tobek stood and steadied himself against a tree that was also one of the supports of the hammock. "That belongs to your siblings who take after your father."

"They're the ones who trapped him there." Bix held up four fingers. "You were correct when you said the number of heralds sent to take each of you was relevant. Four heralds stole you away, my most precious love. Four to represent the fourth of the First Children, Esiw. Esiw is the one to whom he wanted me to pay special attention, because Esiw is one of his jailors. Music is the other. Once I touched the time trap, I knew their magics, and I finally understood Desire's desperate message."

"Your other siblings, they..." He slid his hands over his

face and down his beard with something between a groan and a guffaw. "They imprisoned Eko. They imprisoned Desire. They haven't touched Tempest who is throwing the Devourers at our doorstep. Why?"

"Pity. They pity her."

"Curious how they've proven capable of self-policing, yet they did nothing the forty-two times Tempest and Desire destroyed our home nor when Tempest and Desire drove you to shatter yourself into pieces." He licked a tooth, and his rage glowed even brighter in his eyes. "Some siblings you've got there."

"When I asked them for help directly, they've helped," she whispered, sounding as hollow as she was starting to feel.

"Yeah." He imbued that one word with a wealth of damnation. "Being around others makes you happy, sweetheart, so don't isolate yourself for too long. I'll be at the base whenever you want to join me."

He stepped through the gates, and she closed them behind him. Heartbeats later, she gave in to the emotional crash. It didn't come with the explosion of violence; she was too exhausted for that. Spreading herself over the hospitality World, she became the night sky and finally let herself weep. Tears for old wounds reopened and raw due to her memories being complete. Tears for her precious home that'd become a perpetual battleground. Tears for the lesser beings doing their best against greater forces who held no regard for them. Tears for her dearest friends abused by her selfish siblings. Tears for her family, who should've been there to support each other but were trapped in their own cycles of disillusionment. Tears for the frustration of bearing the overwhelming responsibility for fixing it all. Soft, steady rain fell across the World as she cried, lingering above the tree line while the nightlife of the World went on living, blissfully unaware of all that was raging around it.

It was a relief to be weak for a moment. To admit, at least to herself, that she'd been flattened under the weight of shouldering too much. It was okay to falter and okay to take the time to acknowledge the unpleasant, deflated feelings. But, she wasn't the sort to stay down. She planned. She manipulated. She fought. She fixed. She followed her own path to balance the greater existence.

She still needed more information to formulate a plan to deal with Desire. There were too many unknowns, and now, unexpected players. Just what were Esiw and Music up to, imprisoning Desire? When had that happened? And why had Esiw hidden it from her? Their last conversation had been about Desire. The opening had been right there. Esiw being his usual pompous self or something more? It felt like more, but she couldn't put her finger on the reason.

As the crescent suns struggled to light the sky against her midnight presence, a flutter along one line of starlight and one of darkness at equal strength commanded her attention. Phobos. Summoning her. Mirri must have news about Feng and Cian. At last.

Regaining her composure and drawing on reserves of strength, she descended to the island and locked into her corporeal form. She dressed in the clothes Tobek had left for her, then set off to answer Phobos's call.

CHAPTER 17

L arger than a pro-football stadium, the brightly lit research facility in a formerly forgotten annex of the sprawling subterranean Consortium Headquarters beneath Washington, DC, Primary Mid World, bustled with activity. Thick limestone walls stretched up to barreled ceilings that contained the echoing din of great minds at work. Workstations, not walls, segmented the sprawling space. The leading minds of biology and immunology from myriad races across the Mids labored alongside plague gods and Other World entities trying to find a cure and a vaccine for the disastrous consequence of Devourer blood entering the body of a mortal. Progress had been made in the past months, but the ultimate goal remained elusive.

Phobos summoning Bix *here* was disconcerting, to say the least. This lab, these researchers, the research subjects, everyone under one roof with one shared goal was all Cian's doing. The kid had leveraged his burgeoning personal networks to unite once-combative races to work toward a common solution. He'd called in favors and extended IOUs to secure this location and the gobs of equipment without so much as a whisper to Bix or their team until events had required he tell them. Cian's scientists had had to work in secret from the last Consortium administration, who would've slaughtered everyone involved. Fortunately, Ogun's admin was so supportive, they'd managed to set aside political turf wars to throw everything they had at finding a cure. This chamber was testament to the power of collaboration and innovation.

Heels clacking loudly, Bix made her way down the length of the facility toward resonances she recognized, the gathering of which ratcheted up her concern. Phobos, of course, and Feng with Mirri. A goddess of healing in a place where scientists, soldiers, and spies who'd been turned into fist-sized geodes were being tested on right alongside their healthy counterparts? Made total sense. Archangel Samael rounded out the cadre of familiars. He'd been in lockstep with Cian on this whole facility from the get-go, but him being here instead of in the trenches of battle was worrisome.

Researchers and specimens mumbled hasty salutations as they dodged Bix's path. Phobos stepped squarely into it, wiping ichor from his hand with his plaid pocket square.

"Chimera," he murmured with his usual blend of stoic disdain. He refolded the scrap of cloth before offering her his arm. "I apologize for pulling you away from family matters, but I believe this problem is related."

"I know it causes you actual pain to summon me, so I'm aware you're not abusing the privilege." She wondered where and how he'd harmed himself to summon her, but she wouldn't embarrass him by asking, not in front of an audience. Instead, she looped her arm through his and allowed him to escort her to the back of the huge chamber, making silent note of the extra padding he now had in his sleeves. Either he was taking precautions against her breaking his arm again or her touch was too potent, even for him. "Besides, I figured Mirri had asked you to place the call to me. Hopefully, she has an update on my team. I can feel Feng from here. Any word on Cian?"

"Best you see for yourself." Phobos grimaced ever so slightly and gestured her toward a large crowd gathered under bright lights at the back of the lab.

The dense ring of friends and researchers eight-folk deep parted to reveal a hospital bed surrounded by monitors and machines. There were tubes aplenty leading from bags of assorted solutions into a body encrusted in color-changing crystals. Feet, legs, hands, and arms were completely encased but still in the recognizable shapes of appendages. Thicker crystals covered the shoulders and most of the neck. A third of the face was still flesh and half the scalp still sprouted wayward ginger spikes, but the one uncovered green eye stared lifelessly at the ceiling.

"Oh, Cian," she whispered as her heart broke. She looked to Mirri, then Feng standing side by side across the bed. Although racked with visible concern, Mirri positively glowed in her element. Feng was wan and seemed barely upright. "Was this how he came back?"

"They took his soul," Feng hissed, gripping the bed rail. There was a gray tint to the veins bulging from the backs of his hands that denoted the taint of Devourers expanding through the Mids. "Those things in the future. They took his soul. Their touch accelerated the growth of those damn crystals. I've tried to keep his flesh alive beneath all that, but…"

Mirri folded down the sheet affording Cian a bit of modesty. A raised, polished, hexagonal crystal covered the kid's abdomen. Six points. Six being Desire's sacred number. Her brother needed her help, yet he dared…the most vulnerable of her team. Desire had….

Shadowy vines of thorns slithered from Bix's spine as her malice writhed. Bystanders not of her inner circle retreated quickly from the spreading darkness. Those who actually knew her, knew they had nothing to fear from her night, not as long as they stayed on her good side.

"If they've taken his soul, then he's…" Bix couldn't say the word. Not to describe the kid. She simply couldn't. The word refused to form.

Phobos stepped into the brambles of Bix's shadows, inured to their effects. As a god of fear, he was likely reveling in all the unspoken distress roiling through the lab, yet as a god who cared deeply for a select few, he wasn't devoid of empathy. He offered her his arm again. She patted it but declined. He wasn't a punching bag, and she didn't want to treat him as such.

"The ley lines refuse to cease supporting the kid's body." Feng abruptly let go of the bed and backed away, as if distance might help him regain his composure. "The threads of Fate that once tied his soul to his body are still there, but they're totally crystallized. They're glowing brightly as if to say they're still alive beneath the damn minerals. The foundational elements appear to be holding him in stasis."

"They're waiting on a miracle," Samael rasped from the foot of the bed, where Thárros lay curled by Cian's leg. "On the salvation of an unmoored soul. An extremely rare event."

"What about Cian's Cycle of Soul contract? Is it still intact?" Bix looked to Feng, then Samael. As Mids' superpowers, either of them could read a contract. Bix couldn't because she was too powerful. She'd need to see inside him to read the contract, which would destroy him.

Every Chwed and human was created by the Consortium according to the terms of an individual Cycle of Soul contract. A god provided the soul, a dragon or angel provided the body, and a Fate stitched the soul to the body with threads of destiny that defined the life that soul would lead. Species, magic, caste, lifestyle, all that was laid out in the details of the contract. Cycle of Soul contracts were the glue of the Consortium. The life-forms they created fed the superpowers: negative emotions to the angels, positive emotions to the dragons, expelled magics to the Fates, and fattened souls from a robustly lived life to the gods when that life was over.

Bix wanted the name of the Fate on Cian's soul contract who'd written this ending for him. That Fate would've foreseen Desire's involvement. That Fate's convenient omission would be punished. The Houses of Fate had extensive and complex contracts with the Chimera that absolutely included alerting her to machinations that jeopardized the Mids. After all, Bix had taught the Fates how to earn their freedom from the pantheons eons ago. She hadn't done that for shits and giggles. Any lasting harm befalling an architect of the Mids' defense system qualified as "need to know."

"No one afflicted by the Devourers' blood has a Cycle of Soul contract anymore," Mirri explained, perplexed. During her tenure as the Norse ambassador to the Mids, Mirri had negotiated many a soul contract, so she knew their ins and outs. "The enemy's blood destroys the actual contract. The creations are no longer protected by the terms. If one of the afflicted ever recovers from this rock disease, there's a whole other hurdle about what the Consortium will do with an uncontracted life."

"A lot of that will depend on the condition of the soul, the threads, and the body," Samael noted. "There's a good chance they'll have damage that can never be undone. There's also a chance whatever changes they've undergone will be of massive benefit to the Consortium. No one knows what's on the other side of a cure."

"They'll end up on the execution block or the auction block," Feng said with disgust. His dislike of the Consortium no matter who led it was admittedly merited.

"A problem for after we win the war and secure our home." Bix inhaled slowly as malice banked and made way for the clearer mind required for planning. If the foundational elements weren't giving up on Cian, she wouldn't either. Healing wasn't her calling, but there were plenty of folks around this bed for whom that was their purpose in life. She, however, was very good at finding things. Especially things that were most likely in the possession of her brother. "Okay, then. We need to get Cian's soul back, which is not unrelated to getting the Devourers off our turf. Meanwhile, the researchers shouldn't let up on their efforts to cure Cian's cooties. Feng, I'll need a full debrief of what happened after you and I parted. Give me ten minutes, then meet me in Cian's apartment, all right?"

Feng grunted his agreement, sounding almost relieved for an excuse to depart. He vanished in a surge of native magic.

Chimera, the young Sage's soul was marked for Tartarus, Phobos mentioned into Bix's mind, clearly aware that the abundance of angels in the lab could overhear anything spoken. *The titan had specifically spoken for the boy. Though, according to the contract, the soul would've officially gone to Hades.*

"Naturally." Bix snorted. "If the contract mentioned Cian coming into my life, then certain individuals would want to keep that soul out of the hands of those they deemed unworthy. Thank you for having paid attention to the details."

The boy is the only one of your inner circle with a soul. Of course, I checked his contract when I met him and at intervals thereafter to ensure it was never altered. I've no doubt the Phoenix and the archangel did the same. That they do not admit it leads me to think they do not trust this audience. After all, the wingless archangel is the one who signed the contract for the child's body.

Samael had built Cian's body? He'd never alluded to it, but it did explain why Samael was unusually protective of the kid, in a grumpy uncle sort of way. Also another reason he spoiled Cian rotten. Seeing the kid in this state must be hitting the archangel harder than Samael would like to admit.

"And the Fate?" she murmured under her breath.

The Morrigans.

Formerly of the Celtic pantheon. Their House was small. They didn't ascend new members often. They were extremely adept at weaving destinies of war heroes whose lives ended in great tragedy. Among the Houses of Fate, the Morrigans were notorious for making legends, not new House members.

"Well, they don't get to dictate his ending, not today, not anymore," Bix vowed, filing away a mental note to have a chat with the Morrigans after Cian was set to rights. "Would you ask the leaders of the Under Worlds to keep a lookout for the soul, please? I don't expect it to arrive, but if it does, let me know."

Should Hades attempt to intercept it?

"No. With the current climate in the Unders, that would be unwise. If it gets that far, I'll deal with the relevant party." She didn't name names or titles because of the eavesdroppers doing a terrible job at hiding their nosiness.

If your brother still has the boy's soul, then it is unquestionable leverage, Phobos mused. *Caring for a soul is easier than tending to the fragile body, particularly when time is not fluid. Though it does not explain why he bothered to preserve the boy at all when he had your other loved ones to serve the same purpose.*

"Cian is beloved by the whole team. The others would die to protect him. The chance to restore him pushes them to push me, thus establishing layers of motivation." Bix suspected her brother was holding Cian's soul hostage until he was freed from the time trap. At least she hoped that was the bargain. Desire was already holding the Mids hostage in exchange for his death. What more could he possibly want from her?

Beware, Chimera. An unmoored soul existing without the boundaries of an intended life is already damaged. Unprotected in the hands of a First Child? Uncharted territory. No matter how this ends, the Sage will not be the same boy you knew, even if they succeed in restitching his soul to his eventually decalcified body.

"Our damage can make us into better beings when we stop looking at them as proof of failures and instead embrace them as evolutionary catalysts." Bix refused to entertain the morbid and the morose. She'd already done it, given them their turn to be felt and expressed. She was in planning mode now. Emo and plans didn't go well together. She laid a hand on Phobos's shoulder, a shoulder heavily scarred beneath all his refinements. He'd earned those scars during his demigod trials that had shaped him into the god of fear and future caretaker of the infamous Chimera. "He'll need help adapting, no doubt, but look at who he's surrounded by."

Phobos spared an amber-eyed glance at those still gathered around Cian's bed. With a grunt of acknowledgment, he inclined his head and departed in a fog of mulberry and navy.

"Chimera, before you go?" Samael interjected before she could open gates to Cian's apartment. "The kid's body is not the same as when he left."

"Was it the crystals that gave it away?" she quipped. The flat black-eyed stare the archangel gave her said he did not find her funny, not even a little.

"As in the age of the body. I'd say he's six years older than last I saw him. What happened in those six years that were barely more than six days to us, eh?" Samael crossed his arms and pointedly refused to look at the body in the bed. "I've seen humans in forced labor camps mining toxic ores since their childhood who are in better condition than what's under these rocks."

Six years? That was the time jump neither Phobos nor Tobek could identify. Holy shit. Six years out of sync with time. Six years of complex knotwork that her team had had to break through to get home. Six years in who knew what kind of a future. Those six years were the source of the problems with Feng, with Ashtad and Drew, and with Cian. Desire had dragged them forward in time but hadn't taken the precautions necessary for mortals. One hundred and one reasons she didn't let her siblings play with her toys. Gods, her friends must've believed she'd abandoned them, forsaken them, and discarded them. What horrors had they endured?

When she finally got her hands on Desire…

Temper, temper, she chided herself. This was not the time for anger. It would muddy her mind. She needed to be focused and to pay attention to details. She had a chance to save Cian, she couldn't let her temper get in the way.

"I share your concern, Samael. Six years is not insignificant to a human, even in the best conditions. Believing Cian's soul still exists is the only small comfort we can take right now." Bix reached for the kid but when Mirri smacked her hand, Bix pulled back.

"I'm sorry," Mirri whispered. "You understand why, though, right?"

Too much magic, even with Tobek back in the Mids and absorbing her excesses. "Excess" was defined by what the whole of native magic could tolerate from her, not what an individual mostly human boy could withstand. While she'd been broken, she'd been at a fraction of her power, which had allowed her to touch lesser beings. Now, though, Mid World mortals were off-limits. Especially ones who were "allergic" to magic.

"Please keep up everything you're doing to save him, all of you. It is greatly appreciated. I'm off to do my part." Bix forced a smile and departed via gates to Cian's nearby apartment.

CHAPTER 18

The newly refurbished second-floor apartment in a row house in Southeast Washington, DC, Primary Mid World, was eerily quiet as Bix closed gates. The two bedrooms at opposite ends of the apartment were dark despite the midday sun shining through the long, narrow front windows. Feng leaned against a painted white frame, watching the dearth of traffic below. Hands in the pockets of his tweed trousers, he stood too still and too slouched.

"There used to be a block of dilapidated row houses mixed among the shady restaurants, shabby drugstores, and sketchy salons outside this window. Cars used to slow roll down this street, bass beats rattling windowpanes as deep potholes made shocks groan. Chweds disguised as humans used to shout their greetings while runners smuggled contraband between lookout posts." Feng cupped a shoulder and winced. "Now, it's rubble. The street. The buildings. There are bones in the debris. The stink of decaying flesh is still perceptible."

"Samael's protection of this block ends precisely at the curb. The aftermath of conflict remains as a motivator to fight the war that is far from over. It remains to shame those in the Consortium who chose personal greed over collective survival. There is no political reframing when the proof is still oozing into the streets.

It also remains as a reminder to humanity that what happened here was real and their lives prior to this were an extremely sheltered illusion." Bix perched on one of three barstools set before a quartz countertop in the small galley kitchen of what was now a magazine-worthy modernist bachelor pad normally shared by Drew and Cian, and sometimes Ashtad, or whoever else was in desperate need. After Cian's mom had died, no one wanted the kid to feel alone or isolated, so her team had co-opted his home and made it their base of operations here in the Mids. Even Tobek and his guys used meetings here as an excuse to check on the kid.

The kid who was now, technically, dead, thanks to her brother.

"When the Devourers attacked the District and the Consortium defended it, more lives were saved than lost. Inarguably. But what comes after the war? Who buries the dead who haven't been consumed? Who catalogs the missing? Who decides who gets remembered and who is forgotten?" Feng twitched the cord on the blind, sending white fabric skittering down to thump against the sill.

"Where did the heralds take you, Feng?" Bix gently asked, too easily able to imagine what her delusional and desperate brother had forced him to endure. "What did they make you witness?"

"Is it possible, do you think, for Ashtad and Drew to be here? We spent so long together in each other's constant company that their absence is… I haven't seen them since we were rescued. I'd like to know they're all right." Feng turned toward her, letting her see the ghosts of torture too recent and now compounded. He'd spent years enduring untold agonies as a prisoner in the malicious hands of maniacs, abandoned by the Consortium and branded a traitor. To endure another prolonged imprisonment? How could he not have felt betrayed and discarded yet again? He'd been making good progress living with his PTSD, but he was probably back at ground zero now.

Gods, the breadth of damage Desire's obsession inflicted on those who didn't even know he existed. It was really, really hard not to hate her brother.

"They're in the throes of their own recoveries, but I'll certainly ask their minders. Give me a moment." Bix stretched a thread of darkness through shadows cast by cabinets and connected to the greater pool that was the eternal presence of the Chaos.

Through her mother, Bix could communicate with any chaotic entity who'd trained themselves to use the pool. It was how Bix had accidentally outed herself to her siblings who were aligned to her mother, exposing her progress and lack thereof while repairing herself. That was when Tempest had upped the Devourers' attacks against the Mids. That was also when Eko had reached out to help her. Movement had been beside her throughout her recovery in the Mids, but Bix had been too clueless to understand that the push and pull of native magic had been Movement and Music trying to reassure her without frightening her. As for their mother, to say the Chaos was the hands-off maternal type was an understatement. Unless one happened to be Desire or Tempest and dead.

Ereshkigal immediately answered Bix's call. Ashtad fared too poorly to leave Irkalla, but a compromise involving gates was easy to reach. The blue-black illuminations of Irkalla spilled across the threshold from Ashtad's sumptuously appointed chamber in a modest domicile not far from Ereshkigal's temple. Ashtad sat chest-deep in a steaming, bubbling spring that anchored one side of the chamber. Long screens carved with scenes of ancient masters poring over their studies stood open to the layered mountainside villages and deep ravine towns. The gate connecting Ashtad's chamber to the great room of Cian's apartment allowed for all the scents and sounds to travel between domains.

"Ashtad," Feng sighed with relief, settling on the sleek charcoal-colored couch facing the wall that hosted the huge TV and gaming setup. Today, the gate to Irkalla stood in the space between couch and tech. "It's good to see you."

Ashtad, still too gaunt and pale, raised a soggy, wrinkled hand. "Feng, how's it feel to be home? Did you go out to the edge of the collective and appreciate its vastness like you promised?"

Feng huffed and nodded, the knots in his shoulders visibly loosening as the two of them nattered on like bosom beaus. Odd. They'd been fairly standoffish before their adventure. However, if they really had spent six years in each other's back pockets, then she was fortunate they'd come out fast friends instead of sworn foes.

Bix let them chat undisturbed as she reached through darkness to contact Hel. Not one for idle chitchat, Hel didn't even ask what Bix wanted. Instead, Under World magic flared in the bedroom adjacent to the kitchen, and out trotted a very large, red-eyed, shaggy hound brimming with Other World magic.

"Bixie," the hound cried, managing to reach a gallop in the six steps it took to knock Bix off the barstool. Darkness salvaged Bix's dignity before she hit the floor and set her back on her perch as Drew rubbed his furry self all over her. His Under World constructed body was safeish from the negative effects of proximity to her innate power.

"Drew, you're cogent," Bix gasped through giggles while spitting fur and struggling to maintain her seat.

"Hel don't screw around in times of war." Drew cackled, the sound so dichotomous to the form. "Sparky! Flamer! Mah bois."

Bix watched in curious amusement as Drew darted in and out of Irkalla, up and over the couch in the DC apartment, and round and round across Worlds until Ashtad tossed the dog in the spring. With him. Ashtad. Drew. Same small space? Then again, not as cozy as sharing the same body.

She wanted all the details. The fun ones. The sad ones. The happy and stupid ones. Selfishly, it was a little unsettling no longer to be the hub who bonded them. However, she was content to be the outsider if it meant they were safe and on their way to healthy. Home was relative for all of them, but it seemed to be evolving from a location to an affiliation.

Relationships mattered.

"I'm loath to interrupt the reunion," she interjected at length. "But there are some questions I need answered before I fight to retrieve Cian's soul."

That sobered the trio right quickly. Drew climbed out of the spring, shook the soul-based water from his fur, and wandered to the gate.

"You mean there's a chance for our little herb nerd to come back to us, Bixie?" Drew asked, ears perking as he stretched across the gate's threshold to be in both Worlds at the same time. To be with all friends at once.

"Once upon a time, a human boy danced with a baby ley line and befriended a lonely ancient one," Bix reminded. "Those lines and their kin will not let that boy die. Not if they can help it."

"Putting his soul back in his body in the condition his body is in? That's no kindness, Bix. That's his worst nightmare." Ashtad pushed his wet curls from his face. "If the body can't be cured or replaced, then we owe him the mercy of letting him move on."

Feng grunted an agreement. Drew too.

"Was that part of the death pact you four made?" Bix slid off the barstool and paced behind the couch. "If the heralds kept you isolated and contained, yet left you exposed to the effects of time, then it's only logical you planned for your demise as a group and as individuals."

The look the three of them exchanged wouldn't fool anyone, least of all someone who knew them well. It was a What Happens in the Future Stays in the Future look. It stung to be actively excluded, but they forgot, perhaps, that she didn't need their words to get their truths.

"How long into the six years you were gone did Cian's body finally fail him?"

Again, a shared look and no explanation. But there was sorrow in that shared look. The onset hadn't been instant, then. It'd been slow, enough for them to watch Cian suffer. That meant the journey through time hadn't caused the crystallization. Something else had. Probably the interactions with the heralds. Heralds didn't have mouths to speak. They communicated with the body as a whole, bypassing any possibility of language barriers or mental limitations. That infusion of magic would've collided with the Devourer blood in Cian's system and caused the crystals to grow.

Had Desire planned that prolonged agony or was it a sad coincidence? Hard to know with her brother having set up camp in the future. He should've seen the outcome if he'd been watching the kid. But the kid was just one human boy in the greater existence, so had Desire deigned to notice the details of Cian's illness before the abduction? She needed more info before she could get in her brother's head.

"Which of you asked the heralds to take Cian's soul?" It was a simple question, but a complex one that relied on the old-school spy interrogation method that presumed a fallacy. Unless it wasn't a fallacy at all, which would garner a reaction more than a response.

It worked. Surprise from Ashtad and Drew. Sullen jaw thrust from Feng.

"The kid asked," Bix breathed as assumptions shifted.

That meant Desire's theft of Cian's soul might've been a merciful act, not a malicious one. Might. Could a twinge of conscience actually have penetrated Desire's absolute selfishness? Or had Desire anticipated the request after observing her friends for years? Had he simply waited for Cian to break so he could come out of the situation with a sheen of benevolence? Was this merely part of him laying the groundwork of manipulation for the moment she confronted him? Or was there a spark of something worth redeeming? One single spark could be an avenue to selling her other siblings on her grand plan.

"You overheard him, didn't you, Feng? Your exceptional senses allowed you to eavesdrop on Cian's private moment with a herald." Bix pressed ahead as Feng's temper outed the truth. "That's why you were so mad in the laboratory. You're mad at Cian."

Confusion registered on Ashtad and Drew until they saw what she saw on Feng's face. They were both adepts of the intel-gathering game. They knew how to read body language, particularly a body with whom they'd been sequestered for years.

"He gave up," Feng grumbled. Small flames ignited at the tips of his feathered hair. "I told him native magic wouldn't fail him in *any* time period. He still…he still…"

"Cian was scared and in pain." Drew rested his big head on a paw, ears drooping. "Everybody has a different tolerance. The kid couldn't endure the kind of stuff the rest of us have. It wasn't fair for us to have expected that of him. He's human. He's not even twenty years old. It's easy to forget he's just a kid, but he *is just a kid*."

"They didn't have to kill him," Feng roared. Walls bowed, cabinets opened, and windows cracked. Heartbeats of uneasy silence passed before blue pinpricks of light danced on motes of magic throughout the apartment, restoring everything. "Apologies."

"Heralds aren't killers, Feng." Bix crossed her arms on the back of the couch at the far end from the Phoenix. "They're educators and protectors. Their job is to prepare supplicants for an audience with a First Child, then to shield the fragile entity from the might inherent in a First Child. Any harm suffered at the hands of a herald is to stave off greater damage."

The soul removal had come *after* the full-body spread of the crystals, which explained why the hexagonal crystal over Cian's abdomen was thicker and smooth. It had been spawned atop the initial layer. The heralds had acted to preserve Cian's soul, the essence of what made Cian Cian.

"Is that what you call yourselves?" Feng snarled. "First Children?"

"It's what we are. Energy became sentient and divided into a feminine and a masculine, an encompassing and an exclusionary, a mother and a father. I am the youngest of seven born to those entities. The heralds who took you to meet their master belong to the sixth one of us and the closest to me in birth order."

Bix assumed the heralds had schooled her friends in the facts of First Children as a prerequisite for meeting Desire and to educate them in the enormity of their situation. Time would tell whether that knowledge would lead them astray, but for now, there was no point in evading the truth of her family.

"Their master never showed his face, and they said *you* were the reason we were there." Feng stared at her with the hate born of fear and trauma. She didn't take it personally, having just disembarked from her own emotional roller coaster.

"I think they were trying to surprise us with that last bit." Drew snickered. "They didn't seem to grok that whenever the weirdest shit happens to us, we assume it's someone trying to screw with you, Bixie."

Bix started to apologize, but harmonized grunts of rueful agreement from Feng and Ashtad stopped her.

"The heralds weren't there to teach. They were there to learn from us." Ashtad sank lower in the bath and leaned his head against a smooth rock. "They wanted to see how we would react to witnessing the death of the Mid Worlds."

That made Bix stand up straight.

"Six years from now, three Mid Worlds are all that's left after the Devourers consume the others." Feng rolled his wrist, and holograms of three familiar Worlds spun in the air. "The one we were stuck on was a barren land of sharp rocks and lifeless seas that cried an endless song of mourning. In the evenings, we could see the other World that was a place of constant storms. Totally uninhabitable. The third was a utopia with trees and streams and three crescent-shaped suns. That's the World we tried to get to, but never could."

The hospitality World Bix shared with Tobek and Gurp. No other higher life-forms. The World wouldn't allow strangers to exist there. Bix had had to train it to accept Tobek and Gurp. Desire had been enough of a dick to flaunt that in the faces of her dearest mortals? Why? To make them hope for the unattainable? To make them endure constant failure so he wouldn't be alone in his suffering?

"Those are the three original Mid Worlds," Bix said, wondering if Cian's crystallization had been caused by the World's potency and not the heralds. Perhaps a combination of the two? "Should you have made it to the utopian World, it would've slaughtered all of you and turned you into fertilizer the instant you set foot there. The ley lines couldn't have protected you, just as they weren't able to protect you from the excesses of primordial native magic on the World where you were stranded, particularly since native magic would've been imbued with high levels of the Devourers' toxicity."

"We know all about the dying ley lines and poisonous magic. We lived it." Feng rolled his wrist again, and the holograms winked out. "For six years on our shit World."

"Feng provided food, shelter, and clothing for us," Ashtad explained. "We would never have survived without him."

"Cian was the only one whose emotions I could consume, so I wasn't eavesdropping when he asked to die. His desperation and intention oozed from him toward the end there." Feng braced his forearms on his thighs and sighed. "If Mirri hadn't called out to me when she did, I don't know how much longer I could've lasted before my fire raged out of control in my own death spiral. As it was, without the Fates pulling me down the timeline, we would never have made it out of that hellscape."

Desire could've easily made their stay a pleasurable experience, but he hadn't. Had he been testing their resolve, their drive, their skills? Had their struggle for survival been his way to keep them entertained while he waited for her to figure out his plea for help? Or was he just a sulking, bored cosmic entity playing with someone else's toys until he was released from his time out?

"Bixie, they were really interested in our reactions to you not saving us as the hours dragged to days to months to years," Drew offered, as if reading her mind, though it was more likely her expression. "They wanted to know if we'd blame you. Hate you. Reject you."

"Disavow you," Ashtad added. "They were obsessed with our perceptions of you, often engaging us in what-if scenarios. Whenever we did blame you, we'd laugh, which would lead to telling tales, which would lead to more laughter or the occasional *in memorium* for mutual friends we'd lost."

"Sorry, Bixie, the kid died knowing you weren't perfect." Drew panted a chuckle.

"Damn it," Bix cried with faux affront. "Now I *have* to put him back together so I can correct that egregious misconception and prove you all the fiendish liars you are."

That earned a round of weary chortles.

"In all seriousness, guys, I've missed you. I'm so glad you're home. And I am so sorry for what a friendship with me has cost you." Bix bit her lip to stop the endless stream of apologies that her heart kept producing.

"Wouldn't trade it," Ashtad said, closing his eyes. "I'm about to embark on studies in Irkalla as part of my demigod trials as directed by the Houses of Fate. Training under a goddess who is rumored to be a titaness flies in the face of every rule and convention of the trials. There's no way my ascension to godhood is going to be approved by my pantheon, and without my friendship with you, I don't think the Fates would be prepping me for Plan B."

"Bixie, I wouldn't be here without you." Drew sat up. "Let me rephrase that. I wouldn't *be* without you. The rest is just fodder for an eternity of embarrassing stories I get to drag up at inopportune times. Rest assured, there will be inopportune times."

Feng reached over and patted Bix's hand, ignoring the way the clash of their magics sparked a mix of starlight and embers. "Apex entities, you and I, right? You welcomed me into your chosen family despite my many flaws, despite what tradition dictates our relationship should be. You care about me as an individual, not because I'm the Phoenix. Just…just do what you can for the kid. If his soul still exists, then he's counting on *you* to save him."

"I'll get right on it," she promised. Smiling, she resisted the urge to tackle hug all of them. Full-body contact probably wouldn't end the way it used to. "I promised Ereshkigal I'd close the gate when the sun set, so you guys still have some time together, if you want it."

"I would like to finish my bath in private, strangely enough," Ashtad drawled, waving goodbye. "Don't worry. My first challenge in this place is to establish a cross-World communication link that can be used by the scientists here and the scientists in Cian's lab. My radio silence can't last too long. My dignity is on the line."

"Hel gave me a doody list, so I'm off to catch up with a squad of Valkyries in the 'burbs of Ohio to beat down some incognito Devourers." Drew pushed to his feet and stretched, kicking his soul-water puddle in Ashtad's face. Deliberately. That much hadn't changed during their mandatory bonding. "Call me, Bixie, whenever you've got word about the kid. I want to be there for him when he wakes."

"Speaking of the kid, I'm going to sit with his body and make sure no one gives up on him." Feng stood. "Really good to see you guys alive and alert again. Make sure to live in the moment, right?"

Her friends exchanged their farewells before Bix closed the gate to Irkalla, then opened another for Drew to rendezvous with the Valkyries at a familiar safe house in southwest Ohio. She offered a gate for Feng, but he departed for the lab on his own.

Left alone in the apartment, Bix massaged her skull and groaned. Stranding her friends on the original Mid World built by Music, was it petty or merciful? Or was it just part of the message Desire had wanted Bix to understand? Music had worked with Esiw to trap Desire, so Desire had trapped her friends on Music's World like a big flashing sign pointing to their older sister. On the other hand, her friends could never have survived on the original World that Movement had built nor on the hospitality World crafted by both sisters. Music's World was the only place he could've kept them alive while still keeping them in the Mids.

Was she supposed to be grateful for that? Was she supposed to be grateful that he'd harvested Cian's soul? Probably. Tobek had said master manipulators created emotional situations so they could control the outcome.

She had to stop giving too much weight to the memories of the brother she'd loved as a child. Thirty-six times he'd defeated her because he'd played upon those feelings, twisting them until he'd ignited her temper. If she stopped seeing Desire through the eyes of a little girl and started regarding him as a grown-ass adult, then the information she'd gathered from her team confirmed Desire was a manipulative shit who would always put his fickle wants above everything and everyone. She shouldn't look to Desire holding Cian's soul as a spark of conscience. No, it'd give Desire an opening to her emotions and bite her in the ass. Surely. Right?

Gah.

It was odd, though, that Desire had gotten himself trapped at the end of that particular branch of the Mids' timeline. Of the billions of branches mapping potential futures, why had he been hiding on one that showed neither he nor she getting what they wanted? If, as Tempest had asserted, Desire had been trolling about in the future to see which actions would end in his death, why hadn't he set his bolt-hole on a line in which he'd succeeded? Had Esiw and Music made the choice of which branch of the future would be his prison, or had they simply taken advantage of him lingering there? The latter seemed more likely what with the element of surprise being a requisite for the trap.

The choice of branch was more relevant than the time span, at least when it came to crawling inside Desire's head. His goal wasn't to inflict pain and suffering on her. That was merely the means to his ultimate end. So why had the origin of personal motivation taken his eye off the ball?

Was it jealousy? Was he brimming with enough of it to rival his obsession with death? It was an emotion Tempest had in excess, no doubt, but was the excess coming from Desire through their twin bond? Was it possible Desire coveted the Mids? In the centuries of studying Bix while she repaired her marbles, had he developed an attachment to her sanctuary? Did he feel entitled to it? Was it a prize he'd deemed himself more worthy of possessing than she? Was that why he was watching the Mids' demise instead of his own death?

Well now, that could make the family meeting more interesting, holding it here. Right here in DC, though not Cian's apartment, mind. Every one of her siblings had contributed something to this collective to make it her home. Movement and Music had made the original Worlds, native magic, and the three seeding life-forms of ley lines, dragons, and angels. Eko and Esiw had supplied the gods and Fates, respectively, that were catalysts to the continual growth and development of the Mids. Tempest and Desire had crafted the first humans and Chweds to feed the others' creations, thus establishing the cycle of life for the collective.

What better place to reinforce the power of family collaboration and the misery of family dysfunction than the sanctuary they'd built and were now tearing apart? Desire wasn't the only one who could architect circumstances to leverage emotional control.

Having all seven First Children in the same place at the same time would strain the endurance of the Mids. Maybe. Possibly. A lot depended on Tobek and his evolution. Similarly, native magic had been undergoing its own evolution during this fight against the Devourers. There was a chance playing hostess to her family could be feasible. To everyone outside the family, it would be explained as parley. The leadership of the Mids was already expecting her to call for it. There was no need to identify her siblings as First Children, merely as opposition leaders and mediators.

Yes, that could work. The whole family here in DC, right above Consortium HQ, in the midst of ruins from the battle with the Devourers, in the heart of a significant population of everyone's creations, a breath away from Cian's hollow, crystalized body.

One very special goblin would be ecstatic to arrange a suitable venue. Tobek could manage the logistics. She would manage the party invitations.

Timing was the unknown variable. It depended on how long Tempest took to free her twin. Once Desire returned to the present, things would move quickly and dangerously. The Mids had to be ready.

That meant a stop through the coal plant. Besides, she'd promised Tobek she'd check in once she'd reestablished equanimity. She didn't want him worrying about her when his focus needed to be on his men and the Mids.

CHAPTER 19

The main building of the Berserkers' base bustled with curious activity. Bix closed the gates to the boiler room at the back of the ground floor and listened to the rumbling drone of many masculine voices punctuated by the occasional feminine shout or burst of laughter.

Women? In the bastion of testosterone?

Intrigued, Bix peeked down the long iron-clad hallway that connected the high-tech clinic-morgue at one end to the beer hall at the other. Directly across the hall, merry sunlight spread across the repaired and retinted front windows of the body modification shop Dysmorphic. The artists who manned the shop were deployed fighting anti-gods. It was nonetheless sad to see that the stalls that had once hosted art samples, rolling trays of sterilized gear, and double seating for artists and customers had been stripped down to dull brick-backed administrative workstations. The desks' occupants lacked the overly big, brawny builds common to Berserkers, and they exuded various levels of native magic. Chweds. In the uniforms of the assorted branches of the Mid World Army. That explained the presence of women. Unlike the Berserkers, the MWA was gender inclusive. Also explained why they'd been assigned desks down here rather than upstairs in the Berserkers' operations center.

"You don't have to hide in the boiler room, my lady of darkness," whispered a voice from the other side of the partially opened door. The heavy Welsh accent brought an instant smile to Bix's face.

She sidled out of the room and closed the door behind her, keeping close to the wall as soldiers hustled up and down the corridor. The heady aromas of roasted meats, baked breads, and savory side dishes drifted on the breeze churned by the exposed industrial air ducts. Meals were being served in the beer hall, where many more MWA soldiers mixed with Berserkers.

With one bandaged hand draped atop the doorframe to the boiler room, the unit leader of the Berserkers' green team smiled down at her. His raven-black hair was pulled back in braids, and his thick mutton chops were perfectly trimmed to highlight the amusement dancing in his vibrant blue eyes. He wore the blue-and-black camo of the Berserkers' combat uniform, but it was pristine. He clearly hadn't just stepped off the battlefield.

"Hywl," Bix greeted warmly. The erstwhile angel hunter led the team of Berserkers most often charged with accompanying her on missions. Her affection for him ran deep, especially now that she had her complete memories, including those of him from the days before he'd been recruited into the battalion. She felt like a grade-school teacher encountering a former pupil who was now a wildly successful adult. "I wasn't sure what I'd be interrupting. I'm surprised it's so busy here. You guys were running on a skeleton crew not too long ago."

"Chief shows up after being abducted means we show up for the briefing and the subsequent change in orders." Hywl pointed at the ceiling. "He's in the war room. We both know he'd welcome the visit."

By "chief," he meant Tobek, which was the honorific by which most folks addressed her big blond bear. Bix was the only one who called Tobek by her pet name for him.

"By the way, we're all real sorry to hear about the kid." Hywl straightened and sobered, sadness and frustration darkening his expression. "Runjit drew more blood samples from Chief and the rest of us. He's taken them to the fancy lab. Got the okay to spend some time with the researchers there seeing what else he can contribute to the cure."

Runjit was the battalion's lead medic and Hywl's battle buddy. Like the other guys, he had a soft spot for Cian. The kid had been a temporary ward of the battalion and was an honorary member of the brotherhood. Plus, Cian wasn't the only one afflicted by the crystallization problem. There were soldiers aplenty among the victims. Tobek's evolved blood and possibly that of his men held the basis of a cure.

"Tobek's time away has likely altered his blood in some manner, so it's good Runjit's at the lab. I'm just sorry I missed him." Bix stared down a pair of MWA soldiers slowing to gawp at her. Yes, yes, yes, she was the bogeyman of lore. Here, have a shiver of fear. Never mind the shiver they felt was the instinctual reaction of a lesser being cowering in the heavily filtered presence of a greater entity.

"Oy, show respect," Hywl barked, snapping the soldiers to attention.

They saluted smartly, blurted a series of "sir, ma'am, sirs," and hustled to the beer hall.

"Joint maneuvers." Hywl tipped his head at the desk jockeys in the shop failing to be inconspicuous in their study of her. "MWA is supporting us in the field, so we're hosting their rear echelon here."

The Berserkers were used to Bix, both randomly appearing and her full resonance. Since they were linked to Tobek, she suspected they were nowhere near as affected by her as other mortals. Plus, Gurp had upgraded the structures of the base to help alleviate the pressure of her awesomeness. Both he and Tobek wanted her to move back to the basement apartment the three of them once shared, so efforts had been taken to ensure she wasn't a detriment.

"I'll do my best to give them a wide berth. Don't want to scare the friendlies." She held her hands up in peace.

"Keep them on their toes. It'll do them good." Snickering, Hywl winked and headed for the clinic.

Sparing the MWA troops any more discomfort, she moved via gates upstairs to the hallway outside the huge, dimly lit war room. Green glows spilled out the open door to paint the whole second floor. The green wasn't from Tobek's magic or any triggered wards, but from the wealth of data streaming down movable glass walls and live video feeds from around the Mids. Artifacts from assorted ages sat in floor cubbies beneath clear tiles. Some artifacts provided additional security, while others enabled spell work.

Waddling atop the perpendicular conference tables at the center of the room, Gurp arranged another collection of artifacts, pulling them from huge steamer trunks painted with spells and muttering his inimical opinion of their necessity. A pair of Berserkers hefted another trunk to the last open spot at the tables. Tobek thanked them and laid his hand atop the trunk. Silver spears of magic jutted from his silver hand and pierced the curved lid, popping it open. A rush of Other World magic filled the room along with a theremin song. Tobek handed Gurp a pair of white metal gloves. The goblin rolled his bulging eyes and set about unpacking. He paused with one hand in the trunk as he spotted her.

"Pretty lady, home," Gurp cheered.

"For the briefest of moments, dearest Gurp." Bix sent a stream of starlight to curl around the goblin in a gentle hug. He was inured to her crushing presence due to augmentations that had resulted from lifetimes as the third member of her tiny chosen family. He was afraid of her darkness, though, so she kept him in her light. "Please don't let me interrupt your organizing."

He held up something that looked like writhing driftwood and brought it nearer her light. It screeched. He shook a finger at it, gave her a mischievous grin, then returned to his task.

Tobek pushed aside a stack of moving walls. Before Bix completed a blink, he was in front of her, folding her into his arms.

"Did you just use flash step?" she mumbled into his uniform jacket. Super speed would be new. A possible evolutionary update due to his time with Desire? Speed was a function of time, after all.

"Streaming anime in your free time, are you?" He chuckled against her crown and squeezed her. "Just got back from seeing Cian. Ran into Samael while I was there and managed to pry an update from him. Sweetheart, I am so sorry. I had no idea what your brother was doing to the kid or your friends."

"Thank you, but it's not on you." She peered over his bicep and tried to guess what he and Gurp were up to. "What's with the woo?"

"The base is still under reconstruction from the attack on DC. Additionally, using this compound to anchor the time-travel spell to bring your friends home short-circuited some of the temporary defenses we had in place. Consider it housekeeping."

"I should say I'm sorry, right? For breaking your toys?" She wasn't. The spell had worked thanks to the contributions of many.

"My resources are ever at your disposal. I'm pleased you used them, so is native magic and everyone here. Gurp in particular. Don't let his grumbling fool you. Some of those artifacts require acclimatization and introductions to the other magical elements with which they'll be working. Others must be signed to a blood contract before being incorporated. He's explaining to them what we need from them and what they'll get from us."

"Orientation for artifacts, got it." She shook her head. She didn't get it. "Spell work is weird."

"Indeed." He drummed his fingers against her spine. "I sense you've not quite reset your balance, yet the way you're worrying your bottom lip tells me you're up to something. Did you figure out how I can help with our family issue?"

"Don't suppose we could turn off the mics in here?" She looked pointedly at one of the security eyes in the corner of the room. "I wouldn't dream of taking you out of your men's sight considering they just got you back, so gates are out of the question."

Stepping out of the timeline was an option, but she didn't

want to risk disrupting Tobek's recuperation. He'd only been back for a brief bit.

"Give us the room," Tobek said loudly. A double chirp answered from the security eye.

"Gurp, please stay," Bix called.

The goblin beamed as the Berserkers working in the room left with a nod and a smile at Bix. The hall door swung silently shut, pneumatic locks hissing.

"I promised that once I knew what to ask of you with regards to my family, I would, so this is me asking." She grinned as Gurp made sounds of bubbling interest…or maybe he had gas. Hard to know with a goblin. "I'd like your permission for something that will profoundly affect you, possibly to the point where you will not be of any use to your men in combat."

"You're asking my permission to sideline me during a war?" Tobek worked his fuzzy chin against her head. "I can't wait to hear the why and wherefore of this."

"I want to host a parley here in the Mids, specifically downtown DC, perhaps on the rooftop of what remains of the Kennedy Center for the Performing Arts." She addressed the latter part to Gurp.

The goblin grunted multiple times with interest. Tobek gave in to a fit of coughing that nearly cost him his hold on her.

"You, Tempest, and Desire all in the Mids at the same time?" Tobek wheezed. "I take it you're planning on freeing your brother, then?"

"Both brothers," she clarified, causing Tobek to sputter. "I need all my siblings in attendance to affect the desired outcome. Everyone has to participate. Everyone has to contribute. I can only do the deconstruction of Tempest and Desire. The rest will be up to the elders."

"You need your creationist siblings to manifest the storage vessels of the twins' broken parts." Tobek sucked wind through his teeth. "All seven First Children in the same place at the same time. That's going to be dicey."

"It'll be an epic infusion of evolutionary magics to your system." She craned her neck to look up at him as his heartbeat quickened. "It may render you a block of ice for longer than Gurp's nerves can manage."

"I okay," Gurp harrumphed, pulling more artifacts from the trunk.

"Xipil and I have drafted protocols for such occasions. The battalion has its marching orders anyway." Tobek shook his head. "It's native magic I'm most worried about. I don't know that it will be able to survive all of you."

"This collective is made from Music's and Movement's diluted magics," she reminded. "Plus, we haven't tested your max capacity for absorbing our raw energy, but you survived a time trap that employed Music's and Esiw's undiluted magic while in the presence of Desire himself."

"Add to that your arrival when you broke me out of that prison, and we're suddenly up to four of the seven siblings at one, albeit short, time." Tobek's puckered lips added a bit of pondering depth to their shape. "What about Resen? Will all of you being here overload it? Cause it to short out?"

"It's built to ignore us," she dismissed, playing with his beard. "The potential damage will be on the structures of the Worlds and its denizens if I'm wrong about how much magic you can handle."

"We'll need to warn the Consortium. I will not be the only entity affected by this." The more he spoke, the less down his frown. "In fact, we'll probably need the rank and file of the superpowers to utilize their abilities to the maximum in order to burn up the excess magics your family will be adding to the collective."

"Funny how during a war that might come in a teensy bit handy." Bix held up her finger and thumb separated by a small gap.

"Rules of parley demand peace during the conference," he reminded, mocking an authoritarian tone.

"We're talking about Tempest and Desire here." Bix wrinkled her nose. "She craves the attention from the others. He wants the upper hand. We should absolutely expect an enemy surge while the family is sitting in the middle of the battlefield. Cheaters gonna cheat."

"So it's not parley, it's parlor games? I see." Tobek laughed with delighted anticipation. "I think we should give it our best shot. Though, I have to ask, why here? Why not Eko's prison?"

"Because the Mids is my home, and I want my family to understand what that means and why it should matter to them as much as it does to me." Bix tipped her head at Gurp rearranging his display. "And, if I play this right, this place just might be able to save my family from themselves."

Tobek hooked a finger under her chin and tilted her face up. His lips brushed hers, sending tingles throughout her that caused her starlight to shine like freckles through her skin. When he straightened, his eyes searched her face, and he smiled.

"Then hosting a family get-together is what we'll do."

"Yes, yes. Family. Here. All. You family. We family." Gurp patted his belly. "I do. I fix building. I set everything. Yes?"

"Thank you, both." She snuggled against Tobek. "Gurp, I'm sure I'll have some last-minute requests that only you can deliver."

The goblin nearly exploded with pride. "Yes. Yes. I do. You tell. I do."

"I wish I could stay." She groaned as she untangled herself from her Berserker. "But I have party invitations to extend."

"Fair enough. I'll make arrangements with Ogun and the Consortium for the family reunion and the enemy advance." Tobek grinned so widely, his eyes crinkled at the corners. "The moment word spreads about parley with the Devourer leadership, the Kennedy Center, indeed the entire District, will be practically sentient with all the eyes and spies from lowest Chwed to highest superpower in every building, cloud, and water droplet."

"Until we arrive, and they dissolve on the spot, which will teach them a valuable lesson about spy craft." Bix patted his chest above his Eternal Knot that lay quiet beneath his uniform. "Make sure you include the Chweds in the churning of magics and the humans for grounding. They'll come in handy for dispersing the influence of the youngest twins."

"Anything for you, sweetheart." Tobek squeezed her tightly before letting her go. "How long do we have until this momentous occasion?"

"Until Tempest springs Desire from the time trap, so not long, theoretically. Sorry."

"Anything that shortens the amount of time the enemy has to destroy our home is a good thing. All the luck, sweetheart, and don't forget your own battle prep. You've a long history to come to terms with, and you need to be balanced before you engage your brother." Tobek raised his hand to the security monitor.

"Yeah, off to do that part now."

Blowing a kiss to Tobek then Gurp, she opened gates.

CHAPTER 20

Before Bix could extend the invitations to her siblings for the family meeting, she needed to do as Tobek had advised and get her emotional baggage in order. It wasn't just her history with Desire she had to confront, it was her history with her whole family. The core issue with the terrible twins involved everyone, and Desire knew it. The only weaknesses she could afford in her emotional armor were those she left as bait. Since her emotional extremes tended to cause calamities, she had to work on herself in private. Very, very private. As in nothing living anywhere near. On the World. At all.

That ruled out the hospitality World.

Her favorite place in the Mids to let her mind and magics run amok without having to worry about harming anything was the uninhabited Mid World of Vuornis. It'd once been a prosperous gem of the collective, replete with glorious architecture and technological innovations. Its residents had worshipped a single god with great devotion and extravagance. Then the god had gotten too full of himself and offended the dragons and angels, who stopped replenishing the waters and purifying the air. Crops died. Livestock died. Inhabitants died. Eventually, no one was left who believed in the god, and without believers who had souls, the god soon had nothing to eat. He'd faded, rendered powerless by his own short-sightedness.

The World, however, continued to exist without him. Its complex ruins sufficiently obscured its damaged underground structures, particularly the large bone-dry cistern Gurp had renovated for her. Cubbies and shelves lined the walls, packed with items her subconscious had pilfered while her consciousness had been busy reassembling her mind. The goblin had rebuilt luminescent crystal pillars and had hung Tobek-original artwork in a circular alcove where her hot-pink rocking chair and fuzzy white comforter beckoned to deep thoughts.

Heels echoing along the polished crystal floor of the cistern, she paused to pat the lone life-form that could easily be mistaken for one of the many artifacts it guarded. The large metallic Bi Xie was a creature with a blackened iron head and body of a lion, long stainless steel wings on the scale of a condor's, and golden horns that spiraled upward like those of a kudu. It'd started as a pocket-sized trinket given to her by Ashtad, then it'd been bespelled by Tobek to be a sentient guardian of wherever she called home. It'd once resided in the range hood in the basement apartment of the coal plant that she'd shared with Gurp and Tobek. Now, it kept watch over her thinking space and her collection of arcane gewgaws, doodads, and thingamajigs.

"I brought you some treats, my friend." She reached through a tiny gate and retrieved a handful of soul-made coins from the Greek Under World. A gift from Hades, who knew her well enough to know she'd never be long without some type of bestial companion. The Bi Xie's eyes animated and feline irises focused on the metals shimmering in her palm. Its mighty jaw opened with the quavering drone of metal rippling. Bix set the coins along its tongue and chuckled as the beast noisily chomped its prize.

She ambled down one tunnel lined with her extensive collection of artifacts. At the various times she'd stolen these things, she hadn't understood what they were or why she'd wanted them. Now, however, she knew some of them were simply comfort items from a memory she'd been reliving. Others commemorated history-changing executions. More interesting ones symbolized messages her chipped and misaligned marbles had been trying to send herself.

Of greatest importance was the family collection. Spread in a fan shape on one shelf were the cosmic tarot cards she'd used to reestablish communications with Eko. There was a puzzle box that continually changed its shape and code that contained a small starlight fox that would carry missives to and from Esiw. A navy-blue, softball-sized circular gyroscope with seven constantly swirling gimbals would transport her to Movement if she compacted herself inside. The most undeniably beautiful complex contraption was the seven-cylinder purple music box that passed messages back and forth to Music. Contacting her siblings had been instinctually important to her even before she'd remembered her siblings themselves.

She stopped pacing in front of the cubbies containing a black-and-pewter cat-o'-five tails and a stack of six interlocking ouroboroi continually swallowing their tails. All Bix had to do was flagellate herself with the cat to get Tempest's attention. Yeah, she'd never actually used it, but imagine some poor sod getting their hands on a Tempest-summoning tool. Oof. Had to keep that one close for the sake of the greater existence.

Picking up Desire's copper ouroboroi, she scowled at them. Instead of the heads of serpents or dragons as was traditionally depicted, Desire's ouroboroi stared at her from the aging faces of drus, which some legends called male dryads or green men. Vaguely humanoid, they had hair and beards made of leaves, eyes of blooming seed pods, and dimples like lenticles. The bodies of these ouroboroi were vines sprouting six-pointed ivy leaves. There was nothing smooth or soft about them, which suited their master.

She couldn't avoid a confrontation with Desire, nor did she want to. Her immediate challenge was whether she could harness their complex history and her quixotic emotions to outmaneuver him and the twin he'd spent epochs grinding under his thumb.

As children, Bix, Tempest, and Desire had been thick as thieves. Tempest, as the source of external motivation, had constantly pushed Bix to find her boundaries. Desire had then coached Bix through surpassing them. If there was mischief to be had, Bix had absolutely been the actor, while the youngest twins had been the masterminds. Esiw had chastised the three of them endlessly, while Eko had gleefully encouraged them. Even the eldest twins had gotten in on the action, with Movement showing them how to expand their chaotic proclivities, while Music tried to contain it. Bix's childhood had been a wondrous time, full of love and laughter…until her father had isolated her from the others to begin her training as High Executioner.

By the time Bix had completed her trials and reunited with her family, Tempest had demonstrably despised her. Tempest claimed it was because Bix had *stolen* the position of High Executioner from her. But Tempest had never wanted the job. It was Desire who'd set his sights on the perceived accolade without wanting to do the work. It was Desire who'd failed to achieve his personal goal. It was Desire who'd blamed Bix. But, rather than deal with his own emotions, he'd pushed them off on Tempest. While he outwardly pretended to be happy and supportive, he'd become a seething pustule of resentment continually poisoning his twin.

The about-face in Tempest's affections had been so out of nowhere that for eons, Bix had tried to mend her relationship with Tempest. Of course, Desire had been right there, encouraging Bix to rebuild burned bridges. However, the more she tried, the more Tempest hated her. The more aggressive Tempest was in her hate, the more their other siblings retreated from Tempest. The more Tempest was isolated from the family, the more influence Desire had over his twin. Classic emotional abuse. Sadly, because Tempest and Desire were twins—connected through emotional, magical, and physical bonds—Tempest couldn't escape him or his influence.

Eko and Esiw were spot-on about Desire continually victimizing Tempest, but they were epochs too late in grasping its danger to the whole family and the greater reality. Understandable, though. Desire had been the first in all existence to commit such unseen horrors against his twin, which was why the family didn't know it was a problem in the beginning and didn't know how to stop it while it was still possible. That Eko and Esiw recognized it now was a huge milestone in the family accepting accountability for the role they'd all played in the tragedy. Step One on the path to recovery was admitting there was a problem, right?

It was equally fascinating and annoying that Esiw and Music had taken it upon themselves to imprison Desire in a time tangle. Desire likely had thought he was so slick hiding himself in the future to stay out of Bix's feral reach, but, instead, had run afoul of the elder siblings of order. Though, their intervention at this point was odd. Why, after Desire had helped them imprison Eko and bind Tobek, had they punished him? What inciting moment had she missed while caught up in her own drama? It was recent, no doubt. Super recent, even. And why had it only taken two of them to trap Desire when it had taken five to tether Eko? Was their father helping contain his recalcitrant youngest son while their mother had refused to diminish their eldest son? Or did Desire's situation have more to do with the nature of messing around in the future?

So many questions.

Bix flopped down in her rocking chair and opened tiers of viewing gates to keep eyes on Cian, on Resen, on the galaxy of Uppers, Mids, and Unders, and on the influx of Devourers arriving from the neighboring galaxy. What the gates couldn't cover, her threads of darkness monitored, reaching through the shadows of the cistern to spider throughout the pool of endless night to covertly observe players and places. Her soft tentacles bobbed on the floor, pushing her chair. More shadowy appendages cranked the soul-constructed calliope gifted to her by the titan Tartarus ages ago. A strike of starlight lit the cone of cinnamon and clove incense held in the open maw of a brass chimera she'd purchased at a flea market with Drew in the simpler days when she'd been clueless.

Tossing the ouroboroi from hand to hand, she debated contacting Desire. Assuming it was even possible with the time difference, what would she say? Would she be kind? Cruel? Aloof? How did one engage with a sociopath who was trying to provoke her to do her absolute worst? Particularly one who'd once rivaled Eko as her biggest childhood cheerleader? That was the part of Desire to which she kept clinging. That was the brother she wanted to save. Not the misanthrope on a self-absorbed rampage.

Whenever she'd asserted her independence, Desire had backed her, even when she'd been an epic brat. Desire had never been put off by her querulousness. Because he was the embodiment of personal motivation, he understood better than the others the fight to become her own self on her own path, living by standards *she* defined. He'd wept with joy the day she'd confessed she'd wanted to be more than her father's obedient scythe. Rebelling against the Cosmos hadn't been easy, pleasant, or without catastrophes, but Desire's vocal belief in her had gotten her through the hardest parts. Sure, sometimes his support had been an act, but sometimes it had been genuine. Learning his tells when he pretended was how she'd caught on to his decline into complete psychopathy. It was why seeing him lost to his most recent obsession tore her up, even while he wore her down.

What about Cian's soul? What did Desire want her to make of it? Desire's heralds had taken it because the boy had asked. Since she hadn't heard otherwise from Phobos, she assumed Desire still had the soul. Was her brother holding on to it as a beacon of hope that she wouldn't give up on him? Was he holding it hostage in exchange for his freedom? Was he holding it simply because of the death it symbolized? The act was the same, but his reasoning mattered.

She needed confirmation that Desire's conscience was still functioning, even if he was choosing to ignore it. When she finally broke him into pieces, she had to leave him with one seed of self to balance his primary aspect of motivation and set the trajectory of his recovery. A functioning sense of right and wrong would be ideal.

But. Big, big, *but.* Mistaking any of Desire's cunning gambits for a trace of morality had cost her this collective of Worlds and loved ones forty-two times. It was imperative that she preserve this timeline, the friends she had within it, and the multitude of relationships that made this present more precious to her than the previous ones.

She was no longer capable of being the emotional void she had been in earlier go-arounds. She cared. She empathized. She was Desire's perfect target. Then again, she and he were older than galaxies. They weren't mortals stumbling through finite lives discovering who they were and the reason for their existence only to expire upon the epiphany. There was nothing they hadn't seen, and she'd seen more than her brother due to reset timelines. So, could experience and empathy outmaneuver psychopathy? Was she mentally ready to face her brother? Was she ready to resume the fight for her sanctuary and her family's rehabilitation? Could she direct the storm of her emotions to throw him off his game? Hard to know until she was pushed, but the longer she took, the more ground the Devourers gained in the Mids and the more damage occurred to Cian's unhoused soul.

What was taking Tempest so long to free her twin?

Bix had expected Desire's return to happen while she and Tobek were on the hospitality World. Every moment that passed made Bix suspicious.

Gazing at the view of Tempest still driving the Devourers to assail Resen, Bix sighed. She'd given Tempest a clue how to rescue Desire. She'd even demonstrated a variant of the means, assuming Tempest could think beyond her seething ego. Tempest was either too caught up in her hate, or her sister simply didn't want Desire back in the now. The latter was intriguing, but no longer useful. Bix couldn't effect the escape for them because it relied on their twin bond. She could ask the elders to free him, but they wouldn't have trapped him if they didn't have good reason. Alas, whatever their reason, Esiw hadn't felt inclined to share it with her when he'd had the opportunity. Besides, Desire having to humble himself before the twin he constantly shat on, in order to be free? Desire considered himself a master manipulator, but Bix was a master architect. It was time to get the ball rolling, and all Bix had to do was give the terrible twins proper…motivation.

Stretching a thread of darkness along a filament of starlight, Bix wound them around the copper ouroboroi and waited seven sacred beats for their arboreal mouths to swallow.

"Brother mine, it's past time we met." She let her darkness and light carry her words, hoping the messengers Desire had crafted for her could reach him in the future. "If you can answer, do."

The messenger box with the fox rattled on the shelf and chimes plinked from the music box. Esiw and Music intercepting? Odd. Again, Bix tried to reach Desire, but this time, each ouroboros got its own paired line of communication.

"Desire? Is this getting to you?" Bix asked through the six braided streams of her essence.

The fox box tumbled end over end around the cubby. Six of the seven cylinders in the music box struck discordant notes.

Were the elders of order blocking her transmission, or were they blocking Desire's response? What didn't they want Bix to know? Why didn't they want her communicating with their youngest brother? Did they really think they could stop her? The two-in-one? Fully restored? Pfft.

"Desire, I got your message. There's bupkis I can personally do about freeing you from the future, but I did clue your twin into the sitch. Hope you've been nice to her. Kisses." Bix pushed the message through her starlight that connected her to each sibling of order, then shoved her darkness with great force so that her chaotic parts exploded beyond the confines of all order. Her chaos would travel everywhere, finding any crack or weakness in the elders' blockade, for such was its nature. "P.S. Stay away from my friends. P.P.S. What did you do to piss off Music and Esiw?"

The messenger boxes plummeted from their cubbies and crashed on the floor. The sprouted eyes of the ouroboroi pivoted from horizontal to vertical. Messages broadcasted and received from multiple targets. Excellent. How much Desire could communicate depended on the size of the fissure in his prison her chaos had exposed. It was a small one, apparently, but a gap nonetheless. Had she put a chink in it when she'd sprung Tobek? Hadn't been intentional, but happy accidents were useful ones.

Chuckling with droll anticipation, she returned the messenger devices to their storage spots. Her hand froze on the ouroboroi as the drus shuddered and moaned.

A feeble flicker of light in a dark unsettled expanse of space alerted her threads of sentient night scattered throughout the greater existence. She opened a viewing gate to see better what her distant appendages reported.

A copper sun exploded into being. Bix raised her hand against its brilliance and adjusted her gates, allowing her to spot the pewter rings encircling the sun.

The terrible twins. They'd done it. Desire had bullied Tempest into freeing him. Tempest had surprisingly paid attention to the crumb trail Bix had left. Bix's heart thundered, and chills raked her skin. Ready or not, the key players were now on the field.

The game among First Children could finally proceed in earnest.

CHAPTER 21

Shoring up her biggest weak spot before the skirmish commenced, Bix brightened her starlight and illuminated the timeline of the Mids running through the cistern. Her chaos brushed the line, erasing the present and resetting it. Seven sacred minutes were all she needed to invalidate any advantage Desire had gained from lurking in the future of the Mids. A small glitch in time had reverberating effects on the future. It also succeeded in eliminating any other pesky time knots Desire had thought to lay. She hadn't been able to disarm his booby traps while he'd had her mortal friends with him in the future. Doing so would've severed the timeline, which would've stranded her friends. Now, however, it was a bit like shaking the sand out of a beach towel. Yes, the odds of those seven minutes changing some aspect of Tobek's party prep and the Mid World armies' efforts to fight the Devourers were extremely high. Desire, however, was a greater threat than his creations.

As if summoned by her actions, copper leaves shimmered into being and tumbled throughout the cistern. The groan, keen, and ripple of the metal Bi Xie animating echoed above the wind collecting the leaves into a man-sized tornado twirling closer to the tunnel in which Bix stood. Her homestead guardian reacted whenever it sensed hostility, which forewarned her of her brother's mood. The Bi Xie's heavy footfalls brought it to the mouth of the tunnel. It spread its stainless steel wings to block any chance of a leaf entering her sanctuary.

"Stand down," Bix called to her resident guardian, not wanting it to be harmed by Desire's pique. "This is family. The visit is expected."

The Bi Xie roared but folded its wings. Leaves passed through its metal blockade as though the sentinel didn't exist. Fortunately, the leaves left her guardian undamaged. Bix released a wary breath. Good. At least Desire wasn't on a slaughtering rampage already.

The tornado of leaves stopped outside arm's reach of Bix. Plump, dimpled cheeks took shape first amid the whirl, building outward to make a man's face engulfed by a wealth of leafy hair. Young roots swayed and curled in place of a beard. Dense foliage covered a bulky masculine humanoid body. Everything was a shade of copper, from the palest peach to the bluish-greens of aged patina. Bold copper suns burned as his eyes.

"You killed me," Desire rasped without preamble, his voice soft, yet crackling like a forest floor during a windy, arid autumn.

"Yet here you stand." Bix angled herself away from him, wondering where the hell he'd gotten that info. There was no way he remembered the previous lives or the other timelines. That was the curse of the Cosmos and the Chaos resetting time across the greater existence. She and her parents were the only ones who retained the experiences. That was the root of her malice.

Of the many opening volleys she'd imagined exchanging with her brother, this hadn't ranked. Not a great start to the emo mastery game.

"It's true, then? What the elders told me? You have, in fact, killed me before. More than once, possibly." Desire loomed over her, vines forming armor beneath swaying leaves. "Their stories were inconsistent, yet earnest in their telling, almost desperate."

"Music and Esiw told you," Bix echoed dumbly as her mind searched for explanations for how *they* knew.

Anger spiked.

Her memory assimilations, when they'd helped her through the pandemonium of her subconscious running riot while her consciousness was busy putting her marbles back in the jar. Had to be. But they'd only seen fragments. That was all she'd had. Incomplete stories would've retold mismatched falsehoods until she'd retrieved the last segment of her mind that had restored events into proper factual storylines. Esiw had helped her through assimilations twice. Music once.

What must they think of Bix? Of each other? Of all the other siblings? Events that had happened in those previous timelines were ugly, hateful, horrible things that painted none of the First Children in a good light. An unfun chat with Esiw and Music just moved up the priority list. She had to sort fact from fiction for them before they further exacerbated the problems tearing apart the family.

"That was the reason they gave for trapping me in the future. Said they had to keep you and me apart, lest I drive you to kill me again. I recall no such event, so help me understand, little sister. Have I been the fool of which they accuse me?" Desire took in their surrounds. His attention lingered on the collection of family communication devices.

"Since you've had time to think about such things, perhaps you can remind me why you are so intent on death?" Bix tried to keep the sharpness from her tone and ended up with sarcasm, which wasn't what she'd intended.

"You *still* need to ask why?" Fury sparked in the suns of his eyes before cooling. He picked up Tempest's flogger and stroked the five leather tails, balancing the nasty silver hooks at the end of each tail on his broad fingertips. "I am a failure and have been outed as such ever since Father chose you over me."

Bix blinked rapidly. That was a new answer. She wasn't sure if it was genuine or not, sadly.

"Every one of your great accomplishments places my lacking into stark contrast." He hummed ruefully and pressed one hook of the flogger into his finger, causing wisps of copper light to escape from the injury. "It got to the point Father couldn't stomach my presence. I disgust him, yet he fawns all over you. He made that abundantly clear when he chose you as High Executioner. It wasn't long before his loathing for me spread throughout our family. I can't recall the last time one of them regarded me with anything akin to affection. Tell me why I should want to continue an endless lifetime of constant condemnation?"

Desire couldn't have been more wrong. The Cosmos adored his youngest son. That was why their father kept resetting the godsdamned timelines with the help of their mother. Their parents cared for him to the detriment of their other children. Talk about favoritism. Yeesh. Desire's natural propensity for greed must've made him feel their parents' demonstrations of affection simply weren't sufficient. Or…he was lying about the whole thing.

"If any part of that were true, you would've stayed dead the first time I killed you," she said flatly, wondering if his daddy issues were legit or just a sob story to elicit sympathy for him to manipulate.

"The elders were correct, then. You have killed me before." His smile was small yet wholly cruel as he tapped the remaining flogger hooks into his fingertips with enough force to bury the metal in his woody flesh. He ripped out the hooks with a hiss of pleasured pain.

"Not just you. Tempest dies too," Bix said, intrigued by his actions with the flogger. Intentional or not, he was letting on that he wasn't at peace with Tempest. "Otherwise, you simply retreat into her as an instinctual means of survival. You are twins, after all, two aspects of the same core energy."

"How many times?" He set the handle of the flogger in the middle of his stacked ouroboroi, then fanned each lash so they didn't touch each other, only his supporting rings. "How many times have you given me that for which I've begged?"

"Six," she confessed without remorse. It was hard to have any considering all he'd put her through. She wasn't sure what emotional situation he was trying to construct with this line of interrogation. Her orderly half clamored to find the pattern of his pressure, while her chaotic half leaned into the notion that he was still finding his footing with her.

"Suitable." He huffed a wry note. "And how many times have you resisted me without it ending in my death?"

"Thirty-six."

"At least you keep the resets of time to the proper multiples." He gave her a pained smile. "How many of those times have I destroyed your life in an effort to destroy mine?"

"Every one of them." She started to cross her arms, but stopped herself before committing the obvious defensive posture. She double-checked her pose and position in the tunnel, taking the moment to correct any escapist or cautious body language. She couldn't afford to appear like prey ready to bolt, so she turned away from the opening and opted to take a seat instead. "I derive no pleasure from your suffering. Despite you and Tempest repeatedly siccing your pet army on my sanctuary, I continue to try to help you."

"When the others have given up on me, I inevitably turn to you. In every timeline?" He shambled down the tunnel, inspecting more of her collection.

"Always," she confirmed, rocking slowly with her darkness still out and connected to the pool of eternal night. Just because Desire himself was before her didn't mean his heralds or other creations weren't running amok. "Sometimes you don't bother to start with our siblings. You come straight to me. Others, I am your last resort."

"Always comes back to the two-in-one," he muttered before speaking up. "The six times Tempest and I died, there is no echo within us of time being interrupted. I can identify the thirty-six kinks in my personal history that can be explained by you resetting the timelines. You've always left a clue whenever you play with time, as if to say, 'I was here. Ask if you have questions.'"

"There was a time when you did ask," she reminded. "Before

death became your obsession, you'd want to know what it was I'd taken from you during the reset. You wanted the accounting, being numbers oriented as you are."

She reset time not to deceive, but to supply second, third, or forty-third chances. As High Executioner, she often used time resets as a compassionate alternative to annihilation. Leaving a clue for her order-aligned siblings was the means by which she held herself accountable. Desire, of course, interpreted those clues as her flaunting her skills and rubbing his nose in the fact he'd failed to become High Executioner. He, more so than Music or Esiw, had demanded detailed explanations of what was, in fact, a courtesy. He'd professed his interrogations were rooted in concern for her mental well-being, naturally, being her doting big brother and whatnot. Pfft. As if.

"If you didn't resurrect us, then the only ones who could've are our parents. They are to blame for my lack of eternal rest, not you. My frustration and anger are misplaced. I'm not motivating you to help me, I'm tormenting you," he said with mild regret as he tilted his head back and stared at the tiered viewing gates.

"Our parents, in their own curious ways, care about their children." She understood the Chaos and the Cosmos even though she remained furious with them. She also understood that Desire's apologetic tone was rote, not earnest. "No longer having one or two of us exist is unacceptable to them. They have the power to prevent that loss, so they do."

"They think *you've* made a mistake, so they correct it for you and inform none of us." He harrumphed and resumed strolling. He paused before the gallery of Tobek's original artwork. "Your chosen creation, the one who seeks to be more like us. He said he would've happily died infinite times in increasingly gruesome ways if it meant the child he shared with you could have lived."

Ah, there it was. The manipulation. The application of pressure. Bix's fingers curled on the arms of her chair and her body clenched. Most of those sketches were of her in her various stages of depression after she'd miscarried. Drawing was Tobek's method of processing his grief. It took notable effort to relax her muscles. She'd known this part was coming. She couldn't give Desire the tantrum for which he was probing.

"When he loves, it is fiercely, openly, and without shame. It is something I strive to emulate." Bix dug a nail into the pad of her thumb, trying to block the tears. She'd miscarried centuries ago, yet the pain and hollowness would always be a part of her. That tragedy shaped parts of her, an emotionally crippled cosmic entity. It shaped her relationship with Tobek; the good, the bad, and the What the Hell Just Happened. It shaped the course of events leading up to this moment, a moment that could lead to the healing of her family. Life was gloriously chaotic like that. It was often hard to bear, but the balance of good and ugly was necessary. She didn't want to trade it.

She ceased the act of indifference and let the tears fall. Desire knew she wasn't a void anymore. He'd learned that from her friends. If she suppressed her feelings, it would mean she was ashamed of them and it would give Desire what he was looking for. An emotion to exploit.

"I would like this one." Desire pointed to a picture of her in a feminine state of starlight and midnight staring at the viewer with profound sorrow. "This is how I imagine you looking at me each time I drove you to end me."

"Take it." She wiped her tears, knowing full well her brother secretly derived pleasure from seeing the stoic High Executioner shattered and bereft. Again, she wasn't ashamed of her feelings; she was proud she could finally deal with them. Mostly deal with them. Somewhat? Plus, she had at least a hundred versions of that sketch since Tobek doodled whenever he was deep in thought. Being unable to grieve their loss together had plagued his subconscious. Still did, on occasion. She and Gurp had gathered all of Tobek's scrap papers, from napkins to sales receipts, to duty orders. Gurp had built a hope chest to store them because "hope come after sad," the beloved goblin had explained.

"Tell me, little sister, the grief you still feel for energies that were never born, is it more or less than the mortal boy who expired too soon?" Desire took the sketch off the wall and stared at it.

Bix's lips twitched. Second pressure point being probed. Tobek was right, her brother had no clue what their daughter had meant to them. Desire couldn't make that emotional connection. Similarly, he couldn't figure out if she considered Cian to be more like her child or more like her friend. All his time observing her team and listening to their stories, and he still didn't know where she stood. Fascinating.

"Are you referring to Cian?" She pointed to the viewing gate overseeing the laboratory, Cian's crystalized body, and Feng keeping bedside vigil.

"Your chosen creation does not seem to care as much for the boy as he does for the unborn energy." Desire pressed the picture Tobek had drawn to his chest, and foliage absorbed it. "All his time with me, and he never attempted to get to your favored mortals. I would've let him. He could've saved the boy's body, thus saved the boy himself. However, his obsession was returning to you. He had no interest in them. My heralds told your friends that, of course, after they took the boy's soul."

"Do you still have Cian's soul?" she asked, ignoring his provocation. Her team knew full well Tobek couldn't cure Cian. They'd already danced that dance of hope and had endured the crushing results. As for pitting her friends against her consort, it further exposed Desire's weak spot. He couldn't grok the complexities of relationships. He didn't understand the differences between affection and respect any more than he understood various types of love. No matter how good an actor he was, no matter how many fully supportive partnerships surrounded him, his relationships were dysfunctional. He couldn't fake what he couldn't understand, which meant he couldn't plan for it, which meant he couldn't exploit it.

His weakness was useful.

"Do you still have the will to kill me?" he countered, coming to stand beside her, his attention roaming the viewing gates.

"To what end?" She stretched and folded her arms behind her head. Did she come across as relaxed as Tobek did whenever he lounged like this? She really hoped so. "Mom and Dad will just undo it. If you want it to stick, take it up with them."

History knew she had, multiple times. Alas, the Chaos and the Cosmos had no interest in entertaining her request. They happily left Tempest and Desire as a challenge for all their children to solve. Family bonding and whatnot. Besides, the Chaos enjoyed the mess the youngest twins created. The Cosmos had chided Bix for cheating by unmaking the twins. He'd told her to be smarter, that he was disappointed in her. Frankly, dear old Dad could kiss her starlight-speckled ass. If Eko and Esiw hadn't figured out there was a problem with Tempest and Desire until recently, then smarts were never the issue. Fixing their shit came down to ability, which, sadly, left the onus on Bix, yet again, to clean up her family's messes.

"You don't seem to understand, little sister. Making it stick is *your* responsibility. After all, Father chose you as his favorite child. It's on you to convince him. Otherwise, you know how this ends." Desire flicked his wrist.

Activity in the viewing gates overlooking nearer galaxies drew her out of her chair. Desire's Devourer troops multiplied by the thousands, filling every gap beyond Resen's barriers. Soldiers and supplies connected by Tempest's pewter cords pushed against the perimeters of the Uppers and the Unders, surrounding the collectives and spreading further outward into undeveloped galaxies.

Pressure point three. As expected.

The first time he'd pulled this stunt, she'd learned the hard way how quickly his creations could devastate her home. The third time he'd pulled this stunt, she'd panicked. She'd instantly unmade his army, which had kicked off a series of escalations that she, under no circumstance, wanted to revisit. That was why she didn't personally remove Devourers from the Mids anymore. She might be thick, but she did catch on eventually.

"Oh, Desire," she groaned, looking over her shoulder at him with dismay. "The thing about you sons aligned to order is that you're predictable. Of the forty-two repeats of your relentless bullying, flooding the galaxies with your armies is one of your three favorite gambits."

"That so?" He leaned toward her and sneered. "And the ownership of the mortal boy's soul? Is that something I repeat too?"

"You do still have it. Excellent." She faced him fully and smiled. "That's all I was waiting to hear."

She exploded into her native state and bypassed his pitiful attempt to repel her with armor. She was the two-in-one. The High Executioner. She mercilessly invaded his body. The burnished brass of her starlight met the onslaught of his copper sunlight while her darkness located every tiny atom of chaos that made him a son of two divergent energies rather than a pure replicant of one. Seven sacred beats inflated his chaotic minority until he lost all semblance of balance. Seven more seconds inserted breaks in the structures of his cosmic being, fracturing him into millions of particles.

Desire fell away from her in a cloud of glittering dust, fleeing Vuornis, fleeing to the only sanctuary he had. His twin. Tempest.

Chuckling, Bix pulled herself together into her preferred corporeal form. Threads of sentient darkness crept along the ceiling and walls of the cistern, hissing arcane rebukes.

Those threads did not belong to her.

"Relax, Mother," Bix called as she retrieved the dress she'd shed when switching forms. "I didn't kill him. He's still cognizant. I'm merely reminding him of the importance of relationships and the balance with which they need to be maintained."

The tendrils of the Chaos lingered for an extra beat, then retreated. Bix breathed a sigh of relief. Okay. Her mother was watching, now she knew for sure. Upshot, the Chaos hadn't buddied up with the Cosmos to reset time, so at least one of her parents didn't object to the punishment Bix was inflicting on

Desire. Good. Progress. This was as close as Bix was going to get to permission for her ultimate solution. She hadn't broken Desire's mind. She hadn't deprived him of his awareness or magics. She'd simply one-upped him in a physical fight. She couldn't break him down any further without breaking down Tempest too. That was where it was going to get tricky. Twins against the two-in-one.

Unless she flipped Tempest.

Tossing her dress over her shoulder, Bix lingered in front of the cubby containing Tempest's vicious flogger and Desire's ouroboroi drus. Separating the two communication pieces, she smirked. Desire hadn't realized the clue he'd given her when he'd arranged these as though he were the roots and Tempest the tree whose branches were not permitted to touch. No tangling of thoughts. No notions not fed to them by the roots. He was such a control freak.

Not at the moment, though.

None of her siblings could mend what Bix had shattered. For all that Desire believed he could've been the High Executioner, fact was he didn't have the necessary abilities that came as part of the two-in-one benefit package. As long as the breaks she'd inserted between Desire's energies existed, her brother couldn't pull himself together. He was completely reliant on Tempest.

Yet again, though more boldly, Bix had deliberately shifted who controlled the power in Tempest and Desire's relationship. It was a calculated risk, admittedly, but her confrontation with Desire had cast a different light on Tempest's recent recalcitrance on fetching him back from the future. There was a sliver of a chance her sister was signaling for help. They were signals Bix wouldn't have recognized if she hadn't spent decades as a covert agent whose job it had been to get assets out of complex situations. Ashtad and Drew had taught her to identify such signals when words would've compromised the asset and the mission.

Of course, it was wholly possible Bix was reading more into the situation than was there. Tempest was still her own basket of batshittery and far from innocent. But if her sister was finally ready to stop being Desire's victim, Bix wouldn't ignore her. By taking Desire to the brink of death, Bix had made it clear how she was poised to support her sister: she'd figured out the means to protect Tempest from her twin. True salvation, however, would require a sacrifice on her sister's part.

The next move belonged to Tempest. Would her sister use the Devourer reinforcements Desire had delivered to redouble the attack on the Mids? Would Tempest drag Desire to Bix's doorstep and demand his restoration? Or would Tempest take the out Bix was offering?

Whatever Tempest's decision, Bix needed to be ready.

CHAPTER 22

There were many pieces of Bix's plan that had to be put in place before Tempest either retaliated or surrendered. Bix didn't have much time. There was the matter of getting her family on board and the reckoning with Esiw and Music over their spying on her broken mind while presuming to take actions based on false recollections. She needed to give Tobek and Hades a heads-up on the reinforcements Desire had delivered to Tempest. If Tempest didn't switch sides, her sister now had an infinite army to assail the Mids, the Uppers, and the Unders, and a clutch of titans eager to fight. On top of all that, she had to retrieve Cian's soul in much the same way she'd retrieved Tobek from the time tangle. However, she couldn't touch the kid's soul without irrevocably damaging it, so Phobos would have to join her, being the deity most inured to her potency and the one she trusted implicitly to care for Cian's essence.

First, though, the very mundane act of getting dressed. Downside of not being a creationist was that she couldn't manifest clothes whenever she shifted forms. Yes, modesty was her thing. Her reliance on a caretaker kept her humble. Fortunately, one of the best caretakers she'd ever had was Gurp, who anticipated needs long before the need presented itself.

Gathering the rest of her discarded clothes from the floor of the tunnel, she hurried to the intersection where a collapsed tunnel hosted the bedroom Gurp had made for her, stocked with a full closet and ample shoe selection. The furniture had been lovingly crafted from the bones of this World's forgotten mortals. Mounted in warded crystal and recessed into the side wall were a pair of large, lush, black, feathered angel wings. All claws still attached. Those were Archangel Samael's wings. She'd seized them as a punishment, and Samael had asked her to keep them as a preventive measure should he ever be captured by Devourers again. Theirs was a delightfully strange relationship, bonded by a common drive to protect the Mids and its many denizens. If she hadn't broken herself into pieces, her friendship with Samael would never have happened. Same for Ashtad, Drew, Cian, Ogun, and more. Hell, most of the relationships she valued had sprung up from her being completely vulnerable.

Relationships mattered. Something both Tempest and Desire needed to relearn.

Tossing her flora-dust-streaked clothes in a hamper, Bix dressed in attire that boosted her confidence and amused her malice. There was something about corsets and garters, back-seamed stockings with embroidered demonic beasties up the calves, fitted leather dresses, and platform pumps with heels designed like exposed vertebrae that screamed, *I ate your fairy tale princess.*

Returning to the tunnel of cubbies, she grabbed the puzzle box containing Esiw's fox and released its messenger. The small fox of yellow starlight bounded around the tunnel, quick to explore, leaving a trail of golden lights as it darted to and fro. She leashed it with a thread of bronze starlight to draw its attention. It didn't resist the leash. Instead, it studied her with a curious bright gaze, ears twitching.

"Esiw, you know by now Desire is free of your trap. Your misguided attempt to keep us separated failed. We should discuss the reasons you and Music felt such separation was necessary before you two take further actions. Based on the argument I interrupted between you and Eko, I doubt you want to do this at his prison. Your messenger will tell you where to find me."

With that, Bix unleashed the fox. Its four tails folded around it like petals. In a poof of golden glitter, it vanished.

Next to warn Tobek. She opted not to use gates in case they disrupted the planes on which he and Gurp might be casting spells. Instead, she reached through a mote of darkness to connect to the war room.

A firm hand of night shimmering with cobalt intercepted her.

Shocked, Bix didn't resist the forced detour as her eldest sibling, Movement, hauled her out of the Mids to a galaxy twice removed from the home Movement and Music had built for her. Taking the form of a short, barrel-bodied woman, Movement crossed her arms and licked a tooth. Eyes of cobalt-blue whirlpools raked Bix from head to toe before the first of the First Children announced her decision with a pursed-lip grunt. Bix wondered what had been decided and whether she'd passed. But with Movement, it was best not to rush a moment, lest one find oneself jettisoned across eighteen galaxies before realizing one was even in motion.

"Music's in a tizzy," Movement finally announced. "Seems she's afraid of you."

That took Bix aback and slammed a big crack through her heart. "I would never intentionally hurt her. Ever. I've done dumb shit, particularly recently, but never with the goal of inflicting any harm to her or you. Not only do I love you, but I also respect you both. If I haven't been clear about that, then I will endeavor to do better."

"None of us thought you'd hurt Tempest, but you did, didn't you? To get your champion back. And now you've wrecked up Desire too." Movement sucked one cheek into a hollow. "Music next on your hit list?"

Bix hated that a sister she adored feared her the way lesser beings feared her, but it wasn't unexpected after Music had spied on her broken mind. Credit to Movement, however, for being as measured in her response as Movement was striving to be. Restraint was difficult for a child aligned to the Chaos. If Movement legit believed Bix posed a threat to Music, the first of Firsts would show no mercy. Only a fool would menace the first twins…the youngest twins having been those fools too often in their sad quests for death.

"When a daughter aligned to order tries to make sense of a chaotic mind"—Bix paused and tapped her temple—"in your vast experience, how well has that ended for said daughter?"

"Ha," Movement barked. "I don't let her in my mind anymore because it ends badly for both of us. That's what she did, eh? Went peeking when she knew you were barely functional? It was obvious you were riding your chaotic half hard to figure yourself out. She probably couldn't resist being nosy, though, thinking she could lead you back to your ordered half if she could just understand where you were in recovery. That side of the family, I tell you, they want everything to happen on a schedule. Can't let things unfold at their own pace."

"She means well," Bix defended. "Esiw too."

"Oh, those two are working together on this, are they? That explains a lot." Movement tsked. "Those brain trusts keep thinking isolation will cure what ails us. Give us time to think, to reflect, to repent, and some other bullshit. Look at how well that's going with Eko, eh? I'm guessing by Desire's current discombobulation that it didn't work on him either. They're ignoring what happened when Father did that to you."

"They believe that without Father's challenge, I wouldn't be who I am. They like who I am, most days." Bix didn't dwell on her time in forced isolation. A tiny part of her was still that child, crushed by her father's determination to turn her into an emotionless killing machine. The positive side of that miserable experience had been her siblings always answering her whenever she'd managed to sneak past their father's blockades. Always. Even Tempest and Desire, strangely enough.

"And did it get Cosmos what he wanted? No. It blew up in his face, as well it should've." Movement harrumphed. "Isolation isn't horrible to them because they haven't been the ones isolated. Look at Tempest, eh? Want to see what prolonged isolation does to one of us? Look at her. Oh, sure, she's got Desire, but what a selfish shit stain he is. And yes, Tempest is subject to hearing the pleas of her creations, but she never developed attachments to them because she never developed attachments with us. Our fault, absolutely. We didn't understand attachment or the consequences of a lack thereof. New concept to us all. A pity she had to be the one to discover it."

"Imprisoning Tempest would only make her external reality mirror her internal state of being. It would confirm the worst of her beliefs and solidify her vilest traits. That's likely why they didn't imprison her," Bix said the last with dawning realization and regarded her eldest sister with new respect. For all Movement's gruff bluster, the first of Firsts really did notice the small things.

"Exactly. So, what I'm saying is, you hurting Tempest and Desire to protect what's yours? I get it. Pain is what Tempest understands best, and who knows what gets through to Desire," Movement grumbled. "Music would never push you to retaliate that way."

"Music isn't afraid of me because I hurt the youngest twins. She knows I've killed them in alternate timelines," Bix confessed. "Though, whether or not pain was involved when I unmade Tempest and Desire depends on which time I ended them and how furious I was."

Movement stared at her for long moments…then broke up laughing.

"You caved. Gave them what they wanted, after all, eh?" Movement slapped Bix's back hard enough to make Bix stumble. "Can't blame you. Those two are relentless. Would've done it myself if I had the ability."

"Mother and Father wouldn't approve, should you ever find yourself with the ability," Bix noted dryly, rolling her throbbing shoulder.

"Of course not. We all serve multiple purposes in the greater existence." Movement scowled at Bix as if she'd lost her marbles again. Movement leaned in closer, and Bix tensed, bracing for impact. "Bet it felt good, though. Those short interludes where the motivation twins were wiped off the face of our concerns?"

"In the past, when you'd learned of what I'd done, you ignored me and kept your distance." Bix tipped her head closer to her sister. "But you never came after me. It's not like you to withhold your opinion."

"I was probably jealous but couldn't show it lest it encourage you to try that stunt on the rest of us whenever your temper gets heated." Movement clamped a hand on Bix's nape, jostling her. "Don't even think about trying it on the rest of us. I don't care how crazy your crazy gets, I will make you wish you'd never been born."

"I believe you," Bix assured, pinching the nerve at the base of her sister's thumb to break Movement's grip as Tobek had taught her ages ago. "Your lessons in family cohesion leave lasting impressions, even when Music encourages you to be gentle."

"You need to talk to her. I don't like it when you two fight. She gets depressed and moody, then I've got to cheer her up, and that's not my strength. Feeling her sadness and fear traveling through our twin bond makes me volatile. More volatile than usual, that is." Movement heaved a mighty sigh, and a cluster of planets tumbled like Wiffle balls. "This mess with the youngest twins doesn't help soothe me either."

"I'll go see Music before I visit Eko," Bix promised.

Movement stared at Bix, expression inscrutable. Comfortable silence stretched past awkward to pained. Bix didn't dare break eye contact. Movement would take the opening to beat her ass. Even when Movement was in a good mood, violence was never far from the surface.

"Well, are you going to invite me or not?" Movement demanded. "To the family meeting? You've been plotting it with your consort. Couldn't help but overhear."

It took Bix an extra heartbeat to jump to the new topic. "Resen. You've been eavesdropping via Resen."

"Nah. Don't need Resen for that. I've got the nice little bond link that keeps your pet locked down." Movement waggled her brows. "Admit it, you've merited monitoring of late."

"So we have zero privacy. Good to know." Bix groaned and closed her eyes. "Yes, please come to the family meeting. Primary Mid World. Above Consortium HQ. Attire is suitably humanoid form and size."

"You're bringing all of us into the Mids, eh? You trying to destroy it before the youngest twins can?" Movement sniffed and looked askance. "Already told you, Music and I would build you a new collective whenever you're done with this one."

"Oh, my grumpy but sweet sister, I know you and Music have been up to things in my sanctuary, things that might make it possible for our family to come together without destroying the delightfully chaotic home you made for me and that I still love." Bix hip-checked her sister. "Besides, the lot of you ensured the champion of my Worlds is physically capable of expanding his responsibilities, including running interference with excess magics."

"You're putting a lot of faith in that rotten godling."

"Tobek has earned it many times over." Bix smiled. "I am aware there are risks to our family being in the same place at the same time, not only due to our innate power, but also due to our personalities. However, it is imperative that we—all First Children—collaborate to help Tempest and Desire break out of their self-destructive mindsets and behaviors. No more turning our backs, no more leaving the solution up to just one of us."

"Yeah, we never should've dumped our responsibility on you. Tell me what you need me to do, and I'll deliver." Movement thrust her jaw to the side and grunted again.

"If you've been listening in via Tobek, then you already know my plan." Bix then elaborated on the details of breaking Tempest and Desire into fragments, including their memories and magics.

"And you need me, us, to supply the containers for these fragments?" Movement rubbed her cheek. "Self-protecting and undetectable. Scattered across galaxies."

"The twins will have to work through a prolonged series of trials before they can acquire those packaged pieces of themselves," Bix confirmed. "They have to have the time and the repeated experiences to learn new habits and develop new instincts that will override their current ones once they reassemble themselves at some point in the far distant future."

"Reprogramming. Got it." Movement nodded.

"The twins can't be allowed to reassemble themselves before they've acquired all the containers. Incremental restoration leads to—"

"Fucking disasters," Movement interjected with a laugh. "Yeah, I think we all learned that from your little experiment. You're asking for some fancy stuff there."

"Is it possible? Those kinds of containers? That type of extended lifespan?" Bix had high hopes but no clue.

"Anything's possible. The rest of us just have to wrap our brains around it." Movement bobbed her head from side to side. "I think our parents might actually approve of this plan, even our curmudgeon of a father. You've a devious mind, littlest sister, patchy or whole. It makes me proud."

"There's a chance Tempest may engage in this willingly." Bix held up her fingers a hair's width apart. "Teeny tiny chance."

"Oh, she'll need convincing. Lots of it. Don't fool yourself. Desire's hooks are too deep." Movement shook a finger at the specks of gray Devourers littering the galaxies surrounding the Mids. "I think I've got a way to get through to her, though. Humans have this game they call billiards. Heard of it? It's all about angles and impacts."

Bix choked back a snort as a cosmic cue manifested in her sister's outstretched hand.

"You leave Tempest to me. I know how to get her to listen." Movement twirled the cue, then took aim. "Go talk to Music. She's going to love this."

CHAPTER 23

Returning to Vuornis to send a message to Music offering to meet, Bix drew up sharply upon spotting said sister in a humanoid form kneeling before the Bi Xie. The eldest child aligned to the Cosmos giggled as she fed coins she manifested to the sentient guardian and stroked its leonine mane, cooing ancient endearments to the beast. Music had chosen a curvaceous body, her hair wavy and dancing despite the lack of a breeze. Her skin appeared mottled in shades of purple at first glance, but each color variant was a note of her personal song. Her innate starlight lit each of those notes as it played the gentle, never-ending tune that was Music's soothing presence.

Hearing it was like listening to a cherished lullaby, but it didn't lessen the second surprise awaiting Bix in her pondering palace. Esiw sat in her hot-pink rocker while it bobbed back and forth to the tune of Music's resonance. He'd scaled himself to fit in the chair, atop a yellow pillow protecting his paws from the hard slats of the seat.

Bix hoped Tobek was comfortably handling this influx. This was only three out of seven siblings loitering in the Mids, after all.

"Movement told me you were on your way to find me," Music trilled without rising from her spot nor looking at Bix. "I thought I'd make it easy on you."

"How considerate." Bix sidled past Music, noting with a heavy heart the way her older sister flinched when she passed.

"You sent a message that you and I were to have words, thus, here I am," Esiw preempted. "Since you made no effort to hide your conversations with Desire from us, I can only assume he is the topic."

"I'm ecstatic you've turned to each other for emotional support," Bix noted wryly. "After all, your chaotic twins could never hope to understand why you'd deemed it necessary to force separation between the youngest children of order."

"You *killed* Desire," Music cried, surging to her feet. "How could you?"

"Poking around my fractured mind and you didn't locate my why?" Bix feigned shock as her temper stirred. Her mind and memories had been her greatest vulnerability after she'd broken herself into pieces. She was fiercely protective of them, yet Music and Esiw had exploited her weakness. She'd expected as much from Esiw; hell, he'd admitted it the first time he'd done it. Second time shouldn't have been a surprise. Music, though, Music had been the one to teach her to respect boundaries. For Music to violate her own creed? To steal instead of ask? That hurt. "There are forty-two answers to that question. Yet, I'm not sure how many were complete or factual when you took it upon yourselves to access that which has always been blocked to you."

"What we did isn't the point," Music argued, her lyrical tones striking sharp notes. "Your actions are intolerable. Reprehensible. There is no excuse for fratricide."

"Bullshit," Bix carped. "Remember you're speaking to the High Executioner, trained by the origin of order himself, our father. You're not angry that I killed Tempest and Desire. They're still here, so their deaths aren't really deaths. And, yes, I killed Tempest too, though you and Esiw like to pretend that chaotic disaster isn't part of the family."

Music's indignant gasps were perfectly pitched notes of the G-sharp scale. If Bix pushed her to F-sharp, then Bix would've known her assessment was off the mark. G-sharp confirmed acute embarrassment tinged with anger. Music had taught Bix how to listen and translate the songs of creation and the cycles of life. The prerequisite of those lessons was learning Music's personal notes and compositions. In short, her sister's truths were an open songbook.

"Music, you're scared because you've long found comfort in the misconception that I *couldn't* unmake family members," Bix said with a wealth of pity and disappointment. Yes, she was angry too, but that was tempered by knowing her sister usually acted from a place of broad concern not selfish manipulation. "Snooping revealed that to be a lie, and now you're spinning. You're bordering on hysteria. Movement can't pull you back because that emotion is squarely in the realm of chaos. Do not blame me or Desire for the consequence of your actions."

"Watch it," Esiw snarled. "You're being cruel, little sister."

"I'm being factual." Bix pivoted on her heel and glared at her brother. She loved him dearly, but, man, she wanted to strangle him. "As for you, I distinctly remember warning you rather recently about the dangers of trusting a broken mind filled with partial memories. Still you acted on what you saw."

"It was information I did not have that turned out to be pertinent to the issues you were facing, issues you kept bringing to me for aid," he snapped, hackles rising.

"It was temptation, plain and simple. You had the chance to finally get inside my head, and you couldn't resist it." Bix slapped her hands on her hips so she wouldn't demonstrate how easy fratricide really was. "You even invited Music to have a look through my crazy, knowing it would rock her reality. You're delighting in her tailspin because it confirms who you think I truly am based on the fragments of what I've done."

"You broke yourself into pieces," he derided. "We had to understand why any child of order would succumb to such chaos. We can't help what we can't fully comprehend."

"The flaw of your primary aspect is what it quickly sacrifices in the name of enlightenment." Bix bid her temper to calm. Flying off the handle wasn't the way to reach him. He'd stop listening if she got too emotional for his comfort, and she needed him to listen, to really hear her. "Empathy is the first casualty. It disgusts you when Music acts upon her *feelings* for me, feelings born of *experiences she's amassed* by sharing them with me and by watching over me. You spend too much time trying to convince yourself a child of order should be above the unruly instigators known as emotions."

"Emotions are necessary to our chaotic twins, but they are a detriment to us," Esiw insisted. "A core difference between wild and ordered. I trained you to know better. I'm disappointed you've chosen to ignore those lessons."

Music whimpered a note for exasperation and another for dismay, but Bix kept trying to get through to her pigheaded brother. She needed him to confront his behaviors that had compounded the problem with Tempest and Desire. She needed him to understand the consequences of tough love, especially when no one else could see it was love fueling his actions.

"I spent too much of my life suppressing my emotions, just as you taught me to. It disconnected me from the realities of life. The three centuries I spent not knowing I shouldn't feel?" Bix chuckled as a cavalcade of disparate emotions marched through her, culminating in fondness and satisfaction. "They've been some of *the* most rewarding years."

"You were broken, and the disasters you created in that state are the reasons Music and I could not stand idly by." Esiw whipped his four tails to punctuate his assertion.

"He has a point," Music interjected, wringing her hands. "There are events you set in motion far beyond this galaxy that we could only arrest but not resolve."

"Those disasters pale in comparison to the crisis in which this family is floundering," Bix dismissed, her attention locked on Esiw and his fraying composure. A little further and she might crack through that shield of his. "Dear brother, you patronize Music because she is dramatic while you cling to stoicism as an indicator of superiority, dignity, and enlightenment. She is no less wise than you. She is no less a child of order. However, she and Movement are the embodiments of expression. Sentient energy chose to reproduce, and the first things they made were expressions through action and sound. Why should emotions be different? Demanding anyone suppress what they feel is just you showing your ass."

The answering stunned silence was prolonged. Had she done it? Had she finally gotten through to him?

"I don't believe I've heard the term 'showing your ass.'" Music tittered, breaking the tension. She blushed a charming shade of lavender. "The imagery suits, though. Esiw, how can you think so little of me when your own twin is a beautiful cacophony of sentimentality? Even if you don't want to, you still *feel.* Eko will never allow you to be as cold as you pretend to be. *We* know better. We see through your façade. All of us do. Why maintain the pretense?"

"Emotions compromise analysis," Esiw argued, ears flattening. "They inhibit learning."

"Emotions are a critical component of a complete analysis. Otherwise, you misconstrue motivation," Bix countered, hammering against his misbegotten belief. "The embodiments of motivation and how we've been mishandling them as a family are what brings us together in this current conflict, aren't they?"

Music looked chagrined. Esiw looked...detached. He was shutting her out and shutting her down. Damn it.

"Esiw, I understand you better than you give me credit." Bix softened her stance and sighed. She wasn't getting through. He'd seen what he believed to be facts. This was an uphill battle trying to prove otherwise. Would words be enough? She really wanted them to be, because she didn't want to let him inside her head again. His previous violations still stung.

"Clearly not," Esiw jeered, lip curling. "*You're* the one entertaining hysteria now."

"Not being able to fix Desire? To redirect his self-destructive behavior? It frustrates and infuriates you." She ignored his jibe and leaned into her own disappointments, letting him see how their burden made her shoulders slump and bowed her head. "You think if you keep refining your focus by stripping away another layer of compassion, you'll figure out how to help him. Yet, when you've presented your suggestions to the youngest twins, they've scorned you, which wounded you deeply. You love them, so you keep trying even as you profess to be done with them. You can't resign yourself to losing them, so you build a wall to keep us from seeing how hurt you are, even as you continually toil toward a solution."

"That's not accurate. I'm not... You're misreading..." He stopped and looked away, but the semaphore movements of his ears spoke loudly. They said she'd found the chink in his armor.

"Oh, Esiw," Music wailed, flying at the fox to envelop him in a hug. "I thought you really were done with them. I'm so sorry I didn't try harder to understand you."

"*My* actions do not excuse *your* actions, little sister," Esiw insisted harshly, disentangling from Music and dashing Bix's hope of getting through to him. "Tempest's and Desire's actions do not excuse yours either."

"Your actions are based on culling untruths from a mind trying to heal and failing." Bix threw her hands in the air, and her thorns of malice shot from her spine to wreath her arms. "Why can't you see your bias? Your empirical data is flawed."

"Look at you. Even now, as you profess to be wholly yourself again, you cannot control your temper. Are you thinking of killing me, eh? Am I next? Is Music? Is Eko? Answer me," he barked, body sparking with his rage.

Music jumped back with a squeak and flattened herself against the wall of cubbies. The eldest child of order bounced her attention among Bix, Bix's thorns, and Esiw, obviously struggling with which sibling she was going to side.

For a moment, Bix considered putting away her thorns to assuage their fears. But for just a moment. Instead, she let her darkness crawl along the floor of the cistern, encircling feet and chair legs. This was her home, damn it. She wouldn't let Esiw shame her for being the two-in-one. He'd pulled this authoritarian bullshit when she was a kid because he disdained the tiny parts of himself that came from their mother. What he had in micromeasures, she had in equal measure. Therefore, in his mind, she was innately problematic and had to be callously trained to suppress it. That he'd relapsed into this nugget of comfortable bigotry exposed just how frightened he really was.

Gah.

Calm. Breathe. Think. Don't lose sight of the objectives. Heal her family. Vanquish the Devourers. Save the Mids. Revive Cian.

Words were never going to be enough for Esiw. She couldn't reach him with logic or emotion. He'd seen what he'd seen, and that was that. Period. Worse, if he couldn't get past his fear of her, then he'd reinfect Music with his doubts and concerns... which would spread to Movement through their twin bond. Eko would do his best to fight it, but he'd eventually become tainted too because of his twin bond.

This episode of family dysfunction was getting worse, not better.

She had a choice: let them in her mind to see her full, complete, and factual truths; or give up everything she'd gained in this timeline and reset it. Give up Cian. Give up Ashtad. Lose Drew. Lose Feng. Lose Samael, Phobos, Hades, and the others. Watch Tobek and the Mids devolve. Live alone with the losses only she'd remember.

She'd spent most of her existence distanced from others, which made it easy to fall back into those habits. It was easy to push others away before getting pushed away, but it was also defensive and counterproductive. She was so close to finally healing her family. So. Close. Would she really stop now just because she was hurt by their fear and angered by their distrust? Really? Was she that precious? Had she learned nothing while living unburdened by her past?

Music and Esiw had helped her when she was broken. Maybe not in ways that respected her boundaries, but she was whole and none the worse for their methods. She could trust them. She could pull them close, invite them in, and remind them they had no reason to fear her.

Relationships mattered. If that was her core truth, then the decision was easy.

"As the youngest of us, I grew up studying more than the topics on which each of you tutored me. I grew up studying you as individuals and as twins. I know your tics and tells. I know when you're lashing out in fear, and I understand why you are." Bix extended her hands to her siblings. "Come, look inside my mind at the complete story. See how I applied what all of you taught me. Learn from me as I've learned from you. Please, don't allow partial truths to set us against each other."

"I don't *want* to be afraid of you, little sister. I'm sorry I am. I really am." Music clenched her fists over her chest and eyed Bix's hand…and Bix's darkness. "It is difficult to imagine you forgiving us our trespass and inviting us to do it again. This feels like one of your complex traps. Is your intention to punish us? I have seen so much in your mind that I don't know what to believe anymore."

"No trap. It's a one-time deal, and only if you make the effort to examine the *whole* story," Bix clarified, letting herself feel the unpleasant sadness of being the bogeyman to her beloved siblings. "Following it to the end should reveal the plan I've presented to Movement for how we, as a family, are going to fix this mess that continues to grow around us."

Bix hadn't finished speaking when Music manifested two more rocking chairs, one in purple and the other in teal. The chairs arranged themselves in an equilateral triangle with the pink rocker. With a huff and a resigned grumble, Esiw provided the pillows. Music cast a ray of plum light at the calliope and clapped with delight as it started to play.

Settling in the teal chair, Bix relaxed her hands on the armrests and brightened her starlight. Music did the same. Esiw curled into a tight ball and draped his four tails over his armrests. Rose-gold starlight streamed from Music first, then yellow gold flowed from Esiw. Their lights connected with Bix's burnished-brass starlight and braided around it, following the path into Bix's body. Bix's innate midnight buffeted the lights of order, instinct trying to distract and repel. Esiw's and Music's starlight kept tight to Bix's, seeking the complete histories of forty-two arrested timelines and a forty-third currently in progress.

Now that her mind was whole, only a child aligned to the Cosmos could walk the many branches of her memories to comprehend the complex lattice of relationships overlaying linear events. Her chaotic siblings would get tangled in the elaborate mapping of a mind, so this tour wasn't something she could offer them. She needed them, nonetheless.

More of Bix's darkness slithered from her spine and headed for the cubbies. A thread of night pulled the tarot card of Temperance and rejoiced when Eko answered, maintaining contact. Another thread of darkness tangled around the gimbles of Movement's messenger orb. The first of Firsts responded in kind, holding the connection. Through them, Bix maintained balance as Music and Esiw studied all that Bix had asked. They did her the honor of not exploring more than they had been invited to see.

A tear filled with many emotions dribbled down Bix's cheek. She made no move to wipe it away.

Time was irrelevant as Bix guided her siblings through the process of understanding into healing. She was fully aware Music was sharing information with Movement, just as Esiw was sharing it with Eko. The elder siblings of chaos confirmed it through their connections to Bix. History, emotions, questions, answers, all of it flowed continuously through the web of interconnected First Children. Such was the level of trust Bix had with her eldest siblings.

She did not share the same kind of trust with the youngest twins. She couldn't imagine a future where she would allow

Tempest or Desire this intimacy. It was a point of exclusion the terrible twins would no doubt notice and decry. Bix didn't have a solution for that, and she didn't hide that fact from the elders. The utter lack of trust in the youngest twins could be the biggest sticking point in the grand plan. The elders took her concern under advisement, but offered no immediate solutions, not that she expected any. There was no fast remedy to what Desire and Tempest had ruined.

Eventually, the lights of her siblings' order withdrew from Bix, leaving her feeling a bit hollow. Fingers wrapping over hers made her open her eyes. Music, with tears streaming, squeezed her hand.

"I'm sorry," her sister whispered. "For all of it. I should've realized there was more happening than I chose to see."

"I too apologize." Esiw patted Bix's legs with a tail. "So much I should've known, should've discerned, should've…"

"None of this is about assigning blame or laying guilt," Bix somehow managed to rasp around the lumps in her throat as relief, joy, and love warmed all the cold and empty places within her.

"This is about us acting as a family," Music finished for her with a watery smile. "A loving, supportive family."

"It's high time we exemplified the affiliation." Esiw cleared his throat. "We have our marching orders, yes?"

Music nodded, squeezing Bix's hand again.

"Then, little sister, we shall rendezvous with you at the appointed hour with our contributions at the ready." With that, Esiw vanished in a poof of golden starlight, taking his pillow with him.

Music stood and drew Bix into a long hug, saying nothing. Her sister didn't need to. Their shared tears expressed everything. With a sniffle and a kiss to Bix's forehead, Music departed.

Sending thoughts of gratitude through her shadows, Bix disengaged from Movement's messenger. Her last connection was to Eko. She drew the card of the Fool reversed to show recklessness and crossed it with the Ace of Wands to represent compassion.

Before he could answer, she connected to the shadows thrown by the black gables of his prison.

CHAPTER 24

Knowing her eldest brother would be alone while the others were prepping for the family meeting, Bix followed the indicators of the garnet triangular tiles to a red-lit workshop filled with assorted and incomplete beings in various stages of innovation. It was like walking into a special effects costume warehouse with assorted heads of various sizes on shelves in the corners. Numerous mismatched legs hung in tiers across from myriad torsos along the curved walls. Arms and tails dangled from the vaulted ceiling like icicle lights, while hands, fingers, toes, eyes, horns, antlers, antennae, etcetera, had been sorted into bins and baskets on racks that made concentric circles around the main workbench situated squarely in the middle of the room.

"Eko?" Bix called from the doorway. "May I interrupt your work?"

"You are always welcome to interrupt me, little sister," came the answer. "Always."

There was a hitch in her brother's voice that worried Bix more than the lack of his usual enthusiastic greeting. Using gates to navigate her way through Esiw's obvious influence on Eko's impressive storage and organization, she paused in the opening to the central work zone.

Eko, seated on a plain three-legged stool, hunkered over his workbench affixing feet to an inanimate project. His three tails thumped on the floor without discernable rhythm. Every whump rattled the collection of vials, ampules, waxen pots, hooves, paws, and more feet spread across the table.

"Are you all right?" she asked, trying not to notice how he ducked his head to avoid looking at her.

He huffed and muttered something, hurling the chosen feet across the room. He rifled through the others on the table, still muttering. The third time he chucked a failed appendage across the room, he flattened his hands on the table and stilled.

Only then did she notice his shoulders heaving.

"Eko?" She adjusted her preferred size to suit his and slowly approached the bench. "You can talk to me, you know."

Her beloved biggest brother gradually pivoted on his seat, head hanging so low, he could sniff his navel. His hands fisted on his knees and his tails tucked under his stool. The soft sound of sobbing met the moist streaks running down his chest.

Bix closed her hands over his and sank to her knees, waiting for him to lead the conversation.

"Why don't you hate me?" he whispered at last, still not meeting her gaze.

"There is never anything you could do that would make me hate you." She rested her cheek on her hand that covered his. "I love you too much."

"You don't…you don't know…" He tightened his fists and turned his head away. "You don't know what I did."

"If it has to do with why the others tethered you to a prison, then I just might." She didn't encroach on his personal space any further, even though it felt like a grater was running over her heart with each bloody beat.

He shook his head violently. "No, you couldn't know. You could never bear to be near me again if you did."

"Eko, our siblings, your twin in particular, have a curious penchant for misusing isolation. It's an instinctual reaction to try to separate a victim from anticipated assault." Bix smirked at the cherry-tufted tip of one tail creeping closer to her. "Passive protection, I think we should call it."

He tipped his head, ever so fractionally, toward her. "Instinctual, you said?"

"Your turf, biggest brother." She grinned and swayed until he relaxed his leg, letting her move it from side to side. "Would you agree that it is instinctual, irrespective of to which parent one might be aligned, to want to protect those we love?"

"Of course. It is a primal instinct. Unavoidable, even to those functioning at a higher level of logic." He cupped his three blunt fingers around hers. "It is a core chaotic emotion that exists once we establish connections with anything from a poppet to a...to a..."

His whole body tensed, and his venturous tail retreated.

"A child?" Bix finished for him. "Eko, I know it was you who tampered with Tobek to make the miracle of my pregnancy possible."

"I just wanted you to know the joy," he blurted, turning so swiftly to her that she lost her balance. His tails caught her before she fell over. "From the moment you were old enough to understand the concept of creation, you have marveled at it with such reverence that I wanted you to finally know what it was like. You'd found a favorite toy who'd reconnected you with the exultant chaos of living. I thought if the two of you... I didn't mean to cause you all the pain. I didn't want you to have to know that part. I would've made sure you never had to know that part once it was born."

"That part was inevitable." She stroked his damp cheek and mourned the lack of merry fire in his eyes. There were nothing more than embers floating amid his profound sadness and regret. "I *did* know the joy, and I also discovered a new dimension of grief that had always eluded me. Conceptually, I understood it, but experiencing it has been..."

"Traumatic?" Esiw leaned into her touch. "I'm so sorry, little sister."

"The others, they tethered you here to force you to reflect on what you'd done, yes, but also to know where they should report when the day came that I remembered the loss of my daughter." She stood and knocked his hands off his lap so she could sit there as she had when she'd been a little girl. "They were protecting you from my wrath. Back then, they didn't know they were also protecting you from being unmade. Imagine to what lengths they would've gone if they'd known then what they discovered today."

"I deserved whatever punishment they'd conceived." He thumped his fist against his heart.

"Pfft. No, you don't." She lightly smacked his chest. "I don't think you anticipated the likelihood of what would go wrong with your gift. I know your intentions were good. Never have I ever doubted your intentions."

"You give me too much credit," he mumbled.

"You don't give me enough," she chided. "I have the choice of unmaking time, so your meddling never happens. I also have the choice of unmaking all the memories associated with my pregnancy, so I don't have to recall any part of it. Good or bad."

"You should," he insisted, scratching a horn. "I was wrong to do that to you. You should do everything you can to make yourself feel better. I will help in whatever way you want."

"I've been on such a journey since the day I accepted I was creating a life." She leaned into his big chest, finally relaxing while this bit of ugly history was neutered of its ability to hurt anyone anymore. "I would be a different entity if I erased everything that happened from that moment to now. I like who I am, Eko. I like the relationships I've forged that sprang out of that tragedy. I like that, through that heartbreak, I was able to figure out how to heal our family. And, of greater importance to this moment, I like *you*. Well, I actually love you *and* I like you."

"It is okay if you do not wish to forgive me. I understand the damage my actions have done." He wrapped his arms around her, just as he had every time Esiw had scared her and sent her running to this great big place of constant comfort.

"To be honest, if this were three hundred years ago, we'd be having a very, very different confrontation." She laughed and tangled her feet in his tails. "Just promise me, don't do it again. Tobek and I are okay with our sterility. We accept that we're not going to procreate. We definitely don't want to relive the loss of what shouldn't have been in the first place."

"Promise," he vowed solemnly. "Never again."

"All right, then, I need you to make a decision. A very important decision. Are you ready for this?" She leaned sideways and stared up at him, delighted when the fires of his eyes ignited.

"As long as it is not feet for that new creation, I am ready." He tipped a horn at his workbench.

"I need you to tell me if you want me to unmake the tether keeping you here or if you want me to unmake the whole prison."

He shook his head as if he had water in his ears. "You mean to free me now? But our agreement was for *after* the Devourers were gone from your home."

"Did Esiw not share everything he was supposed to with you? Did he neglect some part of the grand plan?" Bix felt her temper stir, and filaments of shadows unfurled from her spine.

"Esiw permitted me to experience all he did through our twin bond," Eko assured, patting her back. "I just assumed my participation in the family meeting would be based here."

Bix slid out of his lap and wagged a negating finger. "Oh, no, no. You *will* attend in person and in Mids' appropriate size with everything you've been assigned to bring. I insist."

"I am having difficulties with one of the assignments." He glowered at the workbench.

"Fins. For that, I suggest fins, not feet." Bix cast a shadow to retrieve three sets of fins from the collection on the rear wall. "Now, what will it be? The tether or the whole shebang?"

He looked around, studying everything as if from a new perspective. The perspective of freedom.

"Just the tether, I think." He smiled, finally. "I have projects and toys with which I am not yet done."

"Can't forget those toys I sent you. Special delivery and all." She set her hands on his broad shoulders, then danced her fingers up to his bulky neck. "Hold still. This is going to tickle."

She cast the rays of her starlight and the threads of her midnight into his body, searching for the ties that bound him to Esiw and the others. The twin bond was like a neon sign in the depths of an oubliette. The maternal line of the Chaos connecting him to Movement, Tempest, and herself sparkled blue, pewter, and teal. Locating where the filial lines bisected the twin bond revealed Music's and Desire's fine lights. The complex weave of their siblings' influence pegging him to the prison they'd built was a thing of wretched beauty.

Unmaking that weave was a simple matter of rearranging personal bits, regardless of whether the owners wanted her to or not. As the two-in-one, she couldn't be stopped. That was the core of what scared her siblings. Their safety relied on her equanimity. Their peace of mind came down to how much they trusted her. Sadly, imprisoning Eko proved they didn't, even before they'd known she could unmake them. Their father had trained her to be the High Executioner, so it was reasonable that they still clung to a nugget of fear. Not a damn thing she could do to erase that. The pangs from their distrust were moments she had to acknowledge and move past. No point in dwelling on them. Nothing to gain by being angry.

She released Movement and Music from the tethering weave first, then Tempest and Desire.

"Ah, they did not like that, the youngest twins didn't." Eko chuckled. "I can feel Tempest's rippling anger."

"She hates it when I touch her," Bix admitted as she undid the last of the tether, leaving his twin bond fully intact. Esiw, of course, was the greatest influence trapping his twin in this remote existence. That part, she didn't mess with; it was an issue for the twins to resolve between themselves.

Eko inhaled slowly, rolling his shoulders and cricking his neck. His tails reached for the ceiling and fanned. His shadows sprouted from his head and shoulders, filling the room. The flames of his eyes danced, burning the deepest crimson as the full might of his unrestrained presence flooded the area and galaxies beyond. Goose bumps rose along Bix's skin, to her complete and utter delight. Yes, this, *this* was the broad encompassing chaotic power of impulsiveness, recklessness, and joyous abandonment.

"Thank you, little sister," he said, his voice sonorous as it traveled out his mouth and through his shadows.

"Thank *you*, Eko." She let her darkness flow to meet his, playfully batting at him as an annoying little sister ought. "Without your patience and guidance, I would not have achieved this elevated level of balance."

"I am grateful you choose to see my mistakes as opportunities for progress encompassing both of us." He gathered her hands in his and bowed over them.

"All of us," she corrected with a smile as his horns brushed her hair. "The whole family. We keep learning, we keep evolving, we keep being there for each other."

He chuckled as he straightened. "Indeed."

"I'm off to check on Tempest's response to Desire's current affliction, then to fetch a boy's soul from Desire's clutches before the family gets down to business. I'll see you soon." She rocked up to her tiptoes and kissed her brother's cheek. "The greater existence welcomes you back, unfettered son of the Chaos, eldest of knowledge, embodiment of instinct."

Eko cleared his throat, widened his stance, puffed his cheeks, and lifted his chin. "The greater existence celebrates your return, High Executioner, venerated two-in-one, embodiment of balance."

Laughing at their shared mockery of pomposity and the formalities long disused, Bix opened gates and returned to the Mids.

CHAPTER 25

The muted din of multiple battles coalesced in the gate to the war room at the coal plant. Bix stood on the threshold, out of the way of Berserkers rumbling commands through boom mics attached to cordless headphones as they ran overwatch for the pandemonium playing out across the Mids. Modular walls streamed live feeds from Berserker troops partnered with gods engaged in a brutal mix of weapons-versus-magic combat with Devourers. Gofers hustled from the war room down the hall to ops or downstairs, presumably to the MWA support troops in the repurposed body modification shop. More Berserkers sat at the conference table, typing away at tech or communing with artifacts that resonated with various Mids' magics. The artifacts must've been some sort of connection to civilian Chwed teams or remnants of the decimated guilds.

Tobek stood in the middle of four wall screens, bright eyes darting as he issued orders for the conflict he was overseeing. Bix bided her time. He knew she was there. Every man in the room did. Upshot of being the bogeyman was she never had to announce herself. The weight of her presence took care of that. Besides, she'd come for an update on the preparations, and the activity in the room told her something big had happened. She eyed the assorted feeds, testing her knowledge of the locations and how much or how little they'd changed since she'd last observed them. Sadly, war changed everything.

"Sweetheart, perfect timing," Tobek called, not looking away from his screens. "May I trouble you for some gates, please?"

"Of course," she murmured, unwilling to shout. His evolution had taken care of elevating his senses.

"Thank you." He flashed a smile but didn't shift his focus. "Screen twelve, origins. Destination, the parade field out front, if you would."

A Berserker waved to her from across the room, then pointed to the modular wall beside him. Threads of shadows spidered across the ceiling to get the view of a dozen-odd origin sites. Her heart stammered as Chwed refugees, bloodied and bedraggled, some still bearing the tarry spatters of Devourer blood on their skin, some carrying fist-sized geodes close to their chests, ran screaming from hordes of anti-gods plowing through the defenses of the Mids' armies.

Gates opened. Some in the path of the refugees. Some blocking the path of the Devourers. One or two tiny gates opened in the torsos of random Devourers, allowing her darkness to connect directly to Desire's toys. She took a taste, slightly more than a sip, of the anti-gods' essence.

Disappointment slicked through her on the numbing flavor of her prey. These were not the foot soldiers who'd first penetrated the Mids. Oh, the embroidery on their bronze uniforms identified them as the lower ranks, but their power was equivalent to the colonels of the first wave of invaders. These reinforcements could only be tracked by Resen. They couldn't be rebuffed or contained by it.

Desire had cheated. He'd stolen Resen's architects, used his heralds to learn the system's weakness, and delivered unto Tempest reinforcements capable of getting through the defense system. Sadly, no part of this escalated carnage was a surprise. After forty-two rodeos, Bix would've been stupid for this to be anything less than expected. Sure, Resen hadn't existed in the previous timelines, but Desire's and Tempest's chicanery was old hat.

The disappointment stemmed from Tempest choosing retaliation instead of accepting the out Bix had offered. She'd really wanted her sister to finally stand up to Desire's oppression, to stop being a willing victim. Apparently, despite Movement's best efforts, Tempest was committed to her own villainy. Ah well, at least Bix had her answer. Unfortunately, that answer upped the odds of her failure. Twins against the two-in-one meant breaking them down was guaranteed to be almost impossible. Almost. She had a micron of a chance for success. She still had to give it her best. The wellbeing of her friends, her family, and the Mid Worlds as they knew them were on the line.

"My apologies, sweetheart." Tobek offered her a hand down from the gate. "You warned me there would be a surge. It happened earlier than we were prepared for."

Bix stared at his hand, blinking rapidly. He'd done that speedy-walk thing again. She hadn't seen him move from his command post, then, poof, right in front of her.

"Have they invaded the District?" She took his hand and tugged him into the gate rather than step into the room and occupy much-needed space.

He glowered and nodded. "They've tried for here too, but our wards are holding. I'm afraid your offer of parley has been refused."

"It was only a courtesy. The terrible twins don't actually have a choice in attending, not now that the rest of the family is on board." Bix smiled with all teeth and no kindness. "Tell me Gurp isn't trying to rehab the Kennedy Center while conflict rages around it."

"I would be lying." He tucked a lock of hair behind her ear. "It's family. Even if you hadn't asked, he would've done it."

"So the men you need to be fighting these pop-up battles are instead party prepping with a goblin." She smiled genuinely this time and shook her head. "I'm sorry."

"War is war. The enemy needs to be defeated wherever it presents itself." He gestured to the room and his men hard at work supporting the boots on the ground. "If that meeting ends with the Devourers ceasing their attacks on our Worlds, then Gurp is doing exactly as he ought to welcome the heads of the opposing sides who are there to hash out peace."

"Look at you and your political savvy," she joked. "Let Gurp and his protectors know we'll be there soon. I have one stop to make before the full family meets."

"I'll let them know you're coming, but Gurp and the green team will remain. Yes, before you ask, they are aware of the risks and precautions have been taken." Tobek glanced at his metal arm as green magic illuminated the engravings. "Apparently, more First Children are entering the Mids right now."

Unsurprising. She expected her elder siblings to tour the collective as part of their meeting prep. The surprise was Tobek's arm alerting him to the fact.

"Oh, you sneak, Resen doesn't notice us, but this alerts you?" She tapped her fingers against his glowing silver arm.

"If I was shirtless, you'd see it was more than my arm responding," he drawled and added a brow waggle.

"You're a tease, and I love it." Bix patted his chest, feeling his Eternal Knot violently twitching. "Earlier, there were three of us in the Mids at the same time. How did you do?"

"There were *five* of you here at the same time, and there have been two of you here consistently since," he corrected, and tugged the collar of his jacket and shirt to expose a cluster of ice melting on his torso. "I am aware of the fluctuations. The men became aware when we hit five. A bit like being hopped up on amphetamines, but nothing too overwhelming."

So, while she was having the set-to with Music and Esiw on Vuornis, which two siblings had come to the Mids? Not Eko. He'd still been imprisoned. Movement? Had she dragged Tempest here? Or had Tempest brought Desire to DC to plot retribution?

What, oh what, were the terrible twins up to this time?

"Glad that test run worked." Bix puffed her hair out of her eyes as her mind raced. Had she covered all her bases? Was there a weak spot she'd neglected? The plan was in motion. It was too late to second-guess herself now. "Okay, I'm on my way to Cian's research facility to relocate everyone to safety before I fetch his soul, then try to heal him. After that, I'll move to the Kennedy Center, where things will get ugly before I can enforce calm. Now's the time to evacuate all nonessential personnel from the area. If Devourers are roaming the streets, leave them. They're either there by design, or they'll realize their folly soon enough."

"You're *starting* with healing Cian? I thought that was happening in the aftermath of success." Tobek ran his fleshy hand over his face.

"I can't fetch his soul from a brother who will not remember where he put it after I take away his marbles," Bix explained. "Plus, his and Tempest's bits will be too finely scattered for me to hunt via their cosmic persons when all is said and done."

"Right. Of course. My mistake." Tobek glanced with consternation at the war room. "The lab is on lockdown right now. They're reporting an unknown chemical or biohazard event that's affecting all races, even the gods."

"A mysterious something that's affecting the gods, but hasn't killed the Chweds?" Bix rubbed the hairs prickling along her nape. No part of that statement made sense. Appearances were the only loose commonality among the participating races. Gods weren't made from the same cosmic energies as mortals, not even close.

"My best guess is the foundational elements of Resen are involved in shielding the lesser races." Tobek thinned his lips and huffed like an annoyed bull. "The ley lines and Fates' weave are highly protective of Cian, even the hollow shell of his body. Runjit reported the elements building a visible bubble around the boy when the critical event happened. I wouldn't be surprised if unseen actions are also being taken by the lines to preserve all their creations."

"Are Runjit and the rest of your men at the lab also afflicted?"

Tobek shook his head. "They reported feeling an initial wave of discomfort and gross fatigue as their temperatures spiked, but once their rage engaged, it seemed to cure them. They're running aid for those in the lab while coordinating with remote research facilities to investigate and identify the cause."

The Berserkers' rage was the direct line to Tobek, who was neither god nor mortal. Tobek's body could purify the Devourer toxin infecting the ley lines that enabled Mids' magic, the same magic that created Mids' mortals. Tobek probably hadn't even noticed the tug on his magics to cure his men. He was focused on running overwatch for the troops in the field and still adjusting to the aftermath of his tenure in the future.

"And the timing of this malady striking? Don't suppose it coincided with an influx of First Children entering the Mids?" Bix hoped she was wrong, but two of her siblings entering the Mids while she'd been on Vuornis with two other siblings? Now there was a case of mystery cooties in the lab where Cian's husk was being protected by Feng and the ley lines? It would be scratching the bottom of the barrel for any of her siblings, but so was abducting her mortal friends.

"The malady is limited to the lab. I've confirmed that with the Consortium, so it's not a result of too many First Children in the Mids, if that's your concern," Tobek assured. A heartbeat later, his expression darkened. "However, the incident at the lab *did* coincide with a surge of Devourers bypassing Resen."

"A locked-down laboratory means I'm definitely showing up there." Bix massaged her temples. "It was my intention to relocate the researchers before getting to work on Cian in case I irritated the foundational elements. Too late for that now, I guess."

"Sweetheart, regardless of what you find there, you can't touch Cian." Tobek cupped her cheek. "Even I can't protect him from you. His human body can't handle it."

"I know. I know. I'll be using intermediaries." She rolled her eyes, yet the reminder stung. "As you and your early-alert arm have already discerned, my siblings are arriving early for the meeting and have their own side agendas. This is the last chance you and Ogun have to adjust your deployments to compensate for multiple First Children wielding magic in the same area before all seven of us are at the Kennedy Center. I'm sorry to do this during the peak of battle across the Mids, but there will never be a convenient time."

"Understood, and I agree. The faster this is all over, the lower our total casualties." He hopped out of the gate, returning to the war room. "Ogun has the Consortium standing by. He awaits the go from either one of us."

"I'll leave it with you." She took one last look at the Berserkers bent to the task of salvation in cooperation with the Chweds of the MWA and the gods of the Consortium. Pride. In others. In collaboration. It felt good…despite her family being the cause of ruin. "Are there any other gates you need me to open before I go? Anything else I should know? Any gotchas come up while I was away? Any anythings at all?"

"We've got this. Good luck, sweetheart." He smiled with the confidence of a man itching to get back to kicking ass. "Oh, the Berserkers tasked to the lab? Whatever you end up doing with the researchers, keep my men with the scientists, will you? They'll manage the fallout from whatever it is you need to do, and they'll touch base here."

"Will do. Thank you," she called, retreating into the gate.

"Put me through to the Chair," Tobek said into his mic, tossing her a wink. "Parley is happening. Repeat, parley is happening. Ready the area."

CHAPTER 26

T he crisis in Cian's research laboratory was not caused by a chemical nor a cootie. Oh, sure, it looked that way on the surface. Researchers of every race appeared sweaty, sickly, and overly fatigued, from gods to gnomes. Grim determination had replaced the usual vibrant energy of chasing eureka. Even the security reinforcements of demons bedecked in god-forged armor struggled to maintain stiff-spine alertness.

Bix identified the cause before the gates closed behind her. The mix of magical resonances did not align with the magical races. There was an unwelcomed addition scattered throughout.

Desire was here.

Bix licked a tooth as circumstance bit her in the ass. She'd broken her brother into tiny bits, but she hadn't subdued his magics or his mind. Couldn't. Not without dismantling Tempest too, a feat about which she had no reluctance. However, the catch was the twins needed to be in the same place at the same time with the elders standing by to sort and capture the terrible twins' pieces. Otherwise, being the creationists they were, the youngest twins would simply manifest different containers for their parts, or they'd recycle containers already in existence.

Like, say, the researchers.

What a disastrophy.

No point in playing coy. Desire wasn't hiding himself or being sneaky. By occupying the researchers dedicated to curing the disease caused by his toxic creations, her brother was waving a beacon for attention. Now she had to figure out how to extract him from the mortals without killing them. Punting him from the gods would be unpleasant for the deities, but they'd survive. Funny, though, how her brother hadn't been able to take root in the Berserkers once Tobek's magic had flooded his men's bodies via their rage. Evolution was such a fascinating thing, and it gave her a baseline for how much innate power her brother's bits contained. Stronger than a god's, less than Tobek's. That was going to be useful in the long run of her grand plan.

"Bix, thank the greater powers," shouted a Berserker bedecked in PPE from head to toe. He raised his gloved hand in greeting from halfway down the lab. The extra loft beneath his disposable cap was due to his turban, which identified him as Runjit, the battalion's lead medic.

All movement in the lab stopped. Silence fell. As one, every face turned toward her.

"Runjit, you can put away your vials and testing kits. What's going on here isn't a communicable disease or a chemical accident." Bix sauntered down the main aisle of the lab, heading for the rear of the facility and the undulating lattice of blues, purples, and greens forming a ten-foot bubble around Cian's bed. The foundational elements of Resen guarded the kid and his bedside visitors, just as Tobek had said. If Desire couldn't occupy the Berserkers, he couldn't break through the barrier of the foundational elements either. Small favors, considering Feng, Samael, and Mirri were trapped inside the bubble with Cian's body.

"Then what the hell is going on?" demanded Feng, letting imperiousness infuse his polyglot accent as he assumed a wide-legged, cross-armed stance between Cian's body and the rest of the lab. "And why is native magic pinning us down?"

"It's protecting you from an undesired guest." Bix drew up

sharply twenty feet from the bubble as its colors flared and a hum of caution throbbed. The foundational elements didn't want her getting too close to Cian and company either. Okeydokey.

A sprite tittered. A knocker giggled. Nixen and gnomes sniggered. Shifters of assorted beasts yipped merrily. The whole collective of Chweds laughed manically, which kicked off laughter from all races. The sounds, however, did not match the expressions. The expressions of the researchers were of stark panic and terror. Those who were still lucid, that is.

"Very funny, little sister," the Chweds said in ominous unison. "I see what you did there."

"Sister?" Samael cried, throwing his hands up. "Oh, for fuck's sake. There's more of you? No wonder shit's going from bad to worse."

Feng coughed and stared at the ceiling.

So much for trying to keep a lid on the existence of entities greater than gods who liked to screw over the lesser species.

"Poisoning from a greater power does explain many of the physical symptoms," Runjit conceded, subtly signaling his men as he untied a tourniquet from an incognito dragon.

"I told you it was body possession, a destructive cohabitation," Mirri corrected, standing at the foot of Cian's bed and spreading her arms defensively along the footboard as her puppy, Thárros, rested its two heads on her shoulders. There was a shine in Thárros's eyes that revealed Hades watching from the Under Worlds.

Was Hades alone? Probably. Desire's delivery of excessive reinforcements into the yards of the titans had likely ignited multiple crises in the Unders. Not a problem Bix could afford to care about right now, though. Mortals of the Mids weren't resilient like the gods of the Unders. Besides, when it came to the titans, her elder siblings were aware of her concerns regarding their toys.

"Good to know no one here is contagious." Runjit peeled off his face mask and gloves, tossing them in a bin.

"Mids' magic is trying to save its creations from the core entity existing outside this bubble, thus it keeps us all confined to the lab." Mirri caught Bix's eye, even though she seemingly directed her comments to the Berserker.

Bix got the hint. The foundational elements might have been obvious around Cian's bed, but they were active throughout the lab. It was a good thing Tobek wasn't here, or the elements would've used him as a weapon to try to evict Desire from their creations. Such a conflict would not have ended the way anyone wanted.

"Aren't they quaint, little sister? So blissfully ignorant. Acting as if I don't have a thing to do with their existence," Desire's chorus of Chweds jeered in unison. The lack of mimicry by the others said that Desire had parked most of his mind in the Chweds. It figured, seeing as how Chweds had sprung from the seeds he'd planted as part of his contribution to the Mids.

"It's your instigation of their demise that's more of interest to them, I'd imagine." Bix inclined her head to Mirri. Her attention jerked to Samael at his sharp inhalation and the dawning of realization hardening his features. The archangel's black eyes flicked to Feng in question. Feng raised his brows and blinked slowly, confirming the unspoken question. Samael set his jaw and mirrored Feng's wide-legged, cross-armed stance. Together, the apex entities of the Mids gave her a nod. They were ready for her go. Whatever the go might be.

Bix's heart pounded with pride. Trust. Earned. Tested. Rewarded.

"*My* interest of the moment is whether you convinced our father to concede," Desire's chorus bleated. "Will he let time flow forward after you kill me?"

"You mean have I resolved your daddy issues? Is that why you're camping out here?" Bix casually retreated from the bubble, heading for an empty conference table. "Taking refuge when you're so close to death? How very mortal of you, my brother. Is the act of dying not what you'd thought it would be?"

"This isn't dying," Desire decried through his chorus of Chweds. "This is your lame attempt at circumventing the only event that will save your precious sanctuary and its abundant toys."

"Pfft, shows what little you know. Dying is all about the breakdown of one's body, one's mind, and one's well-being. Dying robs you of everything you took for granted. It forces you to notice the little things. It compels you to long for the relationships for which you had no time whilst at your peak. Dying is a necessary step before final death," Bix taunted, less than thrilled to have the Chweds bear the brunt of her brother's occupation. She needed to get him out of those mortal bodies without causing further damage to the researchers. But how? She couldn't touch them, so she couldn't pry out Desire. Those Chweds had voluntarily risked life and limb to help find a cure for the afflictions Desire had caused. This was a shitty reward for their bravery. Her temper spiked, but she caught it before it flipped to rage.

Master manipulators created emotional situations to ensure control of the outcome.

"You think you have the upper hand here, do you? Did you honestly believe distracting me through physical discombobulation would blind me to your theft of the boy's soul? Did you believe I wouldn't notice? Care? *Retaliate?*" Desire's chorus shouted the last word.

Six bursts of Desire's magic blasted copper light throughout the lab, welcoming three pairs of Desire's minions and their respective hostages. A herald partnered with a Devourer to brace Ashtad. Using the herald to infiltrate Irkalla had likely sent Ereshkigal into fits, stirring tensions in the Unders. As for the use of a Devourer, well, the herald wouldn't harm, and the anti-god wouldn't think twice about it. Phobos wore full armor, so the Devourers flanking him had ripped him from a battlefield. As for the two Devourers dragging one of their own by the horns, their prisoner was barely conscious, thoroughly beaten, and oozed Drew's Other World presence. Now she knew what Hel had sent Drew into the Mids to accomplish. Unfortunately for Drew, the enemy had leveled up since the draugr's last tour in a Devourer body. At least her brother had brought her friends to her this time instead of throwing them into the future. His charity was worrisome.

Emotional control. Bix had to exercise hers so her brother couldn't exploit it. Better to focus on his nugget of ire. Someone had stolen Cian's soul from him. That someone wasn't her. Who the hell had it now?

"Everyone all right?" Bix asked as blue and purple streaks of the ley lines along with the green braid of the Fates' weave flared into visibility throughout the lab then faded. Ashtad. The foundational elements of Resen were greeting the second architect. He was back in the Mids and they were happy. That could work to her advantage.

"Peachy, Bixie," Drew groaned, holding up the severed stump of his middle finger to his captors.

Ashtad and Phobos simply grunted their affirmatives as they took in the situation. Their Devourer guards snarled at them, jostling their captives. The foundational elements warbled threateningly. Alas, the Devourers merely licked their lips in hungry anticipation. That magic was delicious food to them.

"Desire, what are you hoping to accomplish by this hostile occupation?" Bix swung her legs, letting her pumps dangle from her toes. Relaxed. Curious. Indifferent. Had to keep those emotions in the forefront. Had to keep chill on display. Had to keep her team informed of the game in play. "If I had Cian's soul, were you going to stop me from implanting it in his crystalized body? Were you going to snuff him out as payback? For giving you exactly what you want? A slow and painful death?"

"You can't kill me without killing Tempest too. Yet you haven't laid a finger on *her*." Desire's chorus shuffled together into a group, their bodies forming a phalanx shield wall.

Apparently, not all his bits were equally distributed. Interesting. Oh, she didn't believe for one moment they were all in the lab either. No, no, but the majority of him was in the area. Evaluating the resonances within a few miles, she pinpointed the battalion of enhanced Devourers directly above them in the ruins of the District. No echo of the Mids' armies nearby, though. Tobek and Ogun must've directed their troops to fall back. Good. The only mortals she needed to worry about were in the lab with her. Well, that and wherever Cian's soul had gotten to.

"Why so eager for me to punish your twin?" Bix cocked her head and pouted, feigning bemusement. She knew full well consequences were more horrible when one had to face them alone. Had to be worse in his case, particularly when he was accustomed to foisting anything uncomfortable on his twin. There was a reason she'd destabilized the terrible twins' power dynamic.

"Because I want the High Executioner's punishment," Tempest answered, her disembodied voice echoing around the laboratory.

CHAPTER 27

Whirling burls of darkness spotted the barrel ceiling of the underground laboratory. Chaotic magics flooded the space as not one, but two feminine forms took shape. Tempest, bipedal with her tentacle headdress lying thick over her mostly humanoid body, solidified next to Chimalma, the erstwhile memory keeper and current general who should've been leading the gods in battle against the Devourers. The goddess wore battle camo dripping with tarry Devourer blood and held a red orb in which a ripe, glowing soul darted to and fro.

Bix's stomach soured as her heart skipped and stilled.

Cian?

"You? You stole the boy's soul from me?" Desire's chorus caterwauled. "How dare you? We are in this together. All the way to the end."

"Together?" Tempest sneered. "Me bearing your burdens. You excused from accountability."

"We are so close to getting what we want," Desire's chorus shrieked. "Don't you dare let the brat come between us now. Hand over the boy's soul, and I'll forgive you."

"Attached to me for life, and you couldn't care less what I want. All that matters to you is that I accept what you've told me I must feel." Tempest clapped a hand on Chimalma's shoulder.

Chimalma flinched at the unfiltered touch of a First Child, but her hold on the soul orb firmed. The Mid World guardian didn't look in Bix's direction. She kept her attention on Phobos. Phobos didn't spare a glance for his peer, but the tip of a pointy canine peeked from the smirk he attempted to suppress.

Bix left the gods to their telepathy and sat back down on the table, trying to figure out Tempest's play. Had Movement actually gotten through to her? Was the troop surge Desire's doing instead of Tempest's? Or was this spat between the twins a false flag to make Bix suffer more before they started ending Worlds and she started ending the two of them? She debated making a grab for Chimalma and Cian's soul, but if she moved on them, what would happen to Drew, Ashtad, or Phobos? She could stop time and make the play, but it wouldn't stop Desire from killing everyone in the lab.

"Ah, I see now," Desire's chorus cooed, tones brimming with concern. The diversity of voices made his artifice painfully apparent. "My dearest sister, you are upset that I've altered your plans. I am sincerely sorry. You have always been so adept at manipulating the bigger picture. My preference for the surgical extraction of the brat's most favored toys was not meant to demean your troop initiatives. Can you forgive me?"

Tempest's expression could've formed glaciers. "Don't simper. It's revolting."

"Don't be angry, please?" Desire's army of occupied bodies shuffled toward Tempest, mewling softly. "Give me the boy's soul. The brat will crumble. She loves him more than her dead child."

Swift gasps from the Berserkers and Bix's friends echoed. Bix kept her attention on her siblings. She might have been the topic, but she wasn't the issue. This was a power struggle between the twins. Tempest was pissed, no doubt, but pissed enough to stop being Desire's pawn? Publicly, these two squabbled as any siblings were wont to do, but Desire was usually quick to mollify

Tempest to regain control over her. Punishment came later, away from witnesses. The way Desire played his twin made Bix sick, but getting in between them only made them unite against her. Bix had to sit this out until Tempest asked for help.

If Tempest asked for help, that is.

Odds were better that Tempest would stab Bix in the chest for the umpteenth time. Hope had cost Bix thirty-six endings of the Mids. Still, she couldn't refuse her sister, not at this juncture. It was a weakness, yes, but at the moment, Tempest was the best chance for the survival of the researchers in the lab. Tempest and Desire were in the same place at the same time, which was all Bix needed to break them down, but everyone in the lab and miles beyond would die in the clash of the twins against the two-in-one. The foundational elements would react, causing more damage that might sink the entire East Coast. Oh, and let's not forget that uncontained bits of an angry First Child had caused this co-occupancy problem in the first place. Trust in Movement and hope for Tempest were all Bix could do without making things worse.

"The soul, the soul," chanted a cluster of possessed researchers lumbering toward Chimalma, hands outstretched and clutching air.

A quiet chuckle drifted from the Mid World guardian as one soul orb became three, then six. Tangible ribbons of red divine magic swirled around the goddess, smacking away grabby hands. Across the lab, a sinister snicker paused further encroachment on Chimalma. Ribbons of mulberry and red unfurled from Phobos. Between his mail-covered hands, orbs filled with souls multiplied. His ribbons thwarted the attempts of his Devourer guards to snatch the souls. At the back of the lab, within the bubble of protection, ribbons of honey and red danced around Mirri. A dozen soul orbs hovered over Cian's body.

In a synchronized move, Feng and Samael slapped their hands on the barrier keeping them safe. The power of the foundational elements surged, flashing with strobe-light intensity to add to the confusion as soul orbs moved among the three gods.

"Enough," brayed Desire's chorus of Chweds. Copper

sunlight erupted like a mushroom cloud, canceling out the effects of the foundational elements. The humans in the lab dropped, desiccated, overwhelmed by the flush of power hiding within them. Copper bulbs no bigger than a firefly's butt flitted from the dead humans.

Disappointment weighed on Bix as amorphous souls rose from the dead, struggling in confusion. Yet again, a lesser race had to pay the price for the games of greater ones. A gust carrying a moirologist's wail ripped through the lab, wrapping the unmoored souls in orbs of their own and adding them to the mix spread equally among the three untainted gods.

Tempest slowly clapped. The malevolence of her laugh put Phobos's trademark one to shame. "Is it done?"

"Yes." Chimalma pushed her palms together, crushing the many orbs she now possessed and draining the souls.

Berserkers gurgled half-repressed objections. The rest of the researchers stared in silent horror as their bodies lumbered without their consent to gather around the Chwedlonol cluster still hosting Desire's mind.

"Yes," Phobos answered. A wave of his hands, and his captured souls vanished, likely returning to the stash he kept on his home World.

"Yes," Mirri crowed, gesturing to a single orb resting upon Cian's unmoving chest.

Bix grinned into her fist. Tempest had wanted this. Tempest had rescued Cian's soul. Tempest had brought Chimalma to be her intermediary with the more fragile species. Chimalma had made the arrangements while Tempest had supplied the distraction. Bix held tightly to the joy bubbling inside her. Hope was paying off. Tempest was finally going to break Desire's grip.

Please, please, please, let Tempest keep whatever courage had finally blossomed.

"Then, my dear brother, it is time we stepped closer to death." Tempest unleashed her darkness. Pewter faces, long and distorted, formed within whirling clouds of the second daughter aligned to the Chaos. "Careless of you to take haven in entities where any chaos exists. Your suffocating presence of order is unwelcome. Get. Out."

The inhuman demand screamed across every sound wave, audible and not. Bodies trembled and convulsed. Swarms of copper fireflies fled from their hosts only to be caught in the gales of swirling darkness.

"Move them now, bratling," Tempest hissed, visibly struggling to absorb the swarm that was her twin.

Bix didn't need to be told twice. A combination of gates and her own darkness removed every living thing that wasn't a First Child or a fragment of them. From god to soldier to researcher to specimen to bacterium, if it lived outside the bubble of protection, it was gone. Devourers got punted to the next galaxy, heralds even farther. Everyone else was relocated to another lab, one beside a lake overlooking a Resen data center. Any issues with sterilization, refrigeration, magical fluctuations, etcetera, could be easily addressed at the other facility. The extra security Ogun had provided here would be useful there too. Runjit and the Berserkers would manage everything on that end.

Ashtad, Drew, and Phobos, she kept with her. She needed them. More importantly, Cian needed them. She placed her friends at the perimeter of the protective bubble. The foundational elements quickly expanded to include the second architect and the god of fear. But not Drew, not until Feng manifested a red-coated weasel. Native magic allowed him to set the small animal just beyond the edge of the barrier. Drew dragged the new body to himself and vacated the damaged Devourer. Drew, in the body of the weasel, was instantly welcomed into the protective fold. Mirri scooped up Drew and grabbed Ashtad's hand, taking them to a better point of view as everyone stared slack-jawed at the violent struggle between Tempest's External Motivation and Desire's Personal Drive.

Bix desperately wanted to jump into the fray. To aid her sister. To give the support Tempest's courage merited. But, this was

Tempest's battle to win. It had to be done on Tempest's terms, not what Bix thought Tempest's terms ought to be.

"If you need me, sister, I am here," Bix murmured.

"I. Will. Not. Be. Cowed." Tempest snarled. Thrashing. Fighting. Fluctuating between states native and corporeal.

"I will not be subdued," Desire yelled through the buzz of insects. "Yield to me, you spineless git. We end our existence on *my* terms. We die because it is *my* wish. My glee will be the last thought you are permitted to have."

"I will die a thousand times if it means you cannot continue to destroy our family." Tempest extended a filament no bigger than a spider's thread toward Bix.

Bix instantly closed the gap with a vast array of threads of darkness and light, there for her sister's taking. Whatever Tempest needed, Bix was willing to give.

Tempest's thread looped around one of Bix's similarly small threads of darkness and another of light, pulling on neither…just making contact.

Bix breathed in deeply and pushed belief and love to her sister. Despite their history. Despite every cruel act and crushing word. Despite everything outside this singular moment. Right now, Bix was one hundred percent in her sister's corner.

Tempest's agonized scream fractured the walls and ceiling. Exploding darkness shattered the confines of the area and forced the ley lines to contract tightly around the protective bubble. Chaotic magic ripped upward through the city ruins and down into springs yet untapped. Eerie stillness followed. Darkness retracted with a rushing, sighing gust, revealing Tempest lying in a heap, the many tentacles of her preferred state twitching.

Bix knelt beside her sister in a mound of dirt and rubble, holding her hand and trying to think of something worthy of uttering.

Chaotic magic surged. Movement took form on the other side of Tempest. The first of Firsts deftly wrangled Tempest's many tentacles before hefting Tempest into her beefy arms. "I knew you could do it, Pesty. All you needed was the confidence of believing we're all backing you."

"Hurry and heal your human boy, bratling," Tempest hissed, her lashes fluttering. "I don't know how long I can keep Desire suppressed. You've no clue how eager I am to shut his whine hole permanently."

Eyes brimming with tears of awe and appreciation, Bix nodded. "Thank you for saving Cian's soul, Tempest. It may seem minor to you, but—"

"The minor creations make you happy," Tempest interrupted, lolling her head along Movement's shoulder. "I want to know what it's like to be happy again too. Movement said your big plan would teach me that, so you'd better deliver."

"I will," Bix vowed. "But you've got to dismiss the Devourers from this galaxy and its neighbors first. That's always been our deal. I will not save you from your twin until the threat to my sanctuary is gone. Completely. Eternally."

"I'll keep my word." Tempest closed her eyes. "Though, the longer you dally here, the more losses your precious toys suffer."

Bix opened her mouth with a retort burning her tongue, but Movement silenced her with a look. Right. No need to have the last word. Instead, Bix simply inclined her head.

"Oy, little lines," Movement called to the ley lines forming part of the protective bubble. "Good job. Music and I are proud of you."

The ley lines flashed blue, then purple as their cocreator vanished in a whirlwind of cobalt chaos.

CHAPTER 28

Nimbi of blues and plums swirled in the massive gaping hole where once the high ceiling and layers of terrain had separated the underground lab from the city streets. Sunbeams stretched long fingers into the clouds of Mids' magic spawning wider and wider as the debris from Tempest's explosive struggle rained upward to plug the hole and outward to firm the walls. Currents of rolling dirt and muck at sub-subterranean levels forced Bix into the surety of stacked gates as the ground filled in the pit and firmed a new floor, this one of lapis lazuli replete with shimmering iron pyrites.

Within the protective bubble of Resen's foundational elements, Bix's team gasped and grinned as native magic continued to repair the lab, making modifications as it went. Mutterings from Feng and loud coaching from Samael refined the details. Ashtad managed to get requests met by magics he couldn't wield but who held him in high regard. Mirri bounced on her toes and quietly clapped while her hound, Thárros, thumped its tail, heads eagerly tracking the progress of restoration. Phobos's expression read bored but the swift movement of his eyes said he was cataloguing the schematics for future use, ever the spy.

Drew alone ignored the wonder of creation unfolding around

him. He'd curled on the hexagonal plate of crystal covering Cian's abdomen, transfixed on the red orb aglow with Cian's restless soul.

Pangs of sadness, sympathy, and hope knocked Bix's pulse out of rhythm. Wincing, she pressed her hand over her heart and whispered, "Soon, Drew. Soon."

The cloud cover of native magic retracted into a long funnel in the center of the structurally restored laboratory. Sparking silver. Then green. In a blinding flash, the balance of magic in the chamber skewed. Clouds cleared.

One big blond original Berserker stood where the funnel had been.

Tobek turned in a slow assessing circle as his innate green and silver magics slithered around him, eager to fight. His rage-bright gaze lingered on the protective bubble before settling on Bix in her box of gates. His silver fingers uncurled from the hilt of the sword still sheathed in ice across his back. The floodlights of his eyes dimmed as he calmed his battle lust. Chuckling, he sauntered to Bix and offered her a hand down from her gates.

"My apologies for crashing your party, sweetheart." He flashed a playful grin.

"Quite all right. It doesn't seem like that was an invitation you could refuse." Bix took his hand and closed her gates. She drew a stabilizing breath as his thumb stroked her wrist, resetting her pulse and bringing it into time with his. "I guess the foundational elements don't trust me anymore. They aren't letting me near Cian's body."

"On the contrary. I believe they're taking a cue from you. That's why they brought me here," he whispered conspiratorially. "Give them a moment to compose themselves. They *are* sentient and have just had the bejesus scared out of them by the antics of the First Children."

Bix raised her brows, one part surprise, one part waiting for him to finish explaining. He didn't, of course, but as they neared the protective bubble, the lattice of ley lines and the Fates' weave dissipated. Thárros leapt off the bed and raced around the lab with an acute case of the zoomies. Feng and Samael groaned with relief as if the weight of native magic had been too much to bear. Even Phobos shuddered as if a burden had been lifted. If Mirri felt any relief, it was lost to her furious blushing as she averted her gaze from Bix's and Tobek's clasped hands.

Ashtad rolled his wrist, calling minor energies to him. A lightning ball crackled in his palm. Instead of the usual bluish white, his magic manifested in the colors of Resen. His lips thinned.

"Bix, if you're planning on fixing Cian here, be aware this is an unstable hot spot. With everything that just went down, adding more magic to the mix will be like jabbing a stick of TNT into a block of C4."

"Shit's gonna fly," Drew cautioned, tapping his tiny foot on the agitated crystals glowing rainbow hues all over Cian's body.

Realization smacked her. Patting Tobek's big bicep, she let go of his hand. All her siblings were in the area. Of course the ley lines and the Fates' weave were overstimulated. They were coping with the influx of primordial power. They'd delivered Tobek for the same reason she was keeping Phobos here. No direct contact with any part of a fragile human. The elements wanted intermediaries. Just to be safe. Which meant they were going to make uncommonly direct contact with their chosen go-betweens.

"Samael." Bix opened gates to her bedroom in Vuornis and let her darkness retrieve a very particular wall decoration. "You're going to need these."

Samael stared at his wings as the warded crystal around them crackled and fell away into sparkling purple dust. "But the war? It's not over. I told you to keep those until the Devourers are gone."

"Right now, the ley lines aren't asking you to protect the masses." Bix handed one massive lush black-feathered wing to Feng. "They're going to use you as their vessel to heal Cian's body."

"I made that kid's body in his mother's womb the first time, but the lines think I'm not going to be able to do it alone this go around?" Samael ripped his shirt over his head and tossed it to

Ashtad. "Then whatever's coming isn't merely healing."

Feng unfurled his own red-to-yellow ombré wings before reverently accepting Samael's black one. Each wing was taller than its owner and contained a lot of power, so Feng stabilizing himself with his own wings as counterweights was understandable. The archangel presented his naked back to the Phoenix. The fat scars from where Bix had cleanly severed his wings split open anew. Blue blood dripped from the wounds as the blue-and-white stumps that had once supported his wings emerged.

Tobek stepped in front of Samael and patted his shoulder. "Use me for balance."

Samael made a face of distaste but clamped his hands on Tobek's shoulders. Blue fire built around Feng's hands as he hefted the first wing and aligned the stump of the severed wing with the stump protruding from Samael's body. Samael screamed through clenched teeth as both stumps bled, shedding their scabs. Moist slurping like live eels in an oil vat accompanied the bonding of angelic parts. Bix handed Feng the second wing, and the process repeated. Blue auras so dark as to seem black seeped from Samael's entire body as the final adjustments took hold and the fullness of his innate magic returned. Samael squeezed Tobek's shoulders, then stepped away from the gathering to expand his wings to their full height and breadth. A few strong beats sent gale-force winds rushing down the center of the lab. A triumphant roar soared from the archangel's lungs and ended on a rowdy guffaw.

"Bloody hell, that's a fine feeling." Samael exposed his wing claws and clutched at the wind tightening around him, ruffling his feathers and releasing the molt. He cut a sly glance at Bix and flicked his wrist, collecting his discarded feathers. He offered them to her. "I know how you like to keep a few on hand."

Delighted, Bix looked to Tobek. Without having to say a word, her Berserker obligingly manifested a simple iron box for her to store the feathers of potent Mids' power. Tobek's creation allowed the feathers to exist in her collection without being a beacon to the unwitting or plain stupid. She curled a tendril of darkness around the box, and Samael placed his gift inside.

"Thank you," she said, sending the box of feathers through a tiny gate to a cubby on Vuornis.

"You took good care of them, so the gratitude is mine." Samael flapped a wing at the body on the bed. "I'm ready for whatever the lines want to do with me."

"Maybe they're going to break down the crystals?" Mirri offered hopefully. "Maybe all we've been through lately has taught them how?"

"Sadly, no. I will unmake the crystals with Phobos as my intermediary." Bix directed a half-apologetic smile at the god of fear. Phobos rolled his eyes and began unbuckling his armor.

"Phobos? But he's an emotion god." Mirri looked at him in confusion then back to Bix. "I'm a restoration goddess. Use me instead."

"There are consequences to permitting the Chimera to use your entirety for whatever needs she may have," Phobos warned, sending his armor home to his minions in a fog of mulberry and navy. "Lasting consequences. Most of them are not pleasant."

Tobek grunted his confirmation, which caused Mirri's blush to deepen to ripe strawberry.

"Cian isn't the only one afflicted by the poison of Devourer blood," Mirri mumbled, head down, hair tumbling over her face. "Combining what I learn here today with what my divinity already blesses me may well empower me to contribute to a cure or, even better, a vaccine. What I learn here can be applied beyond the Mids too. Thus, I gladly accept the consequences."

Again, Bix looked to Tobek. Though he and she had never spoken of her former relationship with Mirri, he was nonetheless aware. Using Mirri as she used Phobos was a different kind of intimacy from that of a sexual partner, and miles from a life partner. Still, because there was a sexual history, she wanted her consort's input. If he had a problem with it, she wouldn't do it. Her relationship with him mattered more. It mattered the most.

Plus, he was an expert when it came to cooties and cures. Mirri could be hopeful but way off base about what she could actually contribute.

Tobek's eyes crinkled at the corners, and he nodded. "I think she has a valid point."

Thank the powers that be, her big blond bear didn't suffer from jealousy.

"Mirri." Bix hooked a finger under the goddess's chin, drawing it up until Mirri looked her in the eye. She hated to be an asshole, but expectations had to be set. "If you let me use you, it means you're never free of me. Whenever I have a need, you will have no choice about complying. So think very seriously about this. This sort of bond is not an avenue to rekindling anything."

"Your instinct will make you think it is," Phobos added as the base layer he wore under his armor morphed into a bespoke three-piece suit. "It will make you long for her. It will make you covetous and possessive. You don't get past it. The only way to keep your sanity and your dignity is to surrender to loving her from afar."

Bix stared at Phobos. She had no idea that was what it was like on the other end. He'd always made it seem their bond was like an aggravating choke collar yanking him this way and that before he was given full leash to roam again.

"That's hardly different from the way I've been since I met her," Mirri confessed, tears welling.

Ah, fuck.

"I'm sorry, Mirri. I can't do that to you." Bix shook her head and let go of the goddess. "Your intentions are good and noble. But I do not want to bring you more harm, certainly not for an immortal lifetime. You've already endured too much because of me."

"Let her learn how to save the mortals, Bix." Feng stepped forward and wrapped an arm across Mirri's shoulders. "I'll help her cope with the consequences. I'm no god of love, but I know there's a path from that all-consuming obsession to healthy respect, even if it takes some long detours through overly eager reverence."

Bix considered Feng, replaying his words and trying not to read too much into them. Surely he hadn't…not for her…not in this lifetime? They'd beaten the piss out of each other the first time they'd met in his current incarnation. She had a hot date to kill him in a century or two. Wait. Was he saying he had those feelings for Mirri? That could be adorbs, assuming Mirri was onboard. Mirri had a thing for her, yeah, but gods were the pansexual epitome. Deities didn't even let species limit their sexual preferences. Dude stood a chance.

"Bixie, babe." Drew sat up on his, erm, her hind legs. "We all got wants we're never going to have and disappointments that turn us into a puddle of embarrassment every time we remember them. That's living. When I think of all those Berserkers who slipped through my fingers, and my dear, dear Runjit…"

Snickers multiplied at Drew's dramatic anguished sigh. Even Mirri managed to giggle.

"Grown-ass adult policy, Bix," Ashtad chimed in. "You're a subscriber, right?"

"Besides"—Samael gestured vaguely to the lab—"Resen's foundational elements brought her here and kept her here. I think she's got their vote, and if we're trying to save the boy, their vote matters, doesn't it?"

"Okay, okay, okay," Bix conceded. "You all are on the hook for reminding Mirri that she asked for this in a few centuries when the luster wears off. Call your hound, Mirri. You're going to want his support during this."

Mirri beamed and clicked her tongue. Thárros bounded to her side as everyone circled Cian's bed. Mirri, Thárros, and Bix stood on one side, while Samael and Tobek stood on the other. Feng took up position at the feet, and Phobos at the head.

"Phobos, would you hold Cian's soul until we're done with the body, please?" Bix asked, and the god of fear immediately obliged. "Ashtad, if you and Drew would—"

"Clear the area?" The demigod grabbed the weasel and backed away.

"Actually, no, get over here." Bix pointed to the space between Samael and Phobos. "You're in charge of the final step."

"Me?" Ashtad glanced to his left and right as he rejoined the ring around the bed. "I've got no skills beyond thoughts and prayers to heal the kid."

"The Fates chose you to be the architect who incorporated the Other World knowledge necessary to build Resen. The ley lines accepted you in that role. Cian was chosen by the lines to receive Mids' knowledge. He was accepted by the Fates." Bix smiled at her former mentor's dumbfounded expression. "You two represent the balance of Resen. The new balance of the Mids. The rest of us will restore Cian's foundations, but it will be up to you to jump-start his life force so that it reconnects to the network the two of you built."

"Reinstating his admin access to Resen," Ashtad said with dawning understanding.

"No pressure there, Sparky," Drew drawled, draping herself over Ashtad's shoulder. "Think of me as moral support. Go, team. Whee."

"What part can I play?" Feng asked, spreading his hands along the footboard.

"To burn through magic as fast as you can to draw down the levels that will turn this hot spot into a massive crater. You're the first one up and last one done. Do you think you can handle it?" Bix knew the question was unnecessary by the puffing of his chest.

"How wide can I go?"

"Is a twenty-mile radius enough play space?" Tobek asked. "Ogun's cleared the Consortium and the Mids' mortals back that far. Otherwise, the only life-forms within the area are pockets of Devourers and her family at the Kennedy Center."

"You mean I can do away with the battle ruins? Reconstruct the District and its suburbs in whatever way I want?" Feng's expression brightened.

"Don't expect your redesign to be the one that lasts after the war is done," Samael harrumphed. "Until then, Candyland, Chutes and Ladders, Jumanji, whatever, have at it."

"Flaaaamer," Drew shrieked. "The pregame entertainment? For the pooh-bahs? For Bixie's family? It's all you and your beautiful crazy. The biggest of the big shows. The weirdest of the weird productions. Ah, I'm dying with envy."

"Guess it's a good thing I spent six years listening to you what-if your perfect seasonal festivals." Feng shucked his sport coat and unbuttoned his collar. "Plans, Drew, plans. We've got them in stock."

Drew rolled on her back, kicking her teeny legs and squealing in delight. Ashtad caught her when she started to tumble and set her back on her perch.

"The process of saving Cian is pretty straightforward, but likely exhausting," Bix cautioned. "Mirri and I will unmake the crystals. Then Samael and the ley lines will rebuild his body. Phobos will place the soul within the renewed body, and the Fates through Tobek will stitch his threads of destiny. Last step is yours, Ashtad. Everybody clear? Any questions? Any doubts?"

A round of thumbs-up answered.

"Okay, Feng. Time to shine."

Feng walked to the middle of the dark, empty lab and shed his humanoid form. The firebird with a barbed dragon's tail grew in size until his feathered head brushed the reconstructed ceiling. A soft caw carried in the silence of anticipation.

Resen's foundational elements responded, gathering once again in the lab to form blue, purple, and green clouds coasting above everyone. The layers of the ceiling, soil, and streets they'd just reconstructed dissolved into sparks, turning the lab into an open-air theater with a view of the starlit sky.

Feng beat his wings up through the clouds, stirring a song of creation that carried through the elements and out into the night as he grew into his full size. Igniting, the Phoenix ablaze soared like a flaming star above the District.

The lapis and limestone of the lab's floor and walls morphed, changing from bubbling brooks in open fields to crags overlooking thundering oceans, to tawny deserts, to sparkling oases, to steel and concrete hardscapes, to crowded city streets lined with balconied row houses, to watery caves. Hollow life-forms changed with the scenery, from insects to whales, elves to kobolds, infants to the wizened. The torrents of the Phoenix's magic carried outward, changing blocks and neighborhoods, cities and counties. At times, the lab was part of a vale and others a dome beneath a sea.

"I don't think LSD will ever again compare," Ashtad muttered in awe.

Bix resisted the urge to open a viewing gate so everyone could see the impressive show of creation Feng was putting on across the greater metro area. Alas, they had to keep their heads and minds focused on the body in the bed.

"This is your last chance to say no," Bix said as she stepped behind Mirri. "Phobos is capable and accustomed. There would be no shame in maintaining your independence."

Mirri lifted her chin and tapped her thigh. Thárros obediently sat on the goddess's feet and leaned into her legs. Mirri took a deep breath and held her arms out from her sides. "I trust you, Bix. I will not resent the bond we are about to forge, nor will I expect more than it is intended to give. I will use the knowledge you are about to share with me for the greater good."

Bix had never doubted that last part. Mirri's almost naïve drive to be kind, curious, and careful with the lesser beings was what had made Mirri so alluring to Bix in the first place. Alas, what they were about to do would be none of those things. At her full power, there was no way Bix could make this a painless experience for Mirri. Mirri would physically suffer, but her divinity would ensure she recovered quickly. Mentally? Good question. At least Mirri had Feng to help her with that aspect.

"Be brave," Bix whispered in Mirri's ear as threads of darkness and rays of light pierced Mirri's body. The goddess gasped and clutched Thárros's heads, but Bix didn't let up. Drawing this out was no good for anyone. Bix paired her darkness and her starlight along the magics sprouting from Mirri's divinity and began the guided instruction.

Ribbons of honey and red spawned from the goddess and snaked around Cian's body, bundling him up like a mummy. From there, it was a matter of identifying source energies, those that belonged to the Mids, those that belonged to the Fates, and those that belonged to the Devourers. Bix then entrusted Mirri with the code to unmake Devourer energy, demonstrated how to apply it, then waited as Mirri made attempts, failures, and finally repeated success. Pleased, Bix uncoupled from Mirri's divinity, allowing the goddess to complete the work on her own while Bix located Mirri's most recent memories and wrapped them in darkness and light, protecting the blossoming knowledge from anyone who might try to steal it from Mirri. There would be many gods and Fates alike who would try to rob her once word got out.

"I, I think I removed it all," Mirri panted, ichor dripping on the bed. "Double-check?"

Bix's threads and rays surged through the ribbons, verifying purification, then pulled back, all the way back, completely free of Mirri's body. Bix gently squeezed Mirri's shoulders. "Well done. Very well done. You can turn him over to Samael now."

Mirri retracted her ribbons from Cian's body, revealing his dreadfully scarred and discolored hide-like skin over bones that had been crushed by the weight of the crystals. Hissed expletives traveled around the bed as the others looked on in horror.

"No wonder he begged for release," Drew whimpered. "Oh, my poor little herb nerd. Oh, how you suffered."

Ashtad slapped his hand over his mouth and viciously rubbed his lips. His cognac eyes burned with helpless fury as he stared at Bix. Yeah, she understood that fury all too well and accepted every ounce that could be attributed to her.

Across the bed, Samael waggled his fingers in the air,

manifesting a white handkerchief. He handed it to Mirri. "Never thought I'd see those damn rocks gone from his body. You did good, goddess. Real good. This shit, I can fix."

"Thank you," Mirri gasped around a sob, taking the kerchief. She blotted her eyes and came away with clumps of clotted ichor. She whuffed a sound of surprise and turned to Bix. The look was not pretty, what with deep gashes through her eyeballs. "How could I not feel the pain of my eyes rupturing?"

"It's the rapture of feeling her inside you," Phobos explained. "Pain and pleasure are the same."

"Uhm, sorry?" Bix offered to both of them. "I tried not to use your eyes to see what we were doing. Didn't seem to stop the damage, though."

"Worth it. They'll heal," Mirri assured, raising a smile to Samael. "Please, archangel. Take the next step."

"Yeah, I wish it was my eyeballs that were going to get blown out by this." Samael shook a leg and adjusted his balls. He stretched his wings high and wide into the clouds of native magic rolling overhead despite the constantly changing environment. "Light me up, lines."

A rope of thick blue power swept down from the clouds and pierced Samael. The archangel shouted as his dark blue aura exploded from him. A second cord followed the first, this one in aubergine. Samael's black eyes flipped white, then mottled blue and purple. He shouldered Tobek aside and slapped his big hands on Cian's body. One hand glowed blue over the kid's gut. The other glowed plum over the kid's face.

Bix watched in rapt fascination as creationist magic split apart Cian's skin on a cellular level and moved the pieces up and out. Veins, muscles, organs, bones, the whole body deconstructed like a complex jigsaw. Twinkles of green denoted the bits of the kid's leaves that marked his trials toward Fatehood. Filaments of blue light zigged and zagged among all the disconnected pieces, chased by dotted lines of purple. Fragments reshaped and filaments tightened, pulling cells together. Cian was being rebuilt as equal parts of native magic: the part Movement had created, and the part Music had created. It made him more akin to Feng than any other creation. As Cian progressed through his trials and absorbed more of Fates' magic, he'd be the first three-in-one of the Mids.

Tobek caught her eye, held up three fingers, and arched a brow. Yep. Same thought. She clutched her fists to her chest and grinned. Tobek scratched his beard and guffawed. Evolution. So amazing. How it happened. When it happened. Why it happened. The chaotic uncertainty of what would be and all its potential.

At length, Cian's body looked once again like a young human man of eighteen years. His wonderfully thick red hair spiked across the white pillow. His pale freckled skin appeared rosy next to the sheet Mirri kindly folded over the kid's groin. His ten toes had wisps of red hair that matched the fringe of red leg hair leading up from boney ankles no longer crushed to powder. The only bits floating separate from his body were the three leaves of his trials.

Ashtad lifted one of Cian's eyelids. "Still green."

"What, you think I forgot the schematics of a kid who spends more time hanging with my choir than he does with you exemplars of personal safety?" Samael grunted and winced as the ley lines disconnected from him. He coughed and tugged his pant legs. His eyes watered and twitched as they returned to black.

"Need some ointment?" Phobos offered superciliously.

Samael rubbed his cheek with his middle finger.

"He doesn't look a day older than when this whole adventure began." Drew sighed happily. "It's like you erased those six years we were prisoners, plus a few more."

"If I could erase those years from his soul, believe me I would." Samael gestured to the red orb glowing with Cian's fluttering soul held firmly in Phobos's hand. "On you now, fearsome."

Phobos pivoted to Tobek. "This part will need to be fairly instantaneous to keep the soul in the body."

"Then we should position ourselves accordingly." Tobek swapped places with Samael.

Phobos murmured apologies to Mirri as he took her place

across from Tobek. Bix moved to the end of the bed and backed up a few steps, allowing those who could heal to keep close to the boy.

Tobek raised his silver hand to the clouds and hovered his fleshy hand over Cian's chest. Like Rapunzel letting down her hair, yarns of Fate tumbled from the clouds and braided around Tobek's silver arm.

"Oh sure, *you* get the gentle touch," Samael griped, crossing his arms over his chest.

Tobek ignored the archangel as magics green and silver flowed around Fates' chosen champion from boot to scalp. Tobek's eyes glowed teal, a mixture of Berserker and Other. His inhuman growl was barely audible when he addressed Phobos.

"On your go."

"Wait," Drew blurted. "This, this isn't going to turn him into a Berserker, is it? I mean, I love you guys, but I don't think the kid is cut out for that lifestyle."

"The boy…" Tobek paused and swallowed rapidly as if struggling to speak around the magic consuming him. "The boy lacks the pit of festering rage that makes a human male a candidate for the brotherhood. It is the rage that enables the binding."

"Oh, good. Good." Drew exchanged a relieved glance with Ashtad. Whatever had happened during those six years of living in each other's back pockets, the topic had apparently come up and Cian hadn't been keen to be recruited. Interesting.

"May we proceed?" Phobos drawled.

"Yeah, yeah. Sorry. I'll be quiet now." Drew pressed her muzzle into Ashtad's shirt.

Phobos extended the orb over Cian's exposed abdomen and met Tobek's bright gaze. "Go."

Phobos crushed the orb, flipped his wrist, and slammed Cian's soul into the waiting flesh suit. Tobek slapped his bare hand to Cian's chest, and his magics dove into the kid's body. Establishing a network neither vascular nor nervous, lines of green destiny spidered throughout, sewing Cian's soul into the body that anchored him to the Mids. Young vines poked up through Cian's arm and snatched the floating leaves of his trial markers, implanting them as multitudinous layers within the soft skin of his inner forearm. At length, the wriggling lines of destiny stilled. A green mist seeped up from his flesh and continued upward to the clouds of the foundational elements.

The braid of Fate unwove from Tobek's silver arm. The surge of his green and silver magics faded along with the rage of the Berserker. Tobek rubbed his palms together and blew out a long breath. Another two heartbeats, and he nodded to Ashtad.

"All you now."

Ashtad passed Drew off to Mirri, then moved to the head of the bed. He locked his bad leg and bent his good one up so he could grab his boot. A brief shock of electricity, and the heel of his boot popped forward, revealing a hollow compartment. He retrieved a curious gem on a fine chain, then closed the compartment. He dangled the chain in the air for everyone to see before looping it around his wrist and over his fingers, so the gem rested in his palm.

"It turns out that the communications device I was building in Irkalla wasn't for cross-collective communications, but cross-consciousness. It's intended for those of us not blessed with telepathy or who would be on the unfortunate end of a gross power disparity." He grinned more with disbelief than delight. "I will never get over how unnerving the prescient acts of the Fates are."

Everyone around the bed groaned in commiseration.

"I'll apologize in advance for this not being quite as awesome or showy as everyone else's contributions." He slid his hand under Cian's neck and cupped the kid's nape.

"When you're dealing with the mind, subtlety is paramount," Phobos assured with a touch of sarcasm.

"Tell Bix that, will you?" Ashtad closed his eyes. "Jump-starting life force and resetting admin access in five, four, three…"

Cian's whole body flushed blue, then purple, then green,

before returning to rosy white. His eyes opened wide, and his back bowed. Ashtad placed his hand on Cian's chest and sent a shock of electricity into the kid's heart. That triggered Cian's deep breath… and sudden coughing. Cian's arms flailed as the kid struggled to sit up. Many hands helped him. Samael manifested a huge mug of what was hopefully water but could've been caffeinated soda and shoved it into the kid's hands. Cian took the mug and blinked rapidly as his eyes watered, snot dribbled from his nose, and drool formed in the corner of his mouth.

Basic human systems working as designed.

Bix breathed a sigh of jubilant relief and retreated farther from the bed as the others crowded closer to the kid, talking over one another, and all laughing with the shared joy of success. It'd take a while for Cian to sort his ups from his downs, and a whole lot longer to figure out what parts of him had changed in what ways. But for now, seeing his broad smile in his easily flushed face, with bright eyes drinking in his found family, well, that was all things good and right and wonderful.

She started as calloused fingers laced with hers. Tobek kissed her hand, then held it to his heart.

"You did it," he rumbled, pride thick in his voice.

"*We* did. All of us. Collaboration. Cooperation. The very things Cian put into action in this lab." Bix gestured to the space that looked nothing like a laboratory as Feng continued his impressive night show. "Now, I have to take those same lessons and apply them to my family."

"May I have the honor of escorting you this evening?" He bowed before her.

"You are the champion of the Mids. It seems only fair you attend parley." Bix feigned snooty royal superiority before dropping the act and gently tugging on his beard. "As my cherished consort and partner in my chosen family, your support would be very much appreciated."

"Good." He straightened and folded her arm around his. "Because if the Phoenix has to burn this much magic just so we could heal the kid, imagine how much more the entire population of the Mids will have to burn once you First Children kick off your antics."

"Are you going to play magical maestro?" Bix looked way up at the burning star that was Feng. His connection to native magic would've informed him of Cian's status. That he still burned brightly meant the threat of too much magic in the area hadn't yet been arrested. He knew better than she what the Mids could tolerate, so she didn't interfere.

"I believe the Phoenix has that role covered." Tobek winked. "Think of me more as a crusty old army general who wants a front-row seat to the enemy's retreat while the woman he adores outmaneuvers the opposition to make it possible."

"Aw, just think, you'll be one of the youngest entities in attendance. That ought to be a novel experience for you, you old fart." Grinning at Tobek's deep laughter, she wrapped her Berserker in darkness, then reached for a mote of shadows to connect to those thrown by the rooftop of the Kennedy Center.

Time to boot the Devourers from the Mids and heal her family.

CHAPTER 29

The wide terrace framing the rooftop level of the Kennedy Center for the Performing Arts in Washington, DC, Primary Mid World, gleamed. The charcoal-gray marble inlaid in white marble frames reflected the light show of the continually changing sky and landscapes spreading far beyond the horizon. Nary a trace of the District that had been a testament to humanity's greatness and ills remained other than the large white-marble square that was the Kennedy Center. Feng's continual reconstruction and deconstruction as a means of burning magic kept everything in a constant flow of change. Joining him from outside the twenty-mile radius, the Consortium and the Chweds added to the symphony of magic in motion building new environments, then transitioning seamlessly into others. Redolent fragrances rode dancing winds that pushed clouds into shapes that swelled into bursts of rain, blossoms, or sand, only to be swept away by strong gusts to set a new stage of performance. Devourers caught in the churning panoramas flailed like fish in the whitecaps of an angry ocean, unable to find purchase long enough to establish a counterattack.

Chaos. Beautiful befitting chaos.

Bix paused on the southwestern corner of the terrace to take in the glory of chaotic collaboration. She grinned and pointed across what was sometimes a river, sometimes a meadow, and sometimes a jungle.

"I spy with my little eye twenty-five acres and a coal plant resisting the beauty of change."

"I don't half-ass my wards." Tobek chuckled and clutched their linked arms tighter to his side. "Besides, Gurp and I had to update the entire compound to accommodate a very special First Child. We keep hoping she'll move in, but…"

"Little sister," cheered a booming voice that rolled actual thunder and shook the building.

Bix spun with a smile as Eko eagerly motioned her up to the roof of the Kennedy Center, where her siblings gathered around a dark teal table in the shape of her sacred symbol: a seven-sided pyramid. The pointed tip served as the base, perfectly balanced and unmoving in the breezes. Her smile faltered as she noted the presence of her elder siblings' heralds in clusters around the edges of the flat roof. Within those clusters stood Hywl and the green team of Berserkers, seemingly unmolested. Protection. The heralds were protecting the green team from the crushing presence of all her siblings. Bless them.

"Did Gurp know I meant the terrace, not the literal roof?" Bix murmured to Tobek as gates moved them to join the others.

"Of course, but your eldest brother had a different opinion." Tobek tipped his head in the direction of Eko's heralds. They made quite the sight what with sentient towers of blackish-red flames surrounding a squat, mottled-green goblin seated upon a large throne with live-ordinance snacks piled beside him. Gurp would never have arranged that for himself. He was far too concerned about others' comforts. The spoiling? Absolute Eko.

Oh, how she loved those two. Eko and Gurp.

"Champion, if you would take your place over there?" Music directed Tobek with a flick of her finger toward a bundle of purple beasts that vaguely resembled giant hawks. Music's heralds.

Tobek squeezed Bix's arm one more time, then bowed to her sister, before taking his designated position.

Drawing a deep breath to balance herself, Bix joined her siblings at the table, noting the open seat across from hers. Tempest still had Desire bottled within her.

"Thank you, all, for coming," Bix began. "Tempest, if you would, please, release Desire."

Tempest glowered at her. "You sure? We're a single package right now. You can carve us up and be done, no worrying about errant sparks."

"Desire forced us to this moment. He needs to stand accountable. As an individual," Bix insisted.

"Okay, but don't say I didn't warn you, bratling." Tempest pushed back from the table and stretched the tentacles of her body and headdress. Pewter chaotic magic swirled from the core of her being and pushed outward, expelling millions of copper fireflies that zoomed off the rooftop.

They didn't make it far. Panels of blue and purple, of red and yellow burst into existence, corralling Desire into a box and forcing him back to the rooftop. The elder twins were having none of his crap today.

Bix dissolved into her native form and entered the box, mixing her midnight and starlight amid Desire's dominant order and overinflated chaos. She removed the breaks among his energies that she'd placed when he'd foolishly confronted her and relieved the pressures on his chaos, restoring the balance of his physical self.

Copper starlight congealed into a body of leaves and roots of humanoid features and size. The box trapping him on the roof dissipated. Desire stood before them in his preferred form, the suns of his eyes blazing with fury.

"How dare you?" he seethed at Bix as she assumed a feminine body, but not of flesh. "I ought to—"

"Apologize," Movement snapped. "You owe every one of us an apology for your unmitigated selfishness."

"All I want is to die and to have it stick. Your bullying means nothing to me," Desire sniped.

Music's personal song struck chords of pure anger at the attack on her twin. "Don't pretend you don't have feelings, Desire. They exist even when you hide from them, even when you force Tempest to own them. Older than time, yet you have the maturity of a child."

"Spare me your precious indignation. Tempest isn't innocent. She isn't helpless. She isn't my *victim*." Desire sneered and regarded each sibling with haughty disdain, all but Tempest, of course. "She is a fully developed, fully cognizant entity who uses me as an excuse for her destructive behavior. Believe me, I'm the one who suffers her presence. Not the other way around."

Tempest made a strangled sound. Eko and Esiw were instantly beside her, taking her hands and exchanging nods of solidarity.

"That's the crux of it all," Esiw said, his tone thick with disappointment. "We don't believe you. We can't. You made sure of that. You made deception the cornerstone of your personality. Shame on us for not realizing it sooner."

Desire tsked and pouted. "Or what? You would've given me a course correction? Tried to bestir my conscience until it mirrored yours? You who find isolation the ultimate solution to conflict? Even for conflicts within yourself? Please, you are no role model."

"Enough," Bix called. "Genuine remorse begins with empathy before branching into acknowledgment and acceptance of our individual motivations and actions. It cannot be forced. Demanding that of Desire is not why we're here today. Would everyone please take a seat?"

"Did you get Father to accept my death?" Desire challenged as the siblings gathered around the table once again. "If not, there is no point to this charade."

"Desire, until you and Tempest permanently remove the Devourers from this quadrant of existence, that is an answer you will not know." Bix took her seat first, and the others followed.

Desire stared at his twin expectantly across the table. "You're the one who brought them here."

"You're the one who upgraded them, then commanded them

to charge en masse just because you were angry she beat you up," Tempest scoffed. "Yet you still think you have what it takes to unseat her as High Executioner."

"My patience is finite, you two," Bix reminded, opening viewing gates of the Mids and another set covering the whole of the galaxy. "Remove the Devourers and any other unwelcome surprises you planted in my sanctuary. Now."

She desperately wanted to include an "or else" but really, with what could she possibly threaten them? Death? Endless life? Each time they indulged in a petty tantrum, they delayed getting what they wanted. Well, make that what they needed.

"Fine," Tempest sighed and flicked her wrist.

In the gates showing the entirety of the Mids, rings of pewter-tinted darkness spawned concentric circles around the collective and outwards beyond the Uppers and the Unders.

"They don't comprehend the concept of retreat." Tempest flapped her hand at Desire. "You actually have to introduce to them the innate drive to leave this place and never return, parasite mine. Their transportation out of the quadrant awaits."

Desire turned his attention to Bix and curled a lip. "If you don't deliver on your end of the bargain, I will flood every galaxy in the greater existence with monstrosities capable of horrors you can't begin to fathom."

Music snorted and looked askance. The others were hardly better at hiding their mirth. Of course *they* thought the threat was funny. Through the earlier group mind-share, they'd seen Desire's assorted monstrosities and the cruel efficiency that had caused Bix to quickly reset timelines. Sadly, those memories were very real to Bix, as was the gutting devastation associated with them.

"This is our forty-third go-around, Desire. I do not question your sincerity," Bix assured.

"How will you do it?" he pressed.

"No answers until the Devourers are dispatched forever," she repeated.

Barking arcane expletives, Desire clapped his hands, then threw them up in the air, tossing copper spears through the atmosphere and beyond the lattice of Resen. Explosions of copper fireworks rocked the collective. Instead of the sparks fading, they stretched into rays of starlight, hooking Devourers and withdrawing them by the hundreds from every corner and core of the Mid Worlds… and the Unders along with the Uppers and Others.

Raucous cheering erupted from the Berserkers watching from within the protections offered by the assorted heralds.

Bix was less than amused.

"All of them, you treacherous shit," she snapped, letting her temper fly. They were beyond the point of emotional manipulations to control situations. He either complied or he failed to achieve his personal goal. Both were problems for him. "Do not mistake my ability to detect their noxious presence in my godsdamned home."

"What?" Desire mocked affront. "No snacks for later?"

"Patience. Fading. Fast." Bix fanned her shadowy thorns of malice around her and capped them with grisly burrs of burnished brass. She was the two-in-one. The High Executioner. The next part of this process didn't have to be painful, but she could absolutely ensure it was.

Tossing his hands in the air five more times, Desire finally completed the extraction of his poisonous creations from the galaxy. All attendees—family and not—watched the gates in varying states of satisfaction as the Devourer army and its multitudinous reinforcements were encapsulated in copper stars and set upon the cloudy rings of pewter to be whisked away beyond the scope of the gates.

Bix would hunt down the Devourers after her home was safe to ensure they were serving their purpose in the greater existence and nothing more.

"Tobek, what says Resen?" Bix called out for the benefit of those eavesdropping from great distances.

"All clear," her Berserker confirmed. "Ground forces reporting in now, corroborating enemy withdrawal."

"Your turn, bratling," Tempest prompted.

"Verify, for the record, that the termination of your existence as you know it is not only what you want, but what you insist on achieving." Bix looked to both Tempest and Desire as she spoke.

"Of course it is," Tempest huffed.

"Those words, spoken from your lips and embedded in your essence, or we stop here." Bix ignored the curious looks from the elder siblings. Fortunately, none of them questioned her insistence. The statement and emotions behind it would matter when the time eventually came for the twins to rebuild themselves. It might be a million or more years, but knowing they'd asked for this rather than having it inflicted upon them would have great effect on their reassimilation and relationships with the family.

The youngest twins repeated their commitment to death. Bix smiled, grateful she hadn't re-formed a heart in her current state, because it would've hammered clear out of her chest. Oh sure, she was presenting calm, collected, and competent, but she had no clue if this drastic resolution would actually work, short or long term. No time like the present to find out.

"You two have long envied mortals and their swift journey to death. You relentlessly pursued the total reset of form and knowledge. You covet the complete severing of old ties and bad habits. Desire, you crave genuine affection, both the ability to feel it and to demonstrate it. While Tempest, you need the absolute freedom from your history in order to become more than your aspirations. That is what death means to each of you. Thus, you will die as mortals do, repeatedly and for time beyond measure." Bix glanced to the eldest and elder twins, who nodded in confirmation and support.

"What trickery is this?" Desire demanded. "I didn't ask to be demoted to a mortal. I could've done that myself."

"Had you done it yourself, you would still be you, retaining all the knowledge of who you are and the magics with which you were born," Esiw elaborated. "That is not death. That is reincarnation. That is not what you've requested."

"It took forty-two attempts and one prolonged tragic

experience to conceive of the means to deliver what you want without upsetting the greater existence." Bix stood and held out her hand to Tempest. "I will break you as I broke myself. I will take away everything from you as you've asked. But, unlike my journey to rebirth, you will live finite lives in fragile bodies that will expire when you least expect. I will come to you in your final moments and remove the memories you've made in that life, then one of the elders will remake you into a different body to live a different life with no recollection of what has come before."

"That is the kind of death that will *stick*," Movement pointed out.

"Death on loop, eh?" Desire fanned his fingers through his beard and raked his twin with a condescending look. "Well, Tempest, at least we'll die together forever."

"No," Tempest said, taking Bix's hand. "Not together. That was my price."

"What?" Desire stilled, then sneered. "We can't be separated. We're the same core cosmic energy, you twit."

"I'm not unmaking your core energy; I'm simply fragmenting it. Hers to hers, and yours to yours. This allows your innate aspects of motivation to live on regardless of your fractured state. True for the greater existence, true for you as individuals in whatever life you're born into. You will always be the driver and the driven. But not together."

"You need to be separated, to cleanse yourselves of the negative aspects fostered by your twin bond," Eko explained. "You must develop new instincts. Healthy ones. Ones that will allow you to respect each other when the time comes for you to reunite."

"That's going to be a long fucking time," Tempest jeered as she led Bix around the table to Desire blustering in his seat. "About an epoch shy of never."

"No, no, you can't do that. That is not what we agreed to." Desire bolted up from his seat, his face a hair away from Tempest's. "We can't be separated. We can't exist *alone*."

"Should've considered that before initiating our death quest. What did you think would happen after we died?" Tempest derided, using air quotes around the word *died*.

"Relationships matter," Bix said, wrapping the twins in starlight and midnight. "You're going to spend lifetimes learning that powerful lesson."

Tempest reverted to her native state, welcoming Bix into her chaos-dominant existence. Desire, on the other hand, reverted and his starlight surged, attempting to overpower Bix and eject her as he wrestled with his resistant twin. Tempest tried to fight him off. The conflict of the twins spawned a storm of wild chaos and scorching starlight that spread beyond the rooftop and across what had been the District. Bix pulled back from the conflict and banded around them, hauling their destructive tantrum up through the atmosphere and out into the galaxy as the three of them surrendered all pretense of being anything less than violent cosmic entities.

Bix was vaguely aware of the elders giving chase, but her entire focus tuned to the skirmish between the youngest twins. She spared a passing thought of gratitude for the twins fighting each other rather than uniting against her. It made breaking them so much easier. The act was swift, yet the effort immense. She started at the edges of their entwined conflict and pushed her way forward, inserting trillions of breaks. The ropes of their twin bond gleamed brightly in streaks of pewter and copper. Without hesitation, Bix broke their bond, splintering it smaller and smaller. Onward she pressed, until she found their core energy and the seed of a single emotion with which to pair it.

Compassion.

Their seed of compassion was underdeveloped and unbalanced. It was perfect for their new beginning. Too much compassion would present as a conflict to their core energy of motivation, but a nascent seed would temper the ill effects of unbridled motivation. It would keep a pathway to empathy that couldn't be closed, not as an origin seed.

Pulling herself into a form of feminine starlit night, Bix cupped the seed of compassion and the core energy of the twins in her ethereal hands. The dust of the teeny glittering pieces of the youngest twins drifted around her, suspended in a place where gravity didn't exist. Beyond the cloud of broken pieces, Movement floated beside Music, Eko alongside Esiw, all in their native states.

"Is this it, then?" Music asked, her song one of sorrow. "Their tragic end?"

"It is the end of their tragedy," Esiw corrected. "Now, their healing can begin."

"These motes are our siblings at their most vulnerable. Treat them kindly, please, as you place each speck into its own container," Bix requested with resigned relief, holding the core energy of motivation and the seed of compassion to her heart. She gasped as the galaxy filled with myriad life-forms exotic, unique, and not a one a replication. Some were minor, small as insects. Some were more massive than whales. All of them glorious.

"Ta, ta, ta, ta," Music sang, and a song of hope and potential built among the creations. Rose-gold starlight danced with cobalt winds, and golden starlight twirled with red glitter as the elders deposited the broken energies of Tempest and Desire into their new homes.

It was beautiful, the family, working together, to heal, to forgive, and to take up the roles of guardians for the youngest twins. They'd all watched her bumble through her reassimilation, ever curious and mindful. Once she'd begun her rebirth in earnest, they'd stepped up to aid her. She had no doubt they'd do the same for Tempest and Desire when the time was right.

The container creations vanished as quickly as they'd arrived, scattering across the greater existence, taking up lives in different galaxies among different cultures and species. All the memories and magics of the younger twins had been reduced to considerably smaller fragments than those into which Bix had broken herself. She'd had seven pieces to reclaim within the sanctuary of her own home. They had billions sprinkled among infinite galaxies. It would be a long, long time before they were ready to rebuild themselves.

"Come, little sister," Eko encouraged. "Let us see them into their first mortal life."

Bix laughed as her elder siblings swept her back into the Mids, back to the rooftop of the Kennedy Center, and back into the warm welcome of her home. As each sibling assumed their preferred or humanoid form, Bix kept to her starlight. Modesty of a noncreationist being what it was and all.

As the elders settled in their seats, Bix opened her hands and allowed the core energy of motivation to float alongside the seed of compassion.

"Amazing. All we are, all the power we wield, grows from that one speck." Movement leaned forward, crossing her arms on the table.

"All the motivation in the greater existence boils down to that small spark," Esiw harrumphed.

"Eko, Movement, I need a seed of life into which I will place Tempest." Bix smiled at her biggest brother as he thrust his hand in the air and waved it wildly.

"Let me, let me," he cheered, bouncing in his seat.

Movement acquiesced with a shrug, chortling. "Let him. It's not as if we don't get to do this every few decades."

With great focus, Eko tapped his fingertips together. A spark of red cleared to a seed pod of darkness.

Bix split the core energy of motivation and the seed of compassion. The pewter motivation of external influence and half the seed of compassion were carefully added to the seed pod Eko balanced between his big fingers.

"Music, the honor of Desire's new beginning is yours," Esiw encouraged.

Music flared her song and snapped her fingers, creating a hollow pod for Desire's copper core of personal ambition and his half of compassion. Bix added Desire to the pod, and Music sealed it.

"They should spend their first lives here, in the Mids, where I can keep an eye on their progress," Bix suggested.

"We'll all be keeping an eye, be sure of that. I've got just the mother for Pesty's seed." Movement smirked and twitched her fingers, taking the pod from Eko. "It's a good family. Water based. Let's start them off with a fair shot at happiness, eh?"

Bix nodded.

"Oh, I think I must insist on Desire's first family." Esiw tapped his finger on the table, and a small orange cat manifested. "Let's see how he does as a pet."

As Music implanted Desire's seed into the cat, Bix summoned Gurp to the table. The goblin quickly scrambled down from his throne, chipmunking a grenade. Music presented the cat to Gurp on a wave of lavender song.

"See that he and his mother find their way to a good family," Bix asked of her beloved goblin.

Gurp cradled the cat to his chest just as the grenade exploded in his mouth, sending plumes of smoke from his nose. A flare of green magic manifested a cat crate at the goblin's feet. Bix grinned as Tobek winked.

"Thank you, one and all," Bix said, rising from her seat. "I couldn't have done this without you. Hopefully, the Chaos and the Cosmos will approve of what we've done here today."

Eko stood and wrapped her in a hug. "Come out to play with me soon, little sister. There is so much I want to share with you."

"I'm looking forward to discussing all you revealed to us on this journey so that I may be a more informed and active participant in the redevelopment of our family as a whole." Esiw stood, his fox tails whipping around him. Bix gave him a hug too before her elder brothers vanished into darkness and starlight, departing the Mids.

"Who wants to place bets on how long it is before Eko shows up here as a dog to harangue Desire?" Movement rapped her knuckles on the table, and it disappeared along with the chairs.

Music gasped and pressed her fingers to her lips. "He wouldn't."

"He would," Bix assured. "That's why we're playing these first few rounds of rebirth where I can keep an eye on things."

"We, little sister, *we* will be watching. We're not going to let you be solely responsible for fixing them. We're all in as a family." Movement gestured to the landscape still in a constant state of change. "I've got to say, I'm impressed by what the creations pulled off here. I can see why you didn't want to give up on this collective."

"I love this home you two made for me." Bix took her sisters' hands and squeezed them. "Thank you for helping me keep it."

"We love you, little sister." Music kissed Bix's cheek. "I can't wait to see how the caretakers rebuild your home."

In a gust of song, Music and Movement departed. Seven beats later, the heralds of each sibling left too. Alone on the roof with Gurp holding a cat in a carrier, the green team of Berserkers, and Tobek, Bix turned to her found family and beamed.

"It's done. It's finally done," she exclaimed a bit more loudly than she'd intended, caught up in the relief and disbelief that she'd pulled it off. Cian was alive. The Devourers were gone. Tempest and Desire were beginning their rehabilitation, and her family had taken the first steps toward healing. So far, her parents were letting it all stand. Phew.

"What say we go home, sweetheart? I think there's a hell of a celebration to be had." Tobek extended his hand to her. The Berserkers and Gurp cheered their colorful opinions.

Laughing with the joy of success, she took everyone home to the coal plant.

CHAPTER 30

Fireworks burst in the clear autumn night sky above Washington, DC, Primary Mid World. Colorful sparks formed mythical creatures and historical sites as part of the grand celebration of the reestablishment of the capital city of the Mid Worlds. Select monuments and landmarks had been rebuilt to mirror what had stood before the Heralded War. Museum row along the National Mall had been expanded to include exhibitions dedicated to a factual history of the Americans, a history that included the active involvement of Chwedlonol. The Consortium had built magnificent offices aboveground that were accessible to the general public, while their underground headquarters had expanded significantly as a city below the city complete with underwater docks leading from the deeply dredged and purified Potomac River.

The revamped neighborhoods surrounding the governmental core had been the subject of months-long heated political debates over whether the city should only be residential for government employees of a certain class and first responders versus expanding to include merchants who supported those offices. What about family-support providers? Maintenance and repair specialists? The list of potential exceptions crossed all communities, and no one was foolish enough to believe there wouldn't be exceptions for sale to the wealthy and influential. The shops and residences that had been built accommodated the wealth of diversity in the city, from ogres to sprites, and of course the dragons, angels, gods, and Fates.

DC wasn't the only city grappling with its new place in a revised World, but it was one of the few that remained in the new World order. The Consortium had claimed DC as its base long, long, long before humans even knew of the area. The superpowers were not going to relinquish it now. No, it would remain the seat of power for the collective.

Other cities and capitols on this and other Worlds didn't have that enduring legacy. Most cities were gone, never to return. Old territorial lines establishing states and nations had been obliterated in the war, rivers and canyons had been redrawn, mountain ranges smoothed or elevated, seas and lakes moved and multiplied, shorelines shifted as oceans divvied up more landmasses to accommodate more water species. The intersections of ley lines that had been formed with the advent of Resen drew human populations to new locations across the Mid Worlds to ground the magic while Chweds followed for the economic benefits. The governments built under the era of Human Delusion were no more, and unsurprisingly, that wasn't sitting well with those unseated from power. Humanity was divided in their acceptance of coexisting with magical beings, while Chweds rightfully refused to buckle or yield to the violence of ignorance.

There was chaos in the aftermath of the conflict with the Devourers. Beautiful, glorious chaos. Evolution of magics, of beliefs, of collaboration, and of identity brought about by the forces of war had shattered traditions, upended power structures, and migrated populations. It would take time for the Mids to find their new balance.

Bix was thrilled to be in the throes of it.

"Ah, sweetheart, that smile of yours still makes me weak in the knees." Tobek tightened his arms around her, snugging her closer to his chest.

They sat in the middle of the grassy parade field at the center of the Berserkers' base, while the troops celebrated with the nascent community regrowing around them. Large camouflage tents stood with flaps peeled back, hosting food and drink buffets, arts and crafts for the young, and relocation information for those interested in moving to Resen data center communities. A band played on a stage at the foot of the parking garage. Performers, both human and Chweds, milled through the crowd, adding to the entertainment. Gurp, waddling behind the scenes, ensured everything ran smoothly, dispatching gofers and issuing orders to Berserkers refilling foods and supplies.

Bix surrounded herself and Tobek in a box of transparent gates, mindful of the danger she presented to the minor races. This was the best she could do to be among them, and that still bugged her.

"Bix, Bix, Bix." Cian skidded to a halt before them as if stealing home plate, face flushed and eyes dancing. "Hey, I want you to try this on."

She cocked her head at the opalescent amulet shimmering in his hand. "New comm piece?"

Tobek took it from the kid as she lifted her hair, allowing her Berserker to latch the pretty chain around her neck.

"Nope. Power imbalance balancer." Cian grinned. "PIB or something. I'll work on the name later. We can't have you skulking around in gates. That's just wrong. You ought to be able to walk freely, right? Buy shoes without melting malls, go partying with Drew without wiping out the city, or, you know, taking me for cross-World trips bundled up in darkness without killing me in the process. That last one is really important."

Bix laughed with delight…then pouted as the amulet dissolved against her skin.

"Damn it." Cian stood up and dusted his pants. "Back to the drawing board. Don't think I'm letting it go. I'm determined."

"You built an entire defense system, Cian. I've no doubt you'll figure this out." She gave him two thumbs-up before he bolted for the tent serving assorted pastries. "His stomach is a bottomless pit these days."

"Well, he is a teenage boy. Mostly." Tobek draped her hair over one shoulder and kissed her neck. "Runjit gives him regular medical checkups. Physically, he reads healthy human male. No lasting effects from all he went through."

"But?" She eyed him over her shoulder.

"It's a veneer. I don't know when it'll crack or what he'll emerge as, but, for now, the ley lines want to keep him as a Sage in the throes of his trials towards Fatehood."

"How are his marbles?" she asked, knowing his physical didn't reflect his mental. His soul had been through a lot, and there was no undoing that trauma.

"Some days are better than others," answered a familiar voice, settling beside one wall of her gate. "But we're there for him. Me, Drew, Ashtad. We'll get him through it, and ourselves along the way."

"Feng," she happily greeted, elbowing Tobek as he grunted with displeasure. "How are you doing? Did you decide whether you're going to accept Ogun's offer to be reinstated as lead investigator for the Consortium?"

"And limit my ability to answer your call? No one who actually knows you believes you're disbanding the team. Devourers or no Devourers, you're always up to something," Feng scoffed indignantly before taking a sip of a tall frosty drink. "I told Ogun I'd work freelance, only jobs that interest me. He seems to think he'll have enough to keep me busy what with the power struggles throughout the redefined castes destined to last for a few centuries."

"I'm surprised you're not with Mirri tonight," Bix said baldly, totally fishing for what might be a non-thing, but could maybe be a thing-thing.

"She and Thárros are with the researchers still questing for a cure to the Devourer toxin. The lab to which you sent everyone has been officially tasked with picking up where Cian's researchers were interrupted." Feng swept his hair from his face, watching the fireworks. "She's happy to be back in the Mids, on the whole. I think she's planning on sticking around."

"Bixie, babe, there you are." Drew alighted in front of them, gossamer wings flapping behind a corona of wild hot-pink curls. "Catch."

"I thought manic pixie dream girl was a trope, not an actual entity," Bix teased, clapping her hands around a small black totem crafted from souls and radiating Other World magic.

"Gurl, Flamer here is indulging my fantasy suits while the powers that be decide the new rules around dealing with the dead." Drew wagged a finger at the tchotchke. "It's a gift from Sparky. He sends his regards from Irkalla."

Bix took another look at the gift and laughed. It was a Bi Xie. Running her thumb along the bottom, she felt the coded notches. A comm piece. A means to stay in touch while Ashtad continued his studies with the titaness Ereshkigal. The warmth of enduring friendship suffused her.

"Thank you for couriering it from the Unders." Bix tumbled the Bi Xie in her hands. "I take it all's well down there?"

"The titans quieted down after the Devourers cleared out. The gods are still processing the delivered souls from the war and doling out the emptied ones from the treasuries for newly contracted lives here in the Mids. So, yeah, busy days in the unlife of the Unders. Hel don't even miss me. Praise be." Drew held out a hand to Feng and bounced on her toes. "Come, dance with me, Flamer. I've worn out all the Berserkers."

That made Tobek and Feng laugh in unison.

"If you'll excuse me." Feng stood and clenched his fist around his drink, causing it to vanish. He offered his arm to Drew. She took it with a squeal of bawdy glee as they headed for the dance floor nearer the band.

Bix leaned into Tobek and wrapped the Bi Xie in his beard, playing. "Safe to say everything is under control here?"

"Very safe," he agreed.

"No immediate crises?"

"No immediate crises."

"So, we could slip away?" She cut a sly glance up at him.

He sat up a bit straighter, a question in his smile. "We could slip away. Was there some place you had in mind?"

"Well, for the things I have in mind, there's really only one place that offers the recommended privacy," she murmured, leaning up to whisper against his lips, "We do have three-hundred-odd years to catch up on, after all."

His guffaw was wholly wicked and the gleam in his eyes shamelessly predatory as gates opened to the hospitality World.

Relationships mattered.

Character Glossary

THE CONSORTIUM

> The governing body comprised of representatives from the four superpower races charged with populating and protecting the collective of Mid Worlds.

THE DRAGON HORDE

> Led by: The Dragon Queens
> Mid World Entities
> Provide bodies for lifeforms native to the Mids
> Feed on positive emotions
> Named Characters: Raspoine, Rummir, Yashanee

THE ANGELIC HOST

> Led by: Archangels
> Mid World Entities
> Provide bodies for lifeforms native to the Mids
> Feed on negative emotions
> Named Characters: Samael, Michael, Ariel

THE HOUSES OF FATE

> Led by: Heads of House
> Other World Entities
> Sages & Oracles strive to ascend to Fatehood
> Provide threads of Fate that secure a soul to a body
> Feed on magic expelled by a soul-tethered lifeform
> Named Characters: Skuld, Sunan

THE PANTHEONS

> Led by: Greater gods who fought their way to the top
> Other World Entities
> Demigods strive to ascend to godhood
> Provide souls for lifeforms native to the Mids
> Feed on enriched souls

Named Characters: Phobos, Hel, Jörmungand, Ereshkigal, Nergal, Deimos, and many more.

✯

CHWEDLONOL (aka "Chweds"): Catch-all term for the myriad magical races native to the Mid Worlds. Created by the Consortium in terms defined by individual Cycle of Soul contracts.

HUMANS: Do not possess magic, they ground magic; unconsciously drawn to magical hotspots. Created by the Consortium in terms defined by individual Cycle of Soul contracts.

✯

BIX'S FAMILY

PARENTS:
  The Chaos: Bix's mother, the feminine welcome, the eternal darkness, the womb of existence
  The Cosmos: Bix's father, the masculine exclusion, the light of order, the rod of control

THE FIRST CHILDREN:

THE FIRST TWINS:
  Movement: First of the First, aligned to the Chaos, cocreator of the Mid Worlds
  Music: Twin to Movement, aligned to the Cosmos, cocreator of the Mid Worlds

THE SECOND TWINS:
  Eko: Eldest son, aligned to the Chaos, also known as Knowledge Innate or Instinct
  Esiw: Twin to Eko, aligned to the Cosmos, also known as Knowledge Amassed or Experience

The Third Twins:

> **Tempest:** Daughter aligned to the Chaos, also known as External Motivation, source of peer pressure, society's expectations, and familial obligations
>
> **Desire:** Youngest son, aligned to the Cosmos, also known as Personal Motivation, source of drive, ambition, and greed

The Twinless Two-in-One:

> **Bix:** Youngest child, equal parts wild and ordered, also known as Balance and the High Executioner for All Worlds

Other Books
by K.A. Krantz

Urban Fantasy
The Immortal Spy Series:
THE BURNED SPY
THE PLAGUED SPY
THE CAPTURED SPY
THE HANGED SPY
THE EXPOSED SPY
THE SHACKLED SPY
THE HERALDED SPY

High Fantasy
Fire Born, Blood Blessed Series:
LARCOUT

Want to be notified when a new book is released?
Subscribe to K.A. Krantz's email newsletter at
kakrantz.com

If you enjoyed this book, please spread the word and
leave a review with the retailer of your choice.

Acknowledgments

To my family: For cheering me on throughout the series and supporting me in all ways. To Jenn Stark: For encouraging the weird no matter how the plots twisted. Thanks for being an excellent friend and CP. To Linda Ingmanson, my development editor: It took me seven books to finally get the hang of "add emotions here." Alas, I'm still hopelessly addicted to Capping All The Things. Sorry. Thank you for your steady guidance. To Toni Lee, my copy editor and fact checker: Thank you for your endless patience with educating me on the rules of hyphens and transitive versus intransitive verbs. Eventually, there will come a book where I've mastered your lessons. Sadly, it didn't happen in this series. To the team at Gene Mollica Studios: Thanks for making Bix visually captivating for every book, regardless of how odd my requests.

About the Author

KAK splits her time between Cincinnati and the DC 'burbs with her faithful hairy beast. When not writing, she indulges in a shoe obsession, conducts a love/hate affair with paint, and makes epic messes in the kitchen.

Visit her website at kakrantz.com for free flash fiction, blog posts about her latest fancies, and more. If you're on Twitter, she'd love to hear from you. Tweet @KAKrantz.